ST.
RY
D0759360
DISCARD

THE BOUNTY KILLERS

Center Point
Large Print

Also by J. A. Johnstone and available from Center Point Large Print:

The Loner series:
The Loner
The Big Gundown
Seven Days to Die
Rattlesnake Valley

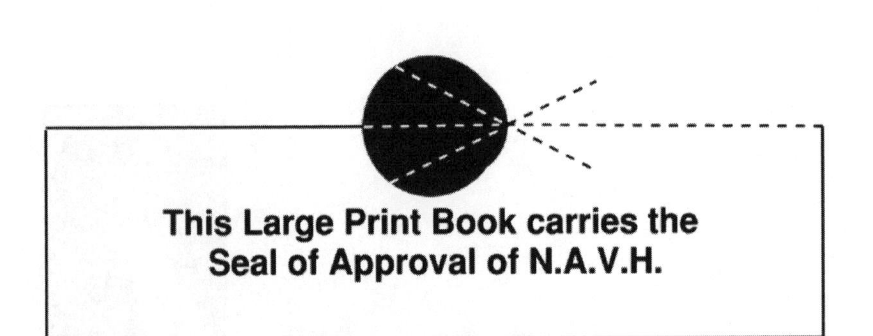

The Loner

THE BOUNTY KILLERS

J. A. Johnstone

CENTER POINT LARGE PRINT
THORNDIKE, MAINE

This Center Point Large Print edition
is published in the year 2013 by arrangement with
Kensington Publishing Corp.

The text of this Large Print edition is unabridged.
In other aspects, this book may vary
from the original edition.
Printed in the United States of America
on permanent paper.
Set in 16-point Times New Roman type.

ISBN: 978-1-61173-642-7

Library of Congress Cataloging-in-Publication Data

Johnstone, J. A.
The bounty killers / J.A. Johnstone. — Center Point Large Print edition.
pages cm. — (The loner)
ISBN 978-1-61173-642-7 (library binding : alk. paper)
1. Large type books. I. Title.
PS3610.O43B68 2013
813′.6—dc23

2012038092

THE BOUNTY KILLERS

Chapter 1

The shot came out of nowhere.

The first warning Kid Morgan had was the whine of a high-powered bullet as it passed his head, followed a second later by a rifle's distant boom.

Instinctively, he kicked his feet out of the stirrups, yanked the Winchester from the sheath strapped to his buckskin horse, and rolled out of the saddle. He hit the ground feet first and running. He ducked behind one of the pine trees growing thick on the Nevada hillside just a few seconds after the slug whipped past his ear.

Another shot sounded in the distance, but the bullet didn't come close enough for him to hear it pass.

The Kid planted his back against the pine trunk, uncertain the tree would shield him, since he didn't know exactly where the bushwhacker was. A moment later a slug thudded harmlessly into the far side of the trunk.

He was safe . . . as long as the rifleman didn't move and get a better angle on him. And unless there were more than one of the bastards stalking him.

The buckskin had run off into a brushy grove. The Kid hoped the horse would be safe. It was possible the man who'd ambushed him might decide to shoot the horse, just to insure that he was set afoot.

It might be wise in the long run to draw the fire away from the buckskin, The Kid decided. Darting out from behind the tree trunk he dashed toward another pine, heading in the opposite direction, away from where the buckskin was going.

The bushwhacker tried to hit him on the run, the bullet kicking up dirt several yards behind The Kid. Breathing a little hard from the sudden exertion, as well as from the fact that after more than a year of drifting in and out of trouble, he still didn't like people shooting at him, he hid behind a second tree.

According to the Kid's father, Frank Morgan, the famous—or infamous—gunfighter known as The Drifter, a man never really got used to dodging bullets.

The distant rifle fell silent. The bushwhacker figured out he wasn't going to be able to hit The Kid.

Maybe he would give up trying.

More than likely, though, he would move and try to get a better shot.

The Kid frowned in thought as the minutes dragged by. He could make a run for his horse, but it was possible the rifleman was waiting for him to do just that. He could call the buckskin to him, but if the bushwhacker figured out what was going on, he would shoot the horse for sure.

Or he could give the would-be killer a little surprise.

The Kid turned to face the tree trunk and tipped his head back. The pine branches above him were heavy with needles and cones, creating a thick layer of greenery. The lowest branch was barely out of his reach. If he jumped he might be able to get a hand on it.

He tossed the Winchester into some brush where he could retrieve it later . . . if he was still alive.

After rubbing his hands together for a second, The Kid bent his knees, gathered his strength, and jumped. He grabbed the branch with both hands and hung on tight. Ignoring the discomfort of the rough bark he pulled himself up. The toes of his boots dug against the trunk helping him climb.

He hooked an arm all the way over the branch and swung a leg up, getting it a little higher with each attempt until he was able to hook it over the branch, too. From there, it wasn't all that difficult to pull himself up so he sprawled on top of the branch, which was about as big around as his thigh.

Being careful to keep himself balanced, The Kid took a minute or so to get used to being in the tree. Then he edged closer to the trunk and grasped it to help pull himself up.

Within seconds, he was standing on the branch, hugging the tree trunk. Branches thrust out from the trunk all around him. He clambered up them, moving carefully to avoid a fall. The last thing he needed with somebody gunning for him was a broken arm or leg.

It was just a matter of waiting for the bushwhacker to get curious enough to ride over there and investigate.

Luckily, The Kid had developed some patience, a quality he'd never had to any great degree when he was still the rich, spoiled young man named Conrad Browning. He had started to grow up a little when he met and got to know his father, but that first meeting hadn't happened until Conrad was nearly grown.

Meeting and marrying Rebel Callahan had helped mature him even more. But Rebel was dead and buried, and once the men responsible for her death had been tracked down and dealt with, Conrad had decided to bury his own past as well.

He had adopted the identity of a gunfighter and became known as Kid Morgan to conceal his true identity and help him in his quest for vengeance. Even though it was no longer needed, he had realized that he would rather continue to be The Kid than go back to being Conrad Browning.

So he had turned his back on what he was and kept drifting. Despite his desire to be left alone with his grief, trouble and danger seemed to seek him out. Being ambushed was the latest instance.

Confident that he couldn't be seen from the ground, at least not easily, The Kid remained motionless. After what seemed like ages but was probably more like an hour, he heard a horse's hoofbeats steadily coming down the hill toward his hiding place.

The rider wasn't in any hurry. He knew that his quarry might be laying a trap for him.

The Kid was counting on the fact that the bushwhacker might not expect any danger from above.

The horse came closer and closer. Carefully, The Kid parted a couple pine boughs, taking pains not to dislodge any cones. He looked down and saw the rider pass underneath the tree.

"Damn it, I know it was somewhere right around here that I saw him last," the man muttered.

The Kid couldn't see the bushwhacker's face, since he was looking almost straight down at the man. All he could see was the top of a broad-brimmed hat and enough of the man's clothes to tell that he was wearing range garb. He carried some sort of long-barreled hunting rifle across the saddle in front of him, which had enabled him to take those long-range shots.

The Kid was fortunate the man's aim had been slightly off on his first attempt. After that, The Kid had been moving enough so the man hadn't been able to draw a good bead on him.

The bushwhacker kept riding. The Kid moved

another branch aside so that he could watch the man. He leveled the Colt and centered the sights on the man's back.

It would have been easy to pull the trigger and blow the man out of the saddle. But that would probably kill him, and a dead man couldn't answer any questions. The Kid wanted to know why someone was trying to kill him. A thing like that could turn out to be important.

The rider kept moving. Since there was no telling where he might go, The Kid holstered his gun and crept out quickly on the branch, until it started to droop under him. Grasping it with his hands, he let his feet drop and swung out, releasing his hold so that he dropped right on the bushwhacker's back.

The unexpected impact knocked the man forward on his mount's neck. The horse shied and lunged ahead. The Kid felt himself falling, and wrapped an arm around the man's neck. Hanging on tightly, he dragged the man out of the saddle with him.

They crashed to the ground, the landing knocking them apart. The Kid rolled over and came up swinging. The bushwhacker, gasping for breath, struggled upright just in time for The Kid's rocketing fist to slam into his jaw.

The blow landed cleanly and knocked the bushwhacker sprawling. The Kid leaped and landed on top of him.

Before the man could fight back, The Kid palmed out his revolver and pressed the muzzle up under the man's chin.

"Freeze or I'll blow your head off," The Kid warned.

"That's good advice, friend," a voice said from behind him. "You'd damned well better heed it."

Chapter 2

The Kid knew the words had the threat of a gun behind them. But he was far from helpless. He said, "Back off, mister. No matter how fast you shoot me, it won't be fast enough to keep me from killing your friend."

The second man laughed. "Friend?" he repeated. "Who said anybody so damned dumb as to get himself jumped on from a tree would be a friend of mine?"

The man had a point there, The Kid supposed.

He could see the face of the man he had tackled. The man's hat had come off, revealing thinning dark hair over an olive-skinned face. The left eye had a peculiar cast to it. Dark beard stubble shadowed his jaw.

The Kid had never seen him before.

Without moving the gun, he said, "Did you fellows ever stop to think that maybe this is all a misunderstanding?"

"Naw, you're the varmint we're after," said the man behind him. "You match the description on the wanted posters."

Bounty hunters! The men were bounty hunters. That explained everything, and they had indeed come close to killing him over some stupid mistake. "Listen to me," he said. "I'm not Bloody Ben Bledsoe. I just look a little like him."

A couple months earlier, The Kid had gone through pure hell because of that resemblance. Bloody Ben Bledsoe was an outlaw who had broken out of prison in New Mexico Territory. The Kid had been captured by a bounty hunter who mistook him for Bledsoe and dragged him back to that hellhole.

It had taken all sorts of trouble to straighten everything out, and a lot of people had died along the way, some innocent, some definitely not.

"Bledsoe?" the man behind The Kid repeated. "I heard Ben Bledsoe got hisself killed down in Arizona. I'm talkin' about Kid Morgan. You're him, and we're takin' you in."

The Kid's breath caught in his throat. He felt like he'd been punched in the gut. "That's crazy. There aren't any charges against me."

"That ain't what the wanted posters say. The Territory of New Mexico wants you for breakin' out of prison and killin' some guards. There's a bounty of ten thousand dollars on your head, Kid. Ten grand, American . . . and Lester and me aim to collect."

"Be . . . be careful, Mack," the man on the ground said. "He could kill me with the twitch of a finger!"

"Well, that'd be a damned shame," Mack said. "But you know, if he did, I don't reckon I'd have to share that ree-ward with nobody, now would I?"

The Kid heard the finality in Mack's voice.

The bounty hunter had decided it would be easier to go ahead and shoot him, no matter what happened to the man's partner.

Knowing that a bullet was about to be on its way to his back, The Kid threw himself aside just as Mack's gun roared.

The other man tried to roll out of the way as soon as The Kid's weight was no longer pinning him to the ground, but he moved too late. The slug sizzled through the space where The Kid had been a shaved heartbeat earlier, struck Lester in the face, and tore half his jaw away.

The Kid landed on his back and spotted a short man with a big beer gut standing about ten feet away. He tried to swing his .44 toward The Kid, but he was far too slow.

The Colt in The Kid's hand bucked as he squeezed off three shots so swiftly the blasts sounded like one long roar. The slugs punched into Mack's midsection, boring through the layer of fat, penetrating deep into his belly. The impact of the bullets knocked him back a step and made his derby hat fall off his bald head. He stayed on his feet for a moment, groaning and staggering to the side as he dropped his gun.

"You . . . son of a . . ."

He couldn't finish the curse. Blood welled over the fingers he pressed to his bullet-ravaged belly. He fell to his knees and then pitched forward onto his face.

The Kid leaped to his feet and swung around to check on Lester.

Moaning and flopping around as he pawed at his ruined face, he was no longer a threat. Dark red blood pooled around his head.

As The Kid watched, Lester went limp and sagged back against the ground. His head flopped to the side, and his glassy eyes seemed to be staring right at The Kid, even though they could no longer see anything.

The Kid hoped there had only been two of them.

Carefully, he checked to make sure both men were dead. Satisfied that they were, he replaced the three rounds he had fired with fresh cartridges from the loops on his shell belt under the tails of the dark coat he wore and then holstered the gun.

He looked around until he found his black, flat-crowned hat that had come off when he first leaped out of the saddle. Picking it up, he slapped it against his leg to get the loose pine needles off, and settled it on his head.

Lester's horse hadn't gone far, and The Kid brought it back to the place where the two men had died. The coppery scent of blood hanging in the air, along with the acrid tang of gunsmoke, made the animal nervous. The Kid tied the reins around a sapling to keep the horse from bolting again.

With that done, he fetched his buckskin and the Winchester and looked around for Mack's horse. He found the animal about a hundred yards up the slope, tied in the trees.

Returning to where he'd been ambushed, The Kid muttered, "You were nothing but a Judas goat, Lester," then chided himself silently for talking to a dead man.

He checked their pockets and found a small amount of money, a deck of greasy cards, tobacco pouches and cigarette papers, and, in a pocket inside Mack's coat, a small silver flask half full of whiskey.

None of that was what The Kid was looking for. He dug into their saddlebags, and in the one on Mack's horse, he found what he sought. He unfolded the piece of paper and smoothed it out. It was a wanted poster, all right, with his name and description on it. In big letters across the top, it declared $10,000 REWARD. The charges were murder, attempted murder, and escaping from prison.

The Kid's pulse pounded like a drum inside his skull as he stared down at the crudely printed poster. The charges were lies, all lies. He had never killed any of those guards at Hell Gate Prison, nor had he tried to kill them.

He had escaped because it was the only way to clear his name. In the end, when the real Ben Bledsoe had been brought to justice, The Kid had been assured there would be no charges leveled at him because of the prison break.

It was all a terrible mistake.

But two men lay dead on the ground at his feet because of that mistake. And with a ten grand price on his head, Mack and Lester wouldn't be the last ones to come hunting The Kid.

He uttered a bitter curse as he thought about what might happen if the bogus reward dodgers had spread across the frontier already. There was no place he would be safe. Ten thousand dollars was enough to put every bounty hunter west of the Mississippi on his trail. And something else on the wanted poster made the situation even worse.

Under his name and description and the list of the charges against him was the legend printed across the bottom of the paper.

In big, bold letters, just like the amount of the reward . . .

DEAD OR ALIVE.

Chapter 3

The Kid left the two dead bounty hunters where they had fallen. He wasn't by nature a callous person, but Mack and Lester had tried to kill him, so he wasn't going to lose any sleep over leaving them for the scavengers.

As he rode away, he pondered his best course of action. He was in the southeastern corner of Nevada, where the state extended in a triangle between California to the west and the territories of Arizona and Utah to the east. The nearest settlement he knew of was the little mining town of Las Vegas, which he had passed through a few days earlier.

A long way off in the mountains to the northwest lay his former home, Carson City, and the mining town of Buckskin, where his father had served for a time as marshal. The Kid had friends in both places, or rather, Conrad Browning did.

But both places also held bitter memories for him, memories that went far beyond the taste of wormwood and gall. Rebel had been abducted from their home in Carson City. Later Conrad had burned it down to make it look as if he, too, had died so the men responsible for Rebel's death wouldn't expect him to come after them.

He wasn't going back to that part of Nevada, he

decided. He might never visit Carson City or Buckskin again, and that would be just fine with him. There was nothing left for him in either place.

It would be a good idea, though, to get in touch with his personal attorney, Claudius Turnbuckle in San Francisco. Claudius would be able to contact the territorial authorities in New Mexico and find out why those wanted posters had been issued. The Kid needed to get the price on his head lifted as soon as possible, before too many bounty hunters set out on his trail.

Las Vegas had a telegraph office, he recalled. He could backtrack and send a wire to Claudius from there, so the lawyer could get started toward clearing up the mess.

The Kid rode east toward the little settlement.

It didn't take him long to reach the edge of the mountains. He paused in the foothills and looked out over the vast sprawl of desert and plains in front of him. He could make Las Vegas in a day if he pushed the buckskin.

But it was too late in the day to start across. The sun was almost touching the rugged peaks behind him. Better to wait and get a fresh start in the morning, he told himself.

His eyes narrowed as he spotted a thin haze of dust hanging in the air. That meant riders. He couldn't tell if they were coming toward him or going away from him.

The Kid's frown deepened as he watched the dust for several minutes. Definitely coming toward him, he thought. More than one or two riders, maybe as many as half a dozen.

Of course, they weren't necessarily looking for him. They could be on their way somewhere else and not have anything to do with him at all. But it wasn't a well-populated or widely-traveled area The Kid was riding through. He was simply drifting. He'd wanted to put Arizona, and his troubles there, behind him.

The sight of that dust definitely made him suspicious. All the more reason to hole up somewhere for the night, he told himself. If those riders *were* looking for him, he didn't want to run right into them.

With that in mind, he rode north along a rocky ridge until he came to a spot where several large boulders clustered, and he could make a small fire without it being seen. There wasn't much graze for his horse, or water for either of them, but his two canteens were nearly full and he had a little grain left in the pouch that he carried. He and the buckskin could get along just fine until morning.

As dusk began to settle over the rugged landscape, The Kid unsaddled his horse and found enough dried brush to build a tiny fire just big enough to boil some coffee. He had jerky and some stale biscuits in his saddlebags. That would do for a meal.

It was a far cry from the times he had dined in the finest restaurants in Boston, New York, and Philadelphia, he thought as he hunkered on his heels next to the fire. Those days had been more comfortable, but he didn't miss them. He felt like he had never been fully alive until he came west.

He couldn't see the dust anymore in the fading light. The riders might have stopped to make camp for the night, or he might have just lost sight of the dust their horses raised. Either way, The Kid didn't care. He wanted to steer clear of them, whoever they were.

And yet, as he finished his meager supper and sipped his coffee, doubts began to nag at his mind. Maybe it would be better to know who the men were. If they weren't looking for him, he could stop worrying about them. If they were . . . he'd have some warning, and he could start figuring out how to deal with that.

To determine who they were and what they were after, he'd have to find their camp. When he gazed along the line of foothills to the south, he picked out an orange glow that came from a campfire. It had to be the bunch he had spotted earlier. There couldn't be two groups of riders spending the night at the edge of those isolated mountains.

Well, there *could* be, he thought, but it was mighty unlikely.

The fact that they weren't trying to conceal

their campfire told him there were enough of them to feel confident they could handle any trouble that came their way. He would be a fool not to stay as far away from them as he could.

Unfortunately, his curiosity nagged at him. He finished off the last of his coffee and cleaned up after the meal. By that time, the last of the sunset's rosy glow had disappeared from the sky. It was full dark, with millions of stars glittering in the sable sky overhead.

The Kid estimated the campfire he saw was about a mile away from the boulders where he had stopped. It was a quiet night. The sound of a horse's hoofbeats would travel a long way in the thin, still air.

If he wanted to spy on the men, he would have to approach their camp on foot. He thought he might be able to work his way close enough to get a good look at them and perhaps even overhear what they were talking about.

He had picketed the buckskin, so the horse couldn't wander. After heaping sand on what was left of the fire to put out any embers, The Kid put his saddle back on the horse, just in case he needed the animal in a hurry. He patted the buckskin on the shoulder and said, "I'll be back after a while."

If anything happened to him, the buckskin would be able to pull loose eventually. From there it would have to fend for itself. Bands of wild mustangs ran free in that part of the country and it might be able to join one of them.

The Kid left all his gear and headed for the camp in the distance. His boots weren't really made for walking, but unlike cowboys who had spent their whole working lives in the saddle, he wasn't totally averse to being on foot now and then.

The darkness and the rough terrain meant he couldn't travel very fast. It took him close to an hour to reach the vicinity of the camp. As he approached he moved slower and more carefully. He didn't want to accidentally stumble right into the middle of them.

Several different aromas told him he was getting close: woodsmoke, food, coffee, tobacco. He paused to listen and heard the murmur of voices, followed by a man's laughter. He couldn't make out any of the words, but he thought he heard several different voices.

As silently as possible, he crept closer. A massive slab of rock leaned away from him, and he thought if he climbed to the top of it, he might be able to look down into their camp.

It was still warm under his hands as the stone clung to the heat of the day. The air had more than a hint of coolness in it, typical of the desert atmosphere. By morning, the temperature would be cold enough to make a man's breath steam in front of his face.

The men gathered around the campfire were still talking, so he counted on that to cover up the tiny scraping noises his boots made against the rock as he climbed. When he reached the top, he took his hat off and set it aside. Carefully, he edged his head higher to peer over the lip of the rock slab.

The men had built their campfire in the lee of the rock. It would reflect heat back and keep the camp warmer during the night. The fire had died down some, but flames still leaped and crackled merrily.

Five men sat around the fire, talking and passing a bottle back and forth. They wore rough range clothes and had hard-planed, beard-stubbled faces.

They were well-armed. Each man sported at least one holstered revolver, and a couple carried two guns. Several Winchesters were stacked nearby, and The Kid saw a Sharps carbine and a shotgun among the long guns, as well.

A sixth figure sat a short distance off, his legs stuck out in front of him and crossed at the ankle. He wore a poncho and leaned back against a smaller rock. Judging by the way his head drooped forward with his hat brim pulled down over his face, he was asleep.

From atop the big rock The Kid could hear what the men were saying, and he didn't like what he heard.

". . . can't be too far ahead of us. He was in Las Vegas a couple days ago."

"Yeah, but who knows how far he could have gotten in two days?"

The first man spoke again. "Everybody we talked to said he didn't seem to be in any hurry. It's been like that ever since we left Arizona."

One of the other men said, "It's almost like Morgan don't know there's a ten grand price tag on his head."

That confirmed it, The Kid thought. The men were bounty hunters, too, and they were on his trail. He had done well to avoid them.

He would continue to do so. As late as it was, they would be turning in soon. He decided he would stay right where he was for the time being, wait until all or most of them were asleep, and then slip away, back to his camp.

In the morning, they would go west, deeper into the mountains, and he would head east toward Las Vegas. He would have to be very careful. Word might have gotten around the settlement that he was a wanted man. He wondered what sort of law they had there.

A new sound intruded on The Kid's thoughts. It came from behind him, and it sent alarm coursing through his veins. It was a deep, throaty, animal growl, full of menace.

The Kid swung around and looked down at the ground on the far side of the rock slab. The silvery illumination of starlight was enough for him to make out the big, shaggy shape crouched at the base of the rock. Whatever it was, it obviously wanted to tear his throat out and gnaw the meat from his bones.

With a surge of muscles and a flash of razor-sharp teeth, the snarling beast bounded up the rock toward him.

Chapter 4

The Kid could have drawn his gun and shot the dog. It wouldn't give away his position since all the bounty hunters could follow the sound of the dog's snarls.

Instead, he took the desperate chance of waiting until the savage brute leaped at him so he could duck under the attack. He fell back as the dog lunged at his throat. The animal's teeth snapped on empty air.

The Kid's hands shot up and grabbed the thick, shaggy body. Using the dog's own weight and momentum against it, he heaved the dog over his head and past the lip of the rock.

The dog howled as it plummeted toward the ground and the fire below.

The men around the campfire yelled in alarm, and although The Kid could no longer see them from where he was, he figured they were on their feet, surprised to see the dog come sailing down out of the night sky at them.

The Kid didn't wait around to see what happened. He took off down the massive stone slab, not bothering to be quiet about the descent. He almost pitched forward out of control as he reached the ground in three giant bounds.

As soon as his boots hit the sandy soil, he caught his balance and headed for the place he'd left his horse. A lot of yelling still came from the camp, but it didn't sound like the bounty hunters were coming after him yet.

A moment later rifles began to crack wickedly. He glanced over his shoulder and saw flashes spurting from the muzzles of the long guns.

The men couldn't see him in the darkness and were firing in the direction they thought he might have gone. The Kid heard a couple bullets hum overhead and another whistled past a few yards to his right, but none of them came any closer than that.

Then he heard the order he'd been expecting. One of the men bellowed, "Get your horses! Spread out and find that son of a bitch!"

In a matter of seconds, hoofbeats pounded behind him. All he could do was keep running.

One of the men shouted, "Over there! I see him!"

The hoofbeats got louder as he galloped after The Kid.

As the horse thundered up right behind him, The Kid spun around. A pistol barked, but the man had fired too quickly. The slug whistled past The Kid's ear.

That decided it. If they were willing to kill him without even knowing who he was, without having any idea that he was actually the man they were hunting, he was willing to return the favor.

His gun leaped into his hand and spouted flame

as he jumped aside to avoid being trampled. The bullet struck the rider in the chest like a sledgehammer and swept him backward out of the saddle.

With his free hand, The Kid made a grab for the trailing reins the man had dropped. He caught them and hung on tightly, feeling like the horse was going to pull his arm right out of its socket, as he ran alongside.

After a moment, his weight caused the horse to stop. The Kid acted instantly, vaulting up into the saddle. His feet found the stirrups and jabbed his heels into the horse's flanks, sending it leaping forward into a gallop again.

Everything had happened so fast, The Kid hoped the rest of the bounty hunters might not realize he had taken their partner's place on the back of the horse. Since he was out in front of the others, he kept moving, hoping they would mistake him for the man he'd shot.

A lot of whooping and hollering came from the men behind him, but they held their fire.

The Kid was a couple hundred yards ahead of them when he reached his camp. He dismounted on the run and never slowed down as he jerked the buckskin's reins free and leaped into the saddle. A heartbeat later, he had the horse running strong, stretching its long legs into a swift gallop.

"What the hell!" one of the bounty hunters

shouted a moment later as they pounded up to the camp. "Here's Jagger's horse!"

Jagger had to be the man he'd blasted out of the saddle, The Kid thought as he leaned forward over the buckskin's neck and urged the animal on to greater speed.

"That fella ahead of us must be the one who was sneakin' around our camp!"

The pursuit was on again.

But The Kid was mounted on a superior animal. He didn't know the quality of horseflesh that belonged to his pursuers, but he was well aware of the buckskin's capabilities. His horse had plenty of speed and stamina and could outrun most horses.

The problem was that the buckskin wasn't fresh. He really hadn't had much chance to rest after being on the trail all day.

Neither had the horses belonging to the bounty hunters, The Kid told himself. They might have a slight edge, but he was still betting on the buckskin.

Betting his life on it, in fact.

The Kid headed east, away from the foothills and across the semi-arid plain that stretched all the way to Las Vegas. The moon had risen, and it cast enough silvery light so the bounty hunters would be able to spot him as they trailed him.

At least they had stopped shooting at him, having figured out they weren't going to hit him unless it was by sheer luck. They were still behind him, though. He saw them when he glanced over his shoulder, dark blobs moving through the glimmering wash of moonlight.

The buckskin was as gallant as ever, running along seemingly effortlessly. The Kid had to trust to luck that the horse wouldn't step in a hole or stumble over something and trip. If the buckskin went down, the fall might kill both of them.

If it didn't, the bounty hunters would soon take care of that.

His horse couldn't run forever. The Kid's only hope was that the mounts of the pursuers would play out first.

His spirits rose as that began to happen. He looked back and saw that the bounty hunters were strung out in a line. Some of them were dropping back, falling out of the chase.

One of the riders in particular wasn't slowing down. In fact, he appeared to have drawn closer, indicating his horse was faster than The Kid's buckskin.

The Kid muttered a curse. Facing one man was better than facing all five of them, but he had hoped to get away without having to kill any more.

Deserved or not, he was in enough legal trouble without having any more fatal shootings attached to his name. Claudius Turnbuckle had plenty to straighten out without that.

It looked like he wasn't going to be able to avoid swapping lead with the man closing in on him. The stubborn rider was close enough The Kid could see he was mounted on a big, dark horse that seemed to be flying over the landscape.

The Kid debated whether it would be better to stop and fight it out. But even if he won, he realized, the delay would give the others a chance to catch up to him. They had fallen far back, but it wouldn't take them long to draw even with him if he stopped.

His best chance was to keep going.

A dark line loomed in front of him, twisting across the ground like a snake. His heart sank as he recognized it as an arroyo. He couldn't see either end of it. Running north and south, it blocked his path as effectively as if it was a rock wall.

The Kid bit back a groan of despair. He wasn't going to give up. He had been through too much in his life simply to surrender.

He hauled back on the reins and brought the buckskin to a skidding halt at the edge of the arroyo. It was a dozen feet deep and almost twice that wide. The banks weren't so steep that he couldn't dismount and lead the horse down them, and probably up and out the other side, but the time needed to do that would allow the bounty hunters to catch up to him.

So it was a fight. If that was what fate had in store for him, so be it.

Swiftly, he dismounted and pulled the Winchester from the saddle boot. Leading the buckskin to the very edge of the arroyo, he swiped off his hat and slapped it against the horse's rump. The buckskin began picking its way down the slope. The Kid wanted the horse out of the line of fire.

He went a short distance down the slope himself and dropped to one knee. The ground itself gave him some cover. The man on the black, fast horse was about fifty yards away.

The Kid levered a round into the Winchester's firing chamber. He brought the rifle to his shoulder, sighted in the moonlight, and pulled the trigger.

Chapter 5

The Winchester cracked and kicked hard against his shoulder. The .44-40 slug passed over the rider's head and screamed off into the night.

The Kid had aimed high, hoping it would turn the bounty hunter back. Charging right at him while he had a good defensive position was suicide.

The rider didn't slow down. If anything, the horse galloped faster. Colt flame bloomed in the darkness as the bounty hunter opened fire with a revolver.

The bullets fell short, but they came close enough to kick up dirt into The Kid's face. He slid down the bank a little as he blinked rapidly, blinded by the grit that stung his eyes.

The big black horse flashed toward him, never slowing. The Kid's vision cleared just in time for him to see the huge animal practically on top of him.

With a startled yell, he jerked backward and lost his balance, rolling down the rest of the bank to the sandy bottom of the arroyo. As he rolled he caught only fragmented glimpses of one of the most amazing things he had ever seen.

With all its powerful muscles behind it, the black horse took off from the bank, sailing up and over the arroyo. As if the animal had somehow sprouted wings, the horse stayed in the air for what seemed like an impossible time. Its front hooves stretched out, out, as the far bank rushed at it.

The Kid came to a stop on his back and watched as those hooves cleared the edge of the arroyo by mere inches, digging in and hauling the rest of the horse's body forward as momentum carried it on. Then somehow all four hooves were on the ground and the horse was slowing, turning. The rider's gun came up, and The Kid knew he was about to be caught in a crossfire.

He had managed to hang on to his rifle as he tumbled down the slope. Rolling onto his side, he propped himself up on an elbow, and fired.

The bounty hunter's handgun belched flame again. The bullet thudded into the arroyo wall several feet above The Kid, as the rider swayed and toppled out of the saddle.

Still a little out of breath, The Kid leaped to his feet. He hoped the hunter wasn't fatally wounded, but he didn't have time to worry about that. The buckskin stood nearby. The Kid grabbed the horse's reins and led him up the far side of the arroyo.

He heard hoofbeats approaching as the other bounty hunters picked their way down the bank as fast as they could.

Shots began to roar again. The Kid ignored them. If one of the bullets was destined to find him, so be it. His eyes were on the big black horse.

The magnificent animal represented his last chance to escape.

The horse had shied away from the crumpled figure sprawled on the ground. In the moonlight, The Kid saw that the man he'd shot wasn't moving. It was the bounty hunter wearing the poncho, he realized. Some of the loose garment was draped over the man's head.

The Kid grabbed the black's trailing reins. For the second time that night, he stole a horse. The black sunfished a little as The Kid swung into the saddle, but his firm hand on the reins settled the animal down. Still leading the buckskin, The Kid kicked the black into a gallop.

The shots from the remaining bounty hunters were coming closer. He felt the windrip of several bullets as they passed close to his head. But none of them found him, and the range instantly grew longer as the black horse lunged over the ground.

Leaning forward in the saddle to make himself a smaller target, The Kid hung on to the buckskin's reins, not wanting to lose the horse. They had been through a lot together. Freed of the burden of having to carry The Kid's weight, the buckskin was able to keep up with the big black. Both horses swept swiftly over the ground.

As the bounty hunters crossed the arroyo and stopped to check on their fallen comrade, The Kid was increasing his lead. For the first time since the chase had begun, he thought there was a good chance he might get away.

Being a bit superstitious he chided himself for thinking such a thing, not wanting to jinx it. But no misfortune befell him as he continued galloping eastward.

After a while, sensing that even the powerful brute beneath him was tiring, he pulled the horses back to a walk, giving him a chance to hip around in the saddle and gaze behind him. He didn't see anything moving through the moonlight and brought both horses to a halt, listening intently.

Nothing. No sound of hoofbeats. He was either so far ahead of the pursuit that it was out of earshot . . .

Or the bounty hunters had given up and abandoned the chase.

The Kid couldn't risk believing that just yet. He gave the horses a few minutes to rest, then started out again at a relatively slow pace, increasing it as they went along until he was pushing them fairly hard again.

Later—long after midnight, judging by the stars and the moon's progression across the heavens—The Kid stopped again to let the horses rest. When he didn't see or hear any signs of pursuit, he had to admit it seemed like he had given the bounty hunters the slip.

Would they try to trail him? Or would they cut

their losses, turn around, and head west again to search for Kid Morgan and the ten thousand dollar reward on his head?

None of them had gotten a good look at him. When he thought back over everything that had happened, The Kid was sure of that. So the bounty hunters didn't know he was actually the man they were after.

He hoped ten grand, American, would be a greater temptation than avenging the two men he'd been forced to shoot. He didn't know for certain that either of them was dead, but it was a strong possibility.

The Kid kept moving all night, stopping only occasionally to let the horses blow. As the eastern sky was turning orange with the approach of dawn, The Kid checked the saddlebags draped over the black horse's back. He thought he might find some clue to the bounty hunter's identity. There might be something he would need to send—anonymously, of course—to the man's family.

He found supplies, ammunition, a spare Colt revolver, a roll of bills that added up to several hundred dollars . . . and an envelope. It was addressed to "L. McCall," in care of a hotel in Tucson.

The Kid turned the envelope over, saw a return address scrawled on the flap. The name on it was Hoskins, and the address was in Kansas City, Missouri.

The Kid didn't particularly want to read McCall's mail, but he decided it would be better to see what was in the envelope. A letter might tell him more about the man he'd been forced to shoot.

Maybe more than he really wanted to know, he thought warily.

But he lifted the envelope's flap, slid a couple fingers inside, and brought out a folded piece of paper. It was blank and had been wrapped around a photograph to protect it. The Kid lifted the picture, turning so the dawn light fell over it.

The photograph was of a little girl, probably four or five years old. She wore a frilly dress, nothing real fancy or expensive, but nice. Long, pale hair fell over her shoulders. She had gazed into the camera with a solemn expression on her face. The Kid supposed she was pretty, although he wasn't much of a judge of such things.

He turned the photograph over, thinking there might be a name or something written on the back. Nothing was there except the name of a photography studio in Kansas City. No hint of who the girl was or how she was related to the bounty hunter named McCall.

As far as The Kid could tell, if anybody had a rightful claim to the money McCall had saved up, it was the little girl. Whoever had sent the picture ought to have it back, too. McCall didn't need it anymore.

When he got to Las Vegas, The Kid decided, as soon as he had sent a wire to Claudius Turnbuckle, he would wrap up the photograph and the cash and send it to Hoskins, whoever that was, at the address in Kansas City. He didn't need or want the money himself. Since it had belonged to a bounty hunter, it might well be blood money.

But the little girl wouldn't know that, and she might need it.

Carefully, The Kid folded the photograph back into the piece of paper, slipped it into the envelope, and replaced it in the saddlebag, along with the roll of greenbacks.

He gave the horses some water, pouring it into his hat from one of the canteens and letting them drink. Then he had a drink himself and splashed some of the water over his head, shaking the droplets away. In the cool morning air, it would help him stay awake and alert, since he hadn't had the chance to get any rest the night before.

That done, he mounted up again, riding the buckskin and leading the black. The big horse was even more impressive in the growing daylight than he had been in the silvery moonlight.

The Kid wasn't sure what to do with the black. People would remember a horse like that. Leading it could draw more attention than he wanted and somebody in Las Vegas might recognize it as McCall's. He was already worried that somebody might recognize him as Kid

Morgan from the description on those wanted posters.

At the same time, he hated to let the black go. A man didn't run into a horse like that every day. Sure, the black didn't belong to him, but he thought the fact that McCall had done his damnedest to kill him ought to count for something.

He would figure it out later, The Kid told himself, when he got closer to Las Vegas.

For now he rode east, into the rising sun.

Chapter 6

In the end, that afternoon he found a place to camp a couple miles outside the settlement and left the black there. It was a little canyon formed by a pair of sheer, rocky upthrusts. A tiny creek trickled through it, no doubt fed by springs higher in the ridges, and hardy grass grew alongside the stream to give the black something to graze on.

The Kid unsaddled the horse and tied the reins to a scrubby bush growing out of one of the canyon walls, making sure they were loose enough so the black could pull away if The Kid didn't ever come back. From there, the horse would probably wander into town.

If it was possible, though, The Kid intended to return and claim the animal for himself. A man who could switch back and forth between two horses like the black and the buckskin could outrun just about anybody.

Riding the buckskin, The Kid headed into Las Vegas. The day had grown hot, so he wasn't wearing his black coat, and the sleeves of his white shirt were rolled up a couple of turns over his tanned forearms.

The town wasn't very big, with only a single main street and a few cross streets. The springs that made Las Vegas a green oasis in the middle of a vast brown-and-tan landscape had attracted many different people over the years, beginning with the Piute Indians. Mormons had established a settlement there, but it hadn't lasted.

The discovery of gold and silver in the nearby hills had made Las Vegas spring to life again, and ever since it had flickered in and out of existence like a candle flame, depending on how the mines were producing. At times it was a bustling settlement, but it went through stretches when it was little more than a ghost town.

The place seemed to be doing all right. A spur line had been built from the main route of the Santa Fe Railroad in the south, and that had brought the telegraph wires with it as well.

Those telegraph wires were what interested The Kid. The sooner he got in touch with his lawyer, the better.

A water tank stood at the far end of the settlement, beside the railroad tracks. The telegraph office was inside the depot. The Kid had to ride the entire length of the street to get there.

No one seemed to pay any attention to him. He didn't hurry, keeping the buckskin at a casual pace, instead.

Halfway to his destination gunfire roared out.

Women screamed and men shouted curses. Everybody in the street and along the boardwalks scurried for cover. The Kid reined in sharply and looked for the source of the shots. Whoever was burning powder didn't seem to be shooting at him.

Several men spilled from the double doors of an impressive two story building constructed of large sandstone blocks. Painted on the wall above the awning over the boardwalk were the words FIRST BANK OF LAS VEGAS.

That and the gunshots were enough to tell The Kid what was going on, even before he saw the bandannas pulled up over the faces of the men who ran out. Smoke curled from the barrels of the guns in their hands.

A bank robbery was none of his business. He had problems of his own. He was willing to let the outlaws get away, though the possibility they might have killed someone during the shootout in the bank nagged at him.

But then a man came running around the corner carrying a shotgun. Sunlight winked off the badge pinned to his shirt.

The four masked men who had just run out of the bank saw him and swung their guns toward the lawman.

The Kid knew they could fire before the man would be able to bring his scattergun to bear and yelled, "Hey!" He palmed out his Colt and squeezed off a shot.

The slug hit one of the outlaws in the back of his right shoulder, shattering bone and spinning him halfway around. He dropped his gun and let out a howl of pain as he staggered into the street clutching the wound and collapsed.

Realizing they were suddenly caught between two fires caused the remaining outlaws to hesitate, giving the lawman time to raise the shotgun and squeeze off both barrels. Flame gushed from the weapon's twin muzzles.

The double load of buckshot tore into two of the robbers, flinging them backward and shredding their flesh. When they landed on the boardwalk, their chests and faces looked like raw meat.

That left only one of the outlaws on his feet, and as The Kid snapped a shot at him, he twisted around and darted back through the open doors into the building. The Kid's bullet missed and chipped dust and stone splinters from the wall next to the door.

The lawman started toward the entrance, obviously intending to pursue the lone remaining robber into the bank. He didn't notice the wounded outlaw in the street had clambered up onto his knees and was fumbling to pick up his fallen gun with his left hand.

The Kid saw the threat and was swinging down from the saddle even as the outlaw finally succeeded in scooping the revolver from the ground.

Moving to where the man could see him, The Kid leveled his Colt and warned, "Don't do it!"

The outlaw hesitated for a heartbeat, then jerked the gun toward The Kid.

Left with no choice, The Kid fired. The slug hammered into the wounded outlaw's chest and drove him over on his back. The gun in his left hand went off, but it was pointed at the sky and the bullet sailed off harmlessly.

The lawman had disappeared into the bank, hot on the heels of the fleeing outlaw. The Kid bounded onto the boardwalk and stepped into the doorway as a woman screamed.

Instantly, his eyes took in the scene. The outlaw had managed to grab a hostage. His arm was looped around the neck of a terrified woman as he dragged her backward. Her body acted as a shield.

The man thrust his gun toward the lawman, who had dropped his empty greener and hauled out an old, long-barreled revolver. It was a standoff as the badge-toter pointed his gun at the bank robber and the hostage.

"Let Mrs. Grimsley go," the lawman warned. "Nobody's dead in here, so you're not facing murder charges, son. But if she gets killed, you'll hang, sure as hell."

"No, I won't," the outlaw insisted. "I'm gettin' out of here, old man. You let me go, or this lady's blood'll be on your head, not mine!"

The lawman shook his head. "It's not gonna work like that, and you know it. The only chance you have of walking out of here alive is to surrender, son."

"Stop callin' me son!" the masked bandit raged. "I ain't your son!"

"No, but you're young enough to be, and I don't want to see you dead."

The outlaw moved his gun back and forth a little, tracking from the lawman to The Kid and back again. "Who's that?" he demanded. "Your deputy?"

The lawman hadn't looked around when The Kid entered the bank. He said, "Somebody back there?"

"Yes, but I'm on your side, Sheriff," The Kid replied. "I'm the one who took a hand in the ruckus outside."

"I'm much obliged for your help, mister," the lawman said without taking his eyes off his quarry. "If you don't mind, why don't you go around back and come in that way? We'll have this varmint between us."

"Sure," The Kid said easily. "Want me to go ahead and put a bullet in him while I'm at it?"

"Sure," the lawman drawled, "unless he wises up and lets the poor lady go."

The trapped bank robber spat out a bitter curse. "All right, all right, damn it," he went on. He angled his weapon's barrel toward the ceiling and lowered the hammer. "I'm puttin' the gun down before I let go of this gal, though. I don't want you trigger-happy lawdogs ventilatin' me."

The Kid didn't bother to correct the outlaw's assumption that he was a peace officer. He kept his Colt level and steady as the man tossed the revolver on the floor. Then he gave the woman a shove that sent her stumbling clear and thrust his hands in the air.

"Don't shoot!" he urged. "I'm givin' up."

A couple sober-suited bank tellers rushed forward to help the woman, who appeared to be a customer who'd been in the bank when the holdup took place. They assisted her through a gate in a wooden railing and onto a chair, where she sat fanning her face, looking like she was about to faint.

The Kid and the local lawman converged on the outlaw from different angles. When the lawman was close enough, he suddenly lifted his gun and smashed it against the side of the robber's head. The man went down hard and didn't move.

"I'm not sure there was any call for that, Sheriff," The Kid said with a frown.

"I'm not the sheriff. I'm the marshal of Las Vegas," the lawman snapped. "And I'm too old to risk this desperado trying any tricks while I'm getting him locked up. He'll be easier to handle this way."

The Kid replaced the three rounds he had fired outside and slid the gun into leather. "I suppose it's up to you how you handle your business, Marshal."

"You're damned right it is. Like I said, I'm obliged to you for your help, but I'll do things my own way."

"Fair enough."

The Kid started to turn toward the double doors, but the marshal stopped him by saying, "Stay right where you are. I want to talk to you." He raised his voice. "Bennett! You and some of your employees lay hands on this bank robber and carry him around the corner to my jail."

A portly, balding man who was probably the bank manager or maybe even the owner pulled out a handkerchief and mopped his perspiring forehead. "Of course, Marshal," he said. He motioned for the two tellers who had helped the female hostage to come with him.

The marshal stepped over to the woman and asked, "Are you all right, Mrs. Grimsley?"

"Yes, I . . . I'm fine," she replied. She was pale and shaky, but appeared to be unharmed. "I was never so frightened in all my life as when that man grabbed me!"

"Well, he can't hurt you now. When I buffalo somebody, he stays out cold for a while."

The men from the bank, aided by a male customer, had taken hold of the unconscious outlaw and lifted him from the floor. They were ready to carry him out. After picking up his shotgun, the marshal moved to accompany them to the jail and jerked his head at The Kid.

"Come along."

The Kid was getting a little tired of being ordered around. From the looks of things, the star packer was used to getting his own way. Not wanting to draw any extra attention to himself, The Kid followed the group of men out the door.

A large crowd had gathered in front of the bank to gawk at the bloody corpses of the dead outlaws. Trying to make the gesture look natural, The Kid reached up and tugged his hat brim lower to shield more of his face. He also kept his head lowered as he fell in step beside the marshal.

"All right, you folks break it up and go on about your business!" the lawman told the crowd. "The undertaker will be here in a minute, and he'll need to get through with his wagon to load up what's left of those ne'er-do-wells."

"Did they get away with any money from the bank, Marshal?" someone in the crowd called.

"They didn't get away, period. What about it, Bennett? Did they get their thieving hands on any loot?"

The banker shook his head as he helped the other men carry the unconscious outlaw. "No, the shooting broke out before they could start emptying the tellers' drawers. They never got around to forcing me to open the vault."

"What started the ball?"

"The ball?" The banker looked baffled for a second before understanding dawned on his face.

"Oh, the shooting! Calvin here grabbed his gun and got off a shot." He nodded toward one of the tellers. "We all dived for cover when they returned the fire."

"Is that true, Calvin?" the marshal asked the man. "You keep a pistol in your drawer?"

"Yes, I do, Marshal," Calvin said. "I got held up once when I was working at a bank over in Flagstaff, and I swore it would never happen again."

"Well, that was mighty brave of you . . . and mighty foolish." The marshal's voice took on a whiplike quality, lashing at the man. "You could've gotten yourself killed, not to mention everybody else in that bank. Next time some owlhoot with a mask on his face comes in, just give him the money and let the law deal with him."

Calvin swallowed and nodded. "Yes, sir. I was just trying to do what I thought was right."

"Let the law do the thinking."

That exchange rubbed The Kid the wrong way, and he had a hunch Bennett felt the same way. Of course, Bennett was grateful the robbery had been stopped and the deposits in his bank were safe.

The Kid didn't like the idea that the marshal didn't want people to defend themselves and their property. Sure, it was necessary to have the law around, but sometimes a man had to stomp his own snakes.

The Kid smiled to himself as he kept his head down. That sounded like something Frank Morgan would say. It had been a long time since he'd seen his father.

Maybe when the mistake about the wanted posters was cleared up, he'd try to find The Drifter. It would be good to visit with Frank again.

Chapter 7

The marshal's office and jail was a squat, sturdy-looking adobe building on one of the cross streets. A frame cottage sat behind it on the same lot, and The Kid wondered if that was the marshal's living quarters.

The lawman led the way inside and directed the men with him to place the unconscious outlaw in one of the four empty cells in the cell block. They lowered the man onto the narrow bunk and filed out of the iron-barred cell.

The marshal checked the outlaw's clothes for another gun or a knife but didn't find any weapons. He stepped out and clanged the door shut.

Bennett said, "Marshal Fairmont, I intend to bring up the subject of hiring a deputy for you at the next town council meeting."

The marshal grunted. "Told you before and I'll tell you again. I don't need a deputy. I can handle things just fine without one."

Bennett used a pudgy hand to point toward The Kid. "Without this young fellow's help, you'd be dead right now, Marshal, and those outlaws would have gotten away."

"You don't know that," Fairmont said, bristling with resentment at the charge.

"I saw everything from inside the bank," Bennett insisted, "and I'm sure plenty of other people in the street did, too. This young man saved your life." He extended a hand to The Kid. "What's your name, friend?"

That sure wasn't the way The Kid had intended for his visit to Las Vegas to go. He kept his face expressionless, careful not to reveal the annoyance he felt, and shook the banker's hand. "Browning," he supplied his name curtly, using the real one for a change since, rightly or wrongly, for the moment Kid Morgan was a wanted man.

"Well, Mr. Browning, I'm grateful to you . . . every citizen of Las Vegas is grateful to you . . . for taking a hand in this affair and making sure those vicious desperadoes were brought to justice."

The Kid shook his head. "No thanks necessary. I just saw the trouble and figured I ought to take a hand."

"Not everyone would have done that. Most people run and hide when the bullets start to fly." Bennett laughed self-consciously. "I know I hit the floor pretty quickly when the shooting started in the bank."

"That's smarter than what I did," The Kid said.

He meant that more than Bennett could possibly know. The Kid hadn't wanted anybody looking at him except maybe the clerk in the telegraph office. Backing the marshal's play had been foolish.

But he hadn't been able to sit there on his horse and let the lawman get killed.

Bennett and the bank tellers were gazing at him with open admiration while Marshal Fairmont regarded him with a shrewd, somewhat resentful frown.

The Kid thought maybe it would be a good idea to get back on the buckskin and ride out of Las Vegas as soon as he could, getting while the getting was good.

"For the next twenty-four hours, your money's no good in this town," Bennett declared. "Whatever you need . . . supplies, a hotel room, food and drink . . . the bank will stand good for it." He slapped The Kid on the back. "You're a hero, my boy, a hero!"

"You'd better get back to the bank so you can see about getting all that bullet damage repaired," the marshal said with a scowl.

Bennett nodded. "That's right." He pointed at The Kid and grinned as he left the marshal's office. "Remember what I said, Mr. Browning. Whatever you want, it's on us!"

The Kid started to follow the group of men out, but Fairmont growled from behind him, "Hold it. I said I wanted to talk to you, Browning."

The Kid half turned. "What is it, Marshal? I have business to tend to."

"Is that so? I'm curious what sort of business brings you to Las Vegas, mister."

The Kid couldn't very well answer that. He said, "Nothing that concerns the law, Marshal."

"Everything concerns the law if it effects the safety of the community. And having a gunfighter in our midst is a definite safety hazard."

The Kid shook his head. "I never said I was a gunfighter."

"You didn't have to," Fairmont replied with a note of contempt in his voice. "I saw how slick you handled that Colt out there, Browning. There aren't very many men who can do that. I admit I haven't heard of any gunfighters with your name . . . but maybe it's not your real name."

"Why don't you just call me a liar while you're at it?" The Kid snapped. He turned to face the lawman as anger boiled in him. "In case you didn't notice, my gun was fighting on your side out there."

"I noticed, all right. I noticed plenty."

For a moment, the air in the marshal's office was thick with tension. Frank Morgan had told Conrad about men like that, star packers who didn't like gunfighters, no matter who they were or what they had done. Frank had been asked to leave many towns where he hadn't caused a bit of trouble, simply because the local law didn't want him around.

Maybe Fairmont would be reasonable, The Kid thought as he struggled to keep a tight rein on his temper. The man was in late middle age, with a weathered face and plenty of gray in his hair. He had probably been wearing a tin star long enough to be set in his ways, firm in his likes and his dislikes. The Kid might be able to take advantage of that.

"Look, Marshal," he said. "I have to send a telegram, and I'd like to wait a little while to see if I get a reply. Other than that, I have no interest in staying in Las Vegas. I won't be here long, and I won't cause any trouble while I *am* here."

"How can you guarantee that?"

"I suppose I can't," The Kid replied with a shrug. "But I promise you I won't be looking for any trouble."

Fairmont frowned in thought as he rubbed his chin with his left hand. His fingertips rasped a little on the silvery beard stubble that had started to sprout.

"Well, I suppose—" he began.

"Dad?" a woman's voice asked from behind The Kid. A quick flurry of footsteps sounded. "Dad, are you all right? I heard all the shooting, but I couldn't get away until now."

The Kid turned his head to look at the woman who had just come into the office. She was in her early twenties, not much more than a girl. Wings of honey-blond hair framed her face. She was tall and slender and moved with a natural grace.

"Carly, take it easy," Fairmont said. "I'm fine."

"I heard talk on the street about some killings."

The marshal nodded. "Four men tried to hold up the bank. Three of them are down at the undertaking parlor by now, I expect. The other one is safely locked up."

"You killed three men?"

"Only two." With a grudging nod toward The Kid, Fairmont added, "This young fella took care of the other one."

She turned to gaze at him. Her brown eyes were open wide with admiration. Despite not wanting to, he took off his hat. The courtesy that Western living had instilled in him demanded it.

"Then . . . you saved my father's life."

"I don't know about that," The Kid said. "Everything happened so fast, it's hard to say."

"I think you're just being modest, Mister . . . ?"

"Browning."

Might as well stick with that name for now, The Kid thought.

She held her hand out. "Well, just in case I *do* owe you my father's life, Mr. Browning, I want you to have supper with us tonight. It's a small price to put on such a debt, but I'd like to do it anyway."

"Now, blast it, Carly—" Fairmont began again.

"By the way," she said, ignoring him, "I'm Carlotta Fairmont, named after Emperor Maximilian's wife. But everyone calls me Carly."

The Kid took her hand. There wasn't much else he could do. Her grip was strong, and her palm was cool and smooth.

"I'm pleased to make your acquaintance, Miss Fairmont."

"Supper's at six." She nodded toward the rear of the jail. "That's our house, back there behind this building." A smile lit up her face as she squeezed his hand. "You *will* be there?"

The Kid felt a little like he'd been caught in an avalanche. A hundred tons of rock sliding down a mountainside wouldn't have taken "no" for an answer, either.

"I suppose so. And I'm much obliged, miss."

"Carly," she insisted. "We're not very formal around here. Las Vegas is just a rough little frontier settlement."

"All right . . . Carly."

The Kid might not have admitted it, but he got a little pleasure out of the glare that appeared on the marshal's face when he said the young woman's name.

She let go of his hand and turned back to her father. "You're sure you're all right?"

"I'm fine," he told her. "You fuss over me too blasted much, girl."

"Somebody has to," Carly said. She lifted a hand in farewell to The Kid. "I'll see you at six, Mr. Browning."

When she was gone, Fairmont said, "I don't

much like the idea of having a gunslinger sitting at my dinner table."

"It wasn't my idea, Marshal. If you want, I'll stick by what I said earlier. I'll ride out of Las Vegas just as soon as I've gotten a reply to my telegram."

Fairmont sighed. "No, if you did that, I'd never hear the end of it. You said you were coming to supper, and you're coming to supper. That's all she'll stand for."

The Kid saw how it was. The marshal bossed everybody in town, and his daughter bossed him.

"You've still got time to send that wire of yours," Fairmont went on.

The Kid put his hat back on. "That's just what I intend to do."

"Try not to shoot anybody while you're going about it."

"Only if they shoot at me first," The Kid said.

Chapter 8

Somebody had tied the buckskin's reins to the hitch rail in front of the bank. The Kid was grateful for that thoughtfulness, although he knew the buckskin wouldn't have wandered very far.

He didn't bother mounting up. Too many people in Las Vegas had seen his face for him to worry about being inconspicuous, and he led the horse down the street to the railroad station. The arrival time of the next train was chalked onto a board beside the door. The sleepy little hamlet only got a couple of trains a week. It wasn't due to arrive until two days later, in the middle of the day.

The depot was built of red sandstone, as opposed to the heavy tan blocks that made up the bank's walls. The atmosphere in the lobby was hot and sleepy, and quiet enough The Kid could hear flies buzzing.

He saw the window of the Western Union office tucked in a corner and headed for it. A gaunt, elderly clerk wearing thick spectacles and a black cap manned it. He looked almost too frail to push down the telegraph key, The Kid thought as he came up to the window and asked for a message form.

"Here you go, sonny," the old-timer said as he

slid one of the yellow flimsies under the wicket. "Stranger in Las Vegas, ain't you?"

"That's right," The Kid said. He picked up a stub of pencil from several that lay there and stepped over to a counter to compose his message.

He thought for a moment about how to word it, then wrote:

REWARD OUT FOR KID MORGAN STOP SHOULD BE NO CHARGES PENDING STOP INVESTIGATE AND QUASH STOP BROWNING

He went back to the window and handed the form to the clerk, who counted the words and named the price for sending the message. As The Kid slid a coin under the wicket, the old-timer said, "Kid Morgan, eh?"

"What about him?"

"Just a funny thing, that's all. I was just readin' about him when you come in."

The Kid stiffened. The old man might have seen one of those wanted posters and recognized him from the description. He might start yelling for help as soon as The Kid stepped out of the station.

The clerk reached down for something, and The Kid's breath caught in his throat. Surely the old fool wasn't reaching for a gun. Did he really intend to apprehend a wanted fugitive himself?

The clerk slapped a thin, yellow-backed booklet down in front of him. The Kid saw the crude drawing and the garish lettering on the front of it.

"Yes, sir," the old-timer cackled, "*Kid Morgan and the El Dorado Gold Train Robbery*. It's one hell of a yarn. Lots of fightin' and shootin'."

The Kid was startled. There were dozens of dime novels about his famous father, but he had never seen one about *him* before. He managed not to grin. When he had chosen the name Kid Morgan, he had thought it sounded like something out of a dime novel.

Now it really was.

He tapped a finger on the booklet and asked, "Where did you get this?"

"Oh, you have to send off for 'em. Some comp'ny back east publishes 'em. There's scads and scads of 'em about all these different quick-gun fellas."

"You think there's any truth to them?"

The clerk pushed out his lips and frowned in thought. "Naw, prob'ly not," he said with a shake of his head. "Some of the folks in 'em are real enough, mind you. I've done read some about Bill Cody and ol' Wild Bill Hickok, and they was real enough, but I know good an' well they never did all the things that've got wrote about 'em."

"No, probably not," The Kid agreed. "Well,

enjoy the rest of your book . . . but send that message for me first, all right?"

"Sure thing, mister. I'll get it on the wire right now."

The Kid waited while the man sat in front of the key and tapped out the message with surprising deftness considering how bent with age his fingers were. When he was finished, he swiveled toward the window and asked, "What if I get a reply?"

"I'm having supper with Marshal Fairmont and his daughter, and after that I suppose I'll be at the hotel," The Kid replied. He dropped a nickel on the counter. "Can you send a boy to bring the reply to me when it comes in?"

"Sure thing."

The Kid looked down at the dime novel again. The illustration on the front cover showed a man with an impossibly huge hat firing two revolvers into a gang of ruffians and outlaws on horseback as he stood on the top of a speeding train.

"Is this supposed to be Kid Morgan?" He pointed to the two-gun man.

"Yep, that's him, all right, defendin' the gold train." The old-timer got a sly look on his wizened face. "I ain't finished the story yet, but I'm sort of figurin' that maybe he's tryin' to fight off that bunch 'cause he wants to steal the gold for his own self."

"You could be right," The Kid said, caring only that the man in the picture didn't look a blasted thing like him. The artist had made it all up, just like the scribbler who had written what was inside the booklet.

He allowed himself a faint smile and a shake of his head as he left the depot. The things people came up with.

It was late in the afternoon but not yet time to head for the marshal's house for supper. The Kid stopped at a general store to pick up a few supplies and replenish his stock of ammunition. As the proprietor got a box of .44-40s off the shelf, he said, "You're the fella who killed those outlaws and saved all the money from the bank earlier today, aren't you?"

"It wasn't exactly like that," The Kid said. "The marshal had a bigger hand in stopping them than I did, and the way I heard it, they never actually made it out of the bank with any money."

"Well, Henry Bennett put the word out that if you wanted anything, we should just send the bill for it over to him. So you don't owe me anything for these goods, Mr. Browning."

The Kid shrugged and nodded. "All right. I'm obliged." He started to leave, then paused and asked, "Say, you wouldn't know a man by the name of McCall, would you?"

The storekeeper frowned. "McCall, McCall . . ."

he repeated. "Nope, can't say as I do. Friend of yours?"

"Not really. Just somebody I ran into, and I thought he might have come through here."

"Lots of people come through Las Vegas and never give their names to anybody. He might've even bought supplies from me without me knowing who he was. What's he look like?"

The Kid had no idea. He had never actually gotten a look at the man, other than the poncho and the broad-brimmed hat he wore.

"Never mind," he told the storekeeper. "It doesn't matter. Where's the post office?"

The man grinned and pointed to a window on the far side of the store. "You're lookin' at it. I'm the postmaster here, too. It's after operatin' hours, but if you've got something you need to mail, you can give it to me and I'll make sure it goes out in the mail bag on the train, day after tomorrow."

"Thanks. Have you got a little box of some kind, and some paper to wrap it up with?"

The storekeeper provided the supplies. The Kid stepped to a corner for some privacy and put the envelope with the picture in it and the roll of greenbacks into the box. He tore the flap with the address off the envelope, then wrapped up the package, tied it with string, and used a pencil to print the address on the outside.

After paying the postage, The Kid took his supplies and ammunition and left the store. He had done what he'd promised himself he would do. His debt to the dead bounty hunter, if such there really was, had been discharged.

He stowed the goods in his saddlebags and led the buckskin toward the middle of the settlement heading to the marshal's house.

He was aware that many of the people he passed were watching him. Loafers sitting in chairs on the front porch of the hotel passed low-voiced comments back and forth. He knew they were talking about the shootout in front of the bank.

Short of collecting a bullet, things couldn't have worked out much worse for him. The last thing he'd wanted when he rode into Las Vegas was attention, and that was practically all he had gotten.

He led the buckskin around the marshal's office and tied the horse to a scrubby tree in the little yard in front of the house. When he knocked on the door, Fairmont answered. The marshal still wore his gunbelt, but he had a pipe in his hand and looked more relaxed.

"So you showed up, eh? Might as well come in."

It wasn't the most gracious of greetings, but The Kid didn't care. He was more concerned with the delicious aromas that floated from the kitchen through the rest of the house.

He hadn't forgotten the days on bread and water

he had spent in Hell Gate Prison. He wasn't sure he ever would. The experience had given him a whole new appreciation for good food.

It was also one more reason he was never going to let himself be sent back to prison, no matter what sort of trumped-up charges somebody had leveled against him.

The Kid took off his hat as he went inside. Fairmont used the pipe stem to point at a hook on the wall where he could hang the Stetson, and ushered the visitor into a nicely furnished parlor. "Want a drink?" Fairmont asked. "I've got a bottle of brandy, but I don't break into it very often."

The Kid shook his head. "No, that's fine, thanks."

Fairmont's teeth clamped down on the pipe. "You get your telegram sent?" he asked around it.

"Yes, I did. I'm just waiting for a reply now. I hope it's all right I told the telegrapher I was having supper here. He's supposed to send a boy with the reply if it comes in."

Fairmont waved a hand and nodded. "Sure, sure, that's fine," he said. "Still plan on riding out as soon as you hear back from whoever you sent that wire to?"

"Well, not this late. I suppose I'll spend the night at the hotel."

"It's a comfortable place, or so I'm told."

The Kid sensed the air of awkwardness in the

room. He knew that Marshal Fairmont didn't like him much. Normally that wouldn't have bothered The Kid at all. Since he had adopted the identity of Kid Morgan and gone on the drift, the opinions of other people didn't concern him much.

The difference was that Fairmont was a lawman, and there were wanted posters out on The Kid. It was an unsettling situation.

"I've been thinking that I've seen you before," the marshal went on.

"Before today, you mean?"

"Yeah."

It was certainly possible. The Kid had ridden through Las Vegas several days earlier, stopping briefly to pick up some supplies in one of the smaller stores. He hadn't talked to anyone except the proprietor, but Fairmont could have seen him riding past and taken note of him because he was a stranger.

That thought flashed through The Kid's mind, but he didn't show it on his face. He just shrugged and said, "It's possible. I've been a lot of places."

"Yeah, but I've got a good memory for faces. It'll come to me."

Before either of them could say anything else, Carly appeared in the doorway of the parlor, untying the belt of the apron she wore.

"The food's ready," she told them with a smile. "Come to supper."

Chapter 9

The food tasted as good as it smelled. Roast beef, potatoes, greens, some of the lightest and best-tasting biscuits The Kid had ever eaten, followed by peach cobbler for dessert. It was a simple meal, but as fine as any Conrad Browning had ever had in those fancy restaurants back east.

The company was a damned sight better, that was for sure, at least where Carly was concerned. She kept up a lively string of conversation. Her father had been a lawman in a number of different towns, so she had seen a lot of sights.

The Kid had too, so they were able to talk about the places they had been.

Fairmont was much more taciturn, and when he spoke up, his questions had an edge to them.

"How come you never stayed in one place very long, Browning?"

"I guess I was always just a little too restless by nature. Fiddle-footed, some men call it."

Then, a little later, "What sort of things have you worked at? You don't strike me as a cowboy."

"It's true, I never got the hang of punching cows," The Kid replied. "But I've worked on railroads and done some mining."

Technically, that was true. As Conrad Browning, he held an interest in several railroads and had overseen the construction of more than one spur line. The Browning financial holdings also included gold and silver mines scattered across the West, including some in Nevada.

"Interesting you use the word 'hang,'" Fairmont commented.

Carly frowned at him. "What do you mean by that, Dad?"

"Oh, nothing," the marshal said.

But The Kid got the message plainly enough. Fairmont was suspicious of him. He was enjoying the marshal's hospitality only because that was Carly's wish.

When the meal was over, Fairmont suggested, "Why don't you step out on the porch with me, Browning, so we can get some air? I can light up this pipe of mine. Carly doesn't like for me to smoke it in the house."

"If you'd burn something in it besides that foul-smelling tobacco, I might not mind," she said with a smile.

The Kid didn't want to add to Fairmont's suspicions of him, so he nodded and said, "Sure, Marshal."

The two men moved to the porch while Carly cleaned up after supper. Fairmont struck a lucifer and cupped the flame in the bowl of his pipe, puffing until it was burning well. He shook out the match, dropped it on the porch, and ground it under the toe of his boot.

"Nice evening," The Kid said.

"It'll be cold by morning," Fairmont replied. He blew a little cloud of smoke in the air.

"More than likely," The Kid agreed.

"You didn't get that reply to your telegram."

"Not yet. It could still come in. I told the clerk at the Western Union office I'd be at the hotel after this, so the boy should still be able to find me."

"I don't suppose you'd like to tell me what business this is about."

The Kid glanced over at his host. "Sorry, Marshal. No offense, but I'd rather keep that to myself."

Fairmont took the pipe out of his mouth. "A man who wears a badge likes to know what's going on in his town," he said. "And a gunfighter's business usually means trouble."

"I never said I was a gunfighter," The Kid pointed out.

"You didn't have to. I'll ask you flat out, Browning, and since you sat at my table and broke bread with me, I expect a straight answer. Did you come to Las Vegas to kill a man?"

The Kid took a deep breath. "Absolutely not, Marshal. I don't want any trouble at all."

Fairmont looked steadily at him for a moment. The light on the porch was dim, but it was enough for The Kid to know the lawman was studying him and weighing his answer.

Finally, Fairmont nodded. "That's good to

know, anyway. Especially since . . . well, the girl's taken quite a shine to you and all."

Suddenly, The Kid realized he might have been misreading the situation all along. Fairmont's suspicions might not come from the fact that he was a lawman as much as they did from him being the father of an attractive young woman.

"I can set your mind to rest about that, Marshal," The Kid said. "The only intention I have toward your daughter is an honorable one, and that's to thank her for a fine meal and some very pleasant company. If you'd like, you can convey those thanks for me, and I'll just get my hat and head on down to the hotel."

Fairmont shook his head. "No, no, she'd never forgive either of us if you did that. Wait a spell. You can say your good nights."

"Thanks," The Kid said, smiling. "I'd like that."

Carly joined them on the porch a few minutes later. "It's a beautiful evening," she said, expressing the same sentiment The Kid had earlier.

"Yes, it is," The Kid agreed, "and that was a fine meal you prepared, miss."

"Carly," she insisted.

"We'll compromise," The Kid said with a smile. "Miss Carly."

"I suppose that'll do. What are your plans now, Mr. Browning?"

"Well, that depends on the answer I get to a telegram I sent earlier. I'll be staying in Las Vegas tonight, but I expect I'll be moving along in the morning."

"So soon?" she asked.

The sound of disappointment in her voice told The Kid that maybe Marshal Fairmont was right to be worried. Carly had taken a shine to him.

But nothing could ever come of that, and it was better that she be aware of it. "I'm afraid so," he said.

"Well, I'm glad we were able to keep you here for a little while, anyway." She sounded disappointed but accepted his decision.

Fairmont spoke up, saying, "Browning, I'm about to make my evening rounds. How about coming along with me?"

The suggestion surprised The Kid a little. Maybe the marshal was more willing to be friendly now that he knew The Kid didn't have any designs on his daughter.

"I suppose I can do that. I need to find a livery stable for my horse before I check into the hotel."

"I can take you right to the best stable in town," Fairmont said. "Just let me get my hat."

He went back inside the house and closed the door. Carly was standing at the edge of the porch, her hands on the railing that ran around it, but she turned quickly and stepped toward The Kid.

Before he could stop her, she put her arms around his neck, came up on her toes, and pressed her mouth to his.

The kiss took him a little by surprise. Instinctively, his arms went around Carly's slim, supple body. Her lips were warm and sweet, and he was human enough to react favorably to what she was doing. Without thinking about it, he returned the kiss.

But only for a moment, and then he reached up and disengaged her arms as gently as he could so that he could step back. "What was that about?" he asked quietly.

"You know good and well what it was about, Mr. Browning," she said. "I just wanted you to know what'll be waiting for you if you ever decide to come back to Las Vegas."

"You plan on waiting for me?"

"That's right."

"Don't," The Kid said. His voice had a brutal flatness to it. "Just don't."

"Why not? Are you . . ." The words caught a little. "Are you spoken for? Do you have a wife somewhere?"

Yes, I have a wife somewhere. She's buried down in New Mexico Territory.

He couldn't say that to her, so he said, "Just take my word for it, Carly. You don't want to wait for me. Find some other young man and marry him. Have a good family and a good life."

"But I—"

"You can't have either of those things with me," The Kid said.

She took a deep breath and said, "All right." Her voice was taut with anger. "If that's the way you feel."

"I'm afraid it is."

She turned away and said, "Good night, Mr. Browning," as the front door opened and her father came out on the porch again.

"Good night," The Kid said.

Fairmont waited until his daughter had closed the door behind her, then said, "It's getting chilly a little sooner than I expected." He handed The Kid his hat.

"Miss Carly didn't like what I had to tell her."

Fairmont held up a hand. "I don't need to know about it. Come on, Browning."

The Kid untied the buckskin and led the horse as the two men walked along the street. Fairmont was as good as his word and took The Kid to a livery stable that looked clean and well cared for. He told the proprietor to take good care of The Kid's horse.

"I sure will," the man said. "And you don't have to worry about paying for it, Mr. Browning. The whole town knows that Henry Bennett is taking care of that."

"I'm obliged," The Kid said. He slung his saddlebags over his shoulder and slid the Winchester from its sheath. He would take them with him to the hotel.

The two of them walked on. Music and laughter came from some of the saloons, and the general stores were still open to serve some late-arriving customers. Overall, though, the town was pretty quiet.

When he said as much, Fairmont replied, "Yes, Las Vegas is a nice, peaceful place most of the time. It's had its wild days in the past, but I think it's settled down now for good. I hope so, because I've had enough of drifting. I'd like to stay on here as marshal until I'm ready to take off the badge for good."

"I'd say the town would be lucky to have you."

They had completed their circuit of the town and found themselves back at the marshal's office. The Kid said, "We didn't stop at the hotel."

"Blast it, I forgot." Fairmont pointed a thumb at his office. "Let's step inside here for a minute, and then I'll take you back down there."

"I saw where it was. No need for you to come along, Marshal."

"Yeah, but there's something in here I want to show you. It's important."

The Kid didn't fully trust the lawman, but Fairmont sounded sincere.

"All right, just for a minute. I'm pretty tired."

"That's all it'll take."

Fairmont opened the door and led the way inside. A lamp with its wick turned down low burned on the desk. Fairmont went over to it and turned it up so that the yellow glow in the room brightened.

"I got to thinking," he said as he pawed through a stack of papers on the desk, "that there might be a reward for those bank robbers, and you're entitled to a share of it, Browning. So I had a look through these reward dodgers for them."

The Kid started to shake his head. "I don't want any reward," he said. He couldn't stop a bitter edge from cutting into his voice. "You can keep all that blood money."

"But look here," Fairmont went on as he turned. "I found those owlhoots—"

He leveled the little pistol that had been hidden under the papers. The barrel pointed right at The Kid's middle.

"And I found something else, too," the marshal went on. "Put your hands up, *Morgan*. You're under arrest."

Chapter 10

The Kid's hands didn't rise, despite the fact that Fairmont thrust the gun at him menacingly.

"You knew all along, didn't you?" he asked coolly.

"That you're wanted for breaking out of prison and murdering some guards over in New Mexico Territory? I've known ever since I went through these wanted posters and found the one about you. I knew you had to be a gunfighter. I just didn't know you were Kid Morgan."

"So you had me to supper at your house?"

"That was the girl's idea," Fairmont snapped. "I was watching you like a hawk the whole time. If you'd tried anything, you would've been sorry."

"I wouldn't have tried anything, Marshal. I told you the truth. I'm not looking for trouble."

"Yeah, tell that to those guards you killed." Fairmont motioned with the pistol in his hand. "Now unbuckle that gunbelt, slow and easy, and put it on the floor."

The Kid made no move to follow the order. "I didn't kill any guards," he said. "Yes, I broke out of prison, but it was because I was locked up unjustly. I was mistaken for an escaped convict named Ben Bledsoe. The authorities in New Mexico *know* this. There are no charges against me. Whoever put out those wanted posters made a terrible mistake."

Fairmont grunted. "Terrible for you, no doubt about that. With a price of ten thousand dollars on your head—and dead or alive, at that—you're going to attract a lot of attention. You'll be safer in my cell block than anywhere else, Morgan. Now unbuckle that gunbelt and get in there."

The Kid thought about how it had felt to have iron bars closing him in. He shook his head.

"Sorry, Marshal. I'm not going to do it."

"Damn it, I'll shoot you if I have to!"

The Kid looked at the gun in Fairmont's hand. "That's a .32 caliber revolver you got so tricky with," he said. "If you put a slug in me, it won't knock me down. I'll have plenty of time to get my gun out. You know what that means."

The marshal paled. "You'd kill a lawman? I thought you said you aren't a murderer."

"I said I never killed any prison guards in New Mexico," The Kid replied with a thin smile. Let Fairmont make of that whatever he wanted.

But as a matter of fact, he *didn't* want to kill the marshal, for Carly's sake, if for no other reason. On top of that, Fairmont believed he was just doing his job. A man didn't deserve to die for that.

"Damn it, Morgan. I can't let you walk out of here. It doesn't matter if you *did* save my life this afternoon. You're a wanted man. It's up to the courts to sort out whether the charges are justified, not me."

"That's why I sent the wire, Marshal. It went to my lawyer in San Francisco. If he's given a chance, I'm sure he'll straighten everything out."

"You expect me to believe that a drifting gunfighter has a lawyer in San Francisco?"

"It's true," The Kid said. "If you're interested in the ten thousand dollars, I can make arrangements to have that amount paid to you." He could have added that he was actually a very wealthy man with business interests stretching from one end of the country to the other, but he didn't think Fairmont was very likely to believe *that*.

The offer appeared to anger the marshal. "I'm a lawman," Fairmont snapped. "I earn my wages by keeping the peace. I don't collect bounties."

"Then you don't have any real reason not to let me go."

"Except the fact that you're a fugitive." Fairmont's hand tightened on the pistol. "There's been enough talk. Are you going to drop your gun and get in that cell, Morgan, or do I have to pull this trigger?"

The Kid sighed. "Take it easy, Marshal." His hands went to the buckle of his gunbelt. "Looks like you've got me—"

Fairmont's eyes dropped, following The Kid's hands . . . just as The Kid had figured they would.

He sprang forward with blinding speed, closing

the gap between them before the marshal could pull the trigger. The edge of The Kid's left hand slashed sideways against Fairmont's wrist.

The pistol barked, but The Kid had already knocked the barrel out of line. The .32 caliber bullet thudded into the front wall rather than finding his flesh.

At the same time, The Kid bunched his right fist and drove it forward. The punch landed cleanly on Fairmont's jaw and rocked the lawman's head back. The lawman fell against the desk and knocked the lamp over.

Flames shot up as burning kerosene splashed over the papers on the desk. The Kid's eyes widened in alarm at the sight of the blaze. He ignored Fairmont for the moment and yanked his hat off, slapping at the flames as he put them out.

From the corner of his eye, he saw Fairmont stagger across the room. The marshal caught himself and shook his head as if to clear it. He had dropped the smaller pistol, but clawed at the butt of the long-barreled revolver on his hip and dragged it out of its holster.

The Kid whirled and flung his charred hat into Fairmont's face as the lawman's gun cleared leather. Instinctively, Fairmont batted the hat away from his eyes, giving The Kid time to leap across the room and close his left hand around the cylinder of Fairmont's gun so it couldn't fire. The Kid drove his other fist into Fairmont's belly.

The marshal doubled over, gasping for breath. He was a tough old bird, but he was no match for The Kid in a brawl. The Kid wrenched the gun out of Fairmont's hand and flung it away behind him. Then he grabbed the front of Fairmont's shirt, jerked him upright, and muttered, "Sorry, Marshal," before he threw another punch. The blow slammed into Fairmont's jaw, and put him out. When The Kid let go of Fairmont's shirt, the marshal dropped senseless to the floor.

Feeling disgusted with himself and the circumstances, The Kid turned away. Somebody would be coming to investigate those shots. He needed to get out of Las Vegas, but hated to leave before he got a reply to his telegram to Claudius Turnbuckle. He would have to get in touch with the lawyer again later, from some other settlement with a telegraph office.

He froze as he came around toward the door. It had opened without him being aware of it as he was struggling with Fairmont. A figure stood there, silhouetted against the light that filtered into the street from other buildings. The Kid instantly recognized the slender figure.

It belonged to Carly Fairmont. And the gun she held in both hands, pointed at him, belonged to her father.

"Dad was right to be suspicious of you," she said savagely. "He told me you weren't who you were pretending to be and that I shouldn't get any thoughts in my head about you. But I didn't believe him. I see now I should have."

The Kid shook his head and told her, "You've got it all wrong, Carly."

"How could I get it wrong?" She took another step into the room. "You attacked my father and tried to burn down his office. I heard shots. Did you try to kill him, too?"

"Just put the gun down and step aside. Your father's not hurt bad. You don't know what's going on here."

"I know enough," she said. "I know you're not going anywhere, Mr. Browning or whatever your name is. Did you lie about that, too?"

"Carly . . ." The Kid took a step toward her.

She screamed and pulled the trigger.

Chapter 11

The muzzle flash from the gun was blinding in the darkened room. The Kid had seen the way the barrel jerked a little just as Carly pulled the trigger, and his superb reflexes enabled him to jump the other way.

The bullet whistled past his ear.

He lunged forward before Carly could fire again. His arm swept the gun aside and knocked it out of her hands. She cried out and tried to get away from him, but he grabbed her so she couldn't retrieve the gun.

"Let me go!" she screamed. "Let me go!"

"Blast it, settle down!" The Kid began, but then he gave it up as a bad job. He wasn't going to be able to make Carly accept the truth. He probably couldn't even stop her from being hysterical. It would be a waste of valuable time even to try.

He had to get out of Las Vegas while he still had the chance. "I'm sorry," he said as he thrust her out of his way.

Arms closed around his legs in a clumsy tackle. "Damn you!" Fairmont yelled. The marshal had regained his senses faster than The Kid had thought he would.

He tried to kick his way free from Fairmont's grip, but Fairmont wasn't a small man and put all his considerable heft into heaving on The Kid's legs. At the same time, Carly planted her hands in the middle of The Kid's chest and shoved as hard as she could. Between the efforts of the two of them, The Kid suddenly crashed to the floor of the marshal's office.

Fairmont clambered on top of him. "Get his gun!" the marshal told his daughter. "Get his gun!"

The Kid made a grab for his Colt, but Fairmont had him tied up too well. He felt Carly pluck the weapon from its holster, but she couldn't use it to shoot at him while he was rolling around on the floor with her father.

Fairmont got a hand on The Kid's neck and tried to choke him. The Kid grabbed the marshal's wrist and ripped the hand away from his throat. At the same time, he bucked up from the floor and threw Fairmont's weight off him. The Kid rolled on top of the marshal and threw a short, wicked jab into the middle of Fairmont's face.

Carly swung the gun at his head. When something exploded against the back of his skull, he knew in a flash of intuition that it was the butt of his own revolver.

As he slumped forward, she hit him again, and the darkness inside the office suddenly got a lot thicker and rushed at him from all sides. He felt his face strike the floor as he collapsed, felt his head bounce a little from the impact.

Then the blackness was all around him, and he didn't feel a thing.

• • •

It wasn't the first time The Kid had been knocked out. Coming to was a slow, painful process, but it brought with it the knowledge that he wasn't dead, which was a relief.

As he became aware of his surroundings, he realized he was lying on a hard, narrow, uncomfortable surface—some sort of cot or bunk. He was positioned on his side, and when he forced his eyes open, he saw a rock wall at close range, only inches away from his face.

Turning his head slightly so he could lift his gaze along the wall, he wasn't surprised to see a small, barred window set into it.

He was in jail, just as he expected.

The light in the cell was dim. The Kid rolled onto his back and looked the other way. The heavy door between the cell block and the marshal's office stood open, and light came from the lamp burning in the office.

Snoring came from across the aisle that divided the cell block into two sets of matching cells, totaling four. That would be the outlaw who had survived the failed bank robbery that afternoon.

The Kid rolled onto his other side so he could swing his legs off the bunk attached to the wall and sit up. As he did so, his senses whirled around crazily for a moment. He felt sick.

He sat there until he felt steadier and the feeling soon passed. When he was confident he wouldn't fall down, he stood up and walked over to the cell door, which was made up completely of iron bars.

A shudder went through him as his fingers curled around the bars. After his experience in Hell Gate Prison had left his back crisscrossed with fading whip scars, he had sworn he would never allow himself to be locked up again.

And yet there he was, behind bars once more.

The Kid drew in a deep breath. "Marshal!" he called. "Marshal Fairmont! Are you out there?"

The would-be bank robber in the cell across the way stirred and muttered in his sleep, but after a few seconds he started snoring again.

With a heavy tread, Fairmont appeared in the doorway. "I thought I heard somebody stirring around back here. You're awake, are you, Morgan?"

"You can see that for yourself," The Kid said. "I tell you again, you're making a mistake, Marshal."

"Not according to that reward poster. But if you're right and it's wrong, then I suppose I'll owe you an apology. It's not up to me to sort that out, though. I've sent a wire to the New Mexico territorial authorities in Santa Fe advising them that I have you under arrest and asking them what they want me to do with you."

The Kid felt an odd surge of hope when he heard that. It was possible that Claudius

Turnbuckle had been in touch with those same authorities, and when Fairmont heard back from Santa Fe, the message might well inform him that all charges had been dropped and The Kid was free to go.

That would be the best outcome for the fiasco. The Kid wouldn't likely know if it was true until morning at the earliest.

"For what it's worth, I'm sorry I had to lie to you, Marshal."

Fairmont nodded. "You see, that's one reason I've got my doubts about you. If you're telling the truth about not being wanted, why did you lie about your name?"

"Think about it, Marshal. You're not the only one who's seen that wanted poster."

Quickly, The Kid told Fairmont about his two encounters with bounty hunters in the mountains west of Las Vegas and the narrow escapes he'd had. There was no longer any point in concealing any of that information.

"So when I rode back into town, all I wanted to do was send that wire to my lawyer, wait for his response, and then get out again without anybody paying any attention to me." The Kid couldn't keep the bitterness out of his voice as he added, "And then those four robbers came running out of the bank."

Fairmont rubbed his jaw. "I reckon you *did* save my life," he admitted. "But then you lied to me, and you made it worse by coming to my house and continuing to lie to me. In my book, that goes a long way toward evening things out."

"If I had told you the truth then, would you have believed me?"

"Well . . ."

"No, you'd have believed what you saw on that wanted poster," The Kid said.

Fairmont jerked his head in a nod. "More than likely."

"So you see, all I was trying to do was save you some trouble."

"You can look at it that way if you want," the marshal said. "To me it seems like you were just trying to avoid being locked up again."

"Locked up unjustly," The Kid said. "For the second time."

"That's for somebody else to sort out, not me. I'm sure that if you really have that fancy lawyer in San Francisco you keep talking about, he'll be able to get to the bottom of things."

"You don't believe me about the lawyer, either, do you?"

Fairmont looked steadily at him and said, "Right now I'm not sure I'd believe anything that comes out of your mouth, Morgan."

"I guess I might as well get some sleep, then."

The outlaw in the other cell had stopped snoring. He said, "Yeah, especially if it means that you'll shut up so the rest of us can sleep!"

• • •

Fairmont spent the night in the marshal's office, explaining that he didn't feel comfortable leaving when he had a couple prisoners. But when The Kid woke up in the morning after a few hours of fitful sleep, Fairmont was gone. He'd probably headed home for some breakfast and maybe a little rest, The Kid thought.

The office wasn't deserted for long. He heard the front door open, then a moment later a key rattled in the lock of the cell block door.

It swung open to reveal Carly standing there. She said, "I've brought breakfast for the two of you."

The Kid stood up and went to the bars. He leaned against them and gave her a sardonic smile.

"What?" she asked after a second. "Why are you looking at me like that, Mr. Browning? I mean, Mr. Morgan."

"Why not just call me Kid?" he suggested. "I was just thinking that you don't *look* like the sort of woman who'd try to bash a man's head in with a pistol."

She frowned at him. "You're lucky I didn't shoot you, after what you did to my father."

"Luck had nothing to do with it," The Kid said. "You tried to shoot me, remember? If I hadn't been fast enough to get out of the way of the bullet, I'd be dead right now."

"And good riddance. Dad said you killed a couple prison guards down in New Mexico Territory."

"That's what the wanted poster says," The Kid corrected. "It's not true."

"If it's not, I'm sure you'll have your chance in court to prove it." She turned away from the door and came back a moment later carrying a tray with a plate of hotcakes, bacon, and eggs on it. "For now you get your breakfast."

She passed the tray to The Kid through the narrow opening in the barred door designed for that.

"Hey, what about me?" the other prisoner asked.

"I have your breakfast, too," Carly assured him. "Just a minute."

She returned to the office and came back with another tray. When she had passed it into the cell, she said, "There's coffee on the stove. I'll get cups."

As she turned back toward the office, the front door opened and a boy about twelve years old came in. He wore overalls and a cap, which, when he saw Carly standing there, he tugged off to reveal a mop of flaming red hair.

"Howdy, Miss Fairmont," he greeted her. "Cyrus down at the telegraph office sent me to look for that Mr. Browning fella who stopped the bank robbery yesterday. Said he'd probably be at the hotel, but they ain't seen him. I figured I'd ask your pa. Is he here?"

"No, he's not, Davey," Carly replied. "But I know where Mr. Browning is." She held out her hand. "If you'll give me the message, I'll see that he gets it."

The boy hesitated. "Well, I dunno . . . Cyrus said to give it straight to Mr. Browning . . ."

The Kid's heart had started to pound harder as soon as the boy announced why he was there. It could be his ticket out of the jail.

He set the breakfast tray on the bunk and stepped quickly to the bars, thrusting an arm out between them.

"That message you have is for me, son," he called.

The boy stepped closer to the cell block, his eyes widening as he peered into the cell and recognized The Kid. "Golly!" he said. "You *are* him!"

"That's right. That telegram is addressed to me."

Davey took an envelope from the pocket of his overalls and squinted at it. "The name on here is . . . Conrad Browning."

The Kid nodded. "That's my real name."

Davey looked at Carly. "Miss Fairmont?"

She sighed and nodded. "He's the one who sent a wire to San Francisco," she confirmed, without addressing the issue of his true identity. "I suppose he has a right to see the reply."

"Thanks," The Kid said dryly.

"All right." Davey advanced hesitantly and held out the envelope to The Kid. "How come you're in the hoosegow, Mr. Browning?"

"It's a long story," The Kid said. "And a big mistake." He felt in his pockets to see if Fairmont had left him any money. Finding a silver dollar, he handed it to Davey and took the envelope.

"Thanks!" the boy said.

"Run along now, Davey," Carly told him.

"You bet!"

He dashed out of the marshal's office, no doubt on his way to the general store to convert that dollar to licorice whips or maybe a pocket knife.

The Kid stood in the cell, paying no attention to Carly or the bank robber in the cell across the aisle. He ripped the envelope open, eager to see what Claudius Turnbuckle had to say.

Chapter 12

The terse words hit him like a hard punch in the gut.

> REWARD GENUINE STOP TERRITORIAL GOVERNOR REFUSES TO DROP CHARGES STOP GOING SANTA FE TO STRAIGHTEN OUT MESS TURNBUCKLE

The Kid sank slowly onto the bunk as he tried to absorb the message.

"Bad news?" Carly asked.

"Bad enough." The Kid crumpled the telegram into a ball and tossed it out through the bars. "See for yourself."

She hesitated for a second before picking up the paper, smoothing it out, and reading what was printed on it.

"Who's Turnbuckle?" she asked as she looked up at him.

"Claudius Turnbuckle, my lawyer. One of the partners in the firm Turnbuckle & Stafford."

Carly tapped a finger on the telegram. "He says he's on his way to Santa Fe."

"Yes, and I have no doubt he'll get everything straightened out like he says. But how long is that going to take?" The Kid shook his head in disgust. "In the meantime, I have to stay here, penned up in this cell."

"Well, for heaven's sake, it's not *that* bad," Carly said. "I happen to know you have a perfectly fine breakfast there. I fix the meals for the prisoners, and I'm a good cook."

"That's a fact," The Kid said with a shrug.

"I'm sure it'll be boring, but if you're telling the truth, in the long run you don't have anything to worry about. You'll be exonerated and released. You'll have lost some time, that's all. Unless you were on your way somewhere in a hurry, that shouldn't be a big problem."

"No," The Kid admitted, "I wasn't on my way anywhere, in a hurry or otherwise."

"Well, there you go," she said with a satisfied nod. "It's just an inconvenience, that's all. You'll be well treated. Consider it just . . . a chance to rest."

That was the sensible way to look at things, The Kid supposed.

But where iron bars were concerned, he wasn't sure he could ever be sensible again.

Marshal Fairmont returned to the jail at mid-morning. He came into the cell block and said, "Carly tells me you got a telegram from some-body in San Francisco."

"My lawyer," The Kid said with a nod from the bunk.

"Well, it just had the fella's name signed to it. There was nothing on there that actually said he was a lawyer."

The Kid laughed and shook his head. "You're determined that I'm not telling the truth, aren't you?"

"She's starting to feel a little bad that she came near to shooting you and then clouted you over the head. She's worried that maybe you didn't deserve it."

"What did you tell her?"

"That until I see proof otherwise, to me you're just another owlhoot on the dodge."

"In other words, I'm guilty until proven innocent."

Fairmont flushed angrily. "It's not like that, and you know it."

"That's the way it sounds to me."

"I'm just doing my job here. If you don't like it, that's too damned bad."

From the other cell, the bank robber asked, "What about me? What are you gonna do with me, Marshal?"

"Now, that's a lot simpler," Fairmont said. "The circuit judge will be through here in a couple weeks. You'll be charged with bank robbery and attempted murder, and I expect you'll be on your way to prison shortly thereafter. It's lucky for you nobody except your partners got killed while all the lead was flying around, or you'd be facing the gallows, son."

The man looked down at the floor and muttered something, probably a curse. He didn't ask any more questions.

The rest of the day passed quietly and uneventfully. It was boring, all right, just as Carly had predicted it would be. But the thick stone walls of the jail retained a little of the coolness from the morning, so as the day heated up it didn't become too unbearable inside the cells.

Carly brought sandwiches made from the leftover roast beef for lunch and stew for supper. After delivering the evening meal, she hesitated outside the cells, and The Kid could tell by looking at her that she had something on her mind.

"What's wrong?" he asked.

"I've been thinking about it all day," she said. "What if I was wrong about you? Growing up with a lawman for a father, I saw a lot of outlaws, and you don't seem like the type to me, Mr. Morgan. Most of them were uneducated louts." She glanced over her shoulder at the man in the other cell. "No offense."

He looked up from the stew he'd been slurping. "Oh, none taken, missy. I'll be the first one to tell you I never had much schoolin'."

Carly turned back to The Kid. "Anyway, I've been worried about that. I hate to see any man locked up who doesn't deserve it."

"What about that wanted poster?" The Kid asked, playing devil's advocate. "According to the wire from Claudius, the territorial authorities in New Mexico meant to issue it and refused to retract it."

"Maybe they don't know the full story of what happened."

"They ought to know. The warden's daughter was going to testify that I was locked up by mistake."

Carly shook her head. "I just have a feeling that there's been a mistake made somewhere, and I'm afraid I may be the one who made it."

After she'd left, taking the empty bowls with her, the other prisoner grinned at The Kid from across the aisle and said, "That gal's gone sweet on you, Morgan. You play up to her, she might just let you outta here."

"It didn't seem much like it last night when she was trying to stove my head in with a gun butt," The Kid said.

The bank robber waved a hand dismissively. "Oh, hell, you can't go by that. I've had gals try to shoot me, stab me, and even bust my skull with a piece of cord wood, but they still loved me." He grinned. "It's because I'm such a roguish bastard. The gals just can't resist me."

"Then maybe you're the one who should be playing up to Miss Fairmont."

The man shook his head. "Naw. Not this one. She's got her eye set on you."

"I think you're wrong," The Kid said.

"Can't hurt to try. Worst she can do is slap you across the mush."

The Kid stretched out and turned his face to the

stone wall. He didn't want to think about what the bank robber had said.

In the first place, he wasn't convinced Carly was smitten with him, and in the second, he wasn't sure he could play up to any woman anymore. Conrad Browning had been quite the ladies' man in his time, leaving a string of broken hearts behind him, but those days were long gone.

Carly was right. What he needed to do was just be patient. He had faith in Claudius Turnbuckle's legal skill.

And Marshal Fairmont had been right, too. With that ten thousand dollar price on his head, he was probably safer in jail—for the time being—than he would be anywhere else.

Five hard-faced men rode into Las Vegas a little after sundown that evening. They headed for the Nugget Saloon, which was the biggest and best of the four saloons in town. They left their mounts at the hitch rail in front and went inside.

The man who carried himself like their leader wore black boots, black whipcord trousers, and a black vest over a dark red shirt. A black Stetson with a tightly curled brim was thumbed back on a rumpled thatch of prematurely white hair above his tanned, angular face.

He stepped up to the bar and rested his left hand on the hardwood. The right stayed close to the pearl-handled butt of the revolver holstered on his hip.

"Whiskey," he told the barkeep without waiting for the man to ask him what he'd have. He angled his head toward his companions as they bellied up to the bar next to him and added, "That goes for my friends, too."

"Sure thing, mister," the apron said. He turned and reached for a bottle sitting on the backbar.

"Not that swill," the stranger snapped. "We'll be needing something better than that." The flinty tone of his voice left no room for argument.

The bartender nodded a little nervously and reached under the bar as he said, "Of course, sir."

He fetched out a different bottle, unwrapped the seal from around its neck, and set glasses on the hardwood. As he studied the five men without being too obvious about it, he wished they had picked one of the other saloons in town to do their drinking.

Standing next to the white-haired leader was a thick-bodied man with a drooping walrus mustache of a muddy shade. To his left was a tall, skinny man with a patchy beard that tried to cover up his weak chin and prominent Adam's apple, but failed. The fourth man was either a Mexican or a 'breed and really shouldn't have been drinking, but the bartender wasn't going to argue with anybody who had such an evil face.

That left the medium-sized, gray-haired man in

black who looked like a preacher, but only if a preacher carried two guns, butt-forward under his coat ready for a cross-draw. His expression was mild, but something about the look in his eyes made the bartender shudder.

The white-haired man tossed back his drink and asked, "Any strangers ride into town lately?"

"Besides you fellas, you mean?"

The man fixed the bartender with an impatient stare. "I don't think I'd be asking about us, do you?"

"No, I, ah, reckon not." The bartender tugged at his celluloid collar. "People come and go in Las Vegas all the time. It's hard to remember 'em all." He paused. "Unless something happens that *makes* you remember them, like that bank robbery yesterday."

"Bank robbery?" the white-haired man repeated.

"Yeah. Well, attempted bank robbery, I guess you'd have to say, since the varmints didn't get away with any loot. Shucks, none of 'em got away, period. Three of 'em are dead, and the fourth is locked up in Marshal Fairmont's jail, thanks to that stranger."

The bartender had relaxed a little as he warmed up to the story he was telling, but a shiver went through him again as the white-haired man asked, "What stranger?"

"He said his name was Browning at first. He helped the marshal stop that robbery, and Henry

Bennett over at the bank was gonna pay for whatever expenses the fella had while he stayed here in town. But then Marshal Fairmont figured out he's really some gunfighter and outlaw called Kid Morgan who's wanted over in New Mexico Territory, so he locked him up. I'll bet he hated to do it, since Morgan helped him, maybe even saved his life, but the law's the law, you know?"

"Yeah," the white-haired man said, "I know. So this Kid Morgan is still locked up in the jail?"

The bartender nodded. "Yep. I don't know what the marshal plans to do with him. Maybe New Mexico's sending somebody to take him back there."

"That's mighty interesting," the man said. He glanced over at his companions and saw the avarice that had appeared in their eyes.

Their glasses were empty. The bartender asked, "You want me to refill those drinks?"

The man spun a coin on the bar. It twirled for several seconds before rattling to a stop. "No thanks."

He turned and headed for the door without motioning for the others to follow him. They did, anyway.

When they were outside, the man who looked like a preacher said, "That's mighty providential, The Kid dropping into our laps like this, Pronto. What are we going to do about it?"

"What do you think?" replied the man called

Pronto. “We can’t collect the reward for him if somebody else locked him up.”

“So what are we gonna do?” the man with the walrus mustache asked.

“The only thing we can,” Pronto said. “We’re going to break him out and then kill him.” His thin lips curved in a cold smile. “Those posters said he was wanted dead or alive, after all.”

Chapter 13

The Kid was dozing on his bunk when he heard Carly's voice out in the office. He wondered why she had come back to the jail—supper had been several hours earlier. He hoped something wasn't wrong.

A few moments later, the front door of the office slammed like somebody had left in a hurry.

The Kid sat up on the bunk and frowned. From the sound of it, Carly had come to the marshal's office to bring her father some sort of urgent summons. Trouble must have cropped up somewhere in Las Vegas.

The key rattled in the cell block door. It swung open, and The Kid saw Carly's slender figure silhouetted against the light in the office. She went quickly into the cell block.

The Kid came to his feet, grasped the bars, and asked, "What's wrong?"

Carly clutched the marshal's big key ring in her hand. She pushed a key into the lock on The Kid's cell and said, "I'm letting you out of here."

"Hold on a minute." The Kid couldn't quite believe he was saying that, but the words came out of his mouth. "What's going on here?"

"I sent some telegrams of my own," Carly said. "I wired Turnbuckle & Stafford in San Francisco and asked if a man named Browning was one of their clients. I also sent a message to a friend of mine in Denver and asked her to check with the newspapers there and see if she could find out anything about Conrad Browning."

"I guess you must have gotten some replies," The Kid said. His mouth was set in grim lines.

"That's right. My God, what terrible things have happened to you! To lose your wife like that, and then to have everyone believe that you were dead—"

"That was my choice," The Kid broke in. "I wanted people to think that Conrad Browning was dead." He paused. "Especially the men who murdered my wife."

"Anyway, I'm convinced those wanted posters are just another terrible mistake, like you said. I knew you . . . you couldn't be a bad man."

The Kid grunted. "I wouldn't be so sure of that. You don't know all the things I've done. But I never murdered any prison guards, in New Mexico or anywhere else, and the only reason I broke out of Hell Gate was to try to clear my name."

Carly turned the key. "That's why I'm turning you loose. So you can clear your name. I told my father some story about being up at the store when I saw a fight about to break out between some cowboys, and he went to see about it. You have to hurry. He'll be back soon."

She swung the door open, but The Kid didn't step out. "What happened to just waiting here until Turnbuckle proves I'm innocent?"

"That was before I knew about everything you've gone through. I-I wasn't sure you could stand being locked up."

The Kid put a hand on the barred door. "I appreciate the sentiment. I really do. But I don't want to get you in trouble with your father. I can stand staying here." He smiled. "As long as you keep providing the meals, that is."

She stared at him and asked, "You're not going to escape?"

"I will," the bank robber said from the other cell. "You can unlock this door, and I'll thank you mighty kindly, ma'am."

"Forget it," The Kid told him. "You go back out in the office, Carly. Take the keys with you. We'll forget this happened, and the marshal doesn't have to know about it."

"But, Kid . . ." she pleaded, and he could tell from the look in her eyes that the outlaw in the other cell was right. Carly had fallen for him, or at least she had convinced herself that she had. She was trying to make this big dramatic gesture in order to prove how she felt about him.

He shook his head. "This isn't right, and you know it."

He could tell she wanted to argue some more, but the sudden opening of the front door in the marshal's office made her jerk around with a sharply indrawn breath.

The Kid expected to see Marshal Fairmont standing there and Carly probably did, too, but instead, a man The Kid had never seen before strode into the office.

He had white hair and was dressed all in black except for a red shirt under his vest. He stopped short as he looked through the open cell block door and saw Carly standing in front of The Kid's open cell.

A grin spread across his hard-planed face. "Well, this is mighty handy," he said. Then his hand dipped and came up with a pearl-handled Colt, drawn smoothly from the black holster on his hip.

"Kid?" Carly said with fear in her voice.

An obscenity slipped from the lips of the bank robber in the other cell. "That's Pronto Pike," he said.

The name meant nothing to The Kid, but he knew a dangerous man when he saw one. He stiffened, one hand still on the barred door.

Pike came across the office, the gun level and rock steady in his hand. "Back away from that cell, miss," he ordered.

Carly was pale with fright, but her chin lifted and she asked with a note of defiance, "What do you want?"

"I want that prisoner," Pike said, nodding

toward The Kid. "I was just going to talk to the marshal and get the lay of the land, but I won't pass up a chance like this." His voice hardened. "Step back out of the way."

"Do what he says," The Kid told Carly.

Her eyes darted toward him. "But what about you?"

"Don't worry about me." He smiled faintly. "You wanted me to escape, remember?"

"Not like this," the bank robber said. "That's Pronto Pike, Kid! He's a bounty hunter, and from what I've heard, he never takes his prisoners in alive."

"Shut up," Pike snapped at the man as he advanced into the cell block. His gaze was fastened on The Kid. "You're Kid Morgan, the man who's worth ten grand. I recognize you from the description on those wanted posters. When some stupid bartender told me you were locked up in here, I wasn't sure whether to believe him, but it's true. You must not be much of an outlaw to let a two-bit marshal in a backwater town like this lock you up, Kid."

"It's all a mistake," The Kid said, not expecting Pike to believe him.

Not only that, but after his experiences in New Mexico, he was getting damned tired of having to tell people they were wrong about him. "You'll never collect that reward," he went on, "because there are no real charges against me."

"The Territory of New Mexico says different," Pike shot back. "Come on the rest of the way out of that cell, Morgan. You're leaving with me."

Carly moved to get between The Kid and Pike as she spoke. "No! You can't—"

Pike moved like a striking snake, lashing out with his left arm and backhanding her across the face. She cried out in pain as she fell across the aisle and came up against the bars of the bank robber's cell.

The Kid lunged toward Pike, but before he could reach the bounty hunter, Pike leaped back and leveled the gun again. The man's lips drew back from his teeth in a snarling grimace.

"Come on, Morgan," he said. "Dead or alive, it doesn't matter to me."

The Kid froze, knowing the trigger of Pike's gun needed just a hair more pressure on it to make it go off. He might have risked the jump anyway, if a burst of gunfire hadn't sounded outside in the street just then.

Pike's head jerked toward the blistering racket, giving The Kid his chance. He plunged forward and slashed his left arm at Pike's gun.

The revolver exploded just as The Kid hit it. He had knocked the barrel off-line just enough to send the slug burning across his left side instead of burying itself in his body. In the next heartbeat, The Kid crashed into Pike, knocking the bounty hunter off his feet. He yelled in alarm as he went over backward.

The Kid grabbed the wrist of Pike's gun hand and rammed it against the floor. At the same time, he hooked a hard right into Pike's midsection. He brought his elbow up under Pike's chin with stunning force. The blow bounced the back of Pike's head off the floorboards.

The bounty hunter went limp. He might not be out cold, but at least he was stunned.

The shooting was still going on in the street outside. The Kid snatched Pike's gun from the bounty hunter's fingers and surged to his feet.

"Kid," Carly gasped behind him. "My father's out there somewhere!"

The Kid had the same thought. With all the shooting going on, chances were the marshal was mixed up in it. If Pike had partners they might have opened fire on Fairmont as they saw him returning to the office while Pike was in the jail.

The Kid knew there was only one way to find out. But he wanted his own gun before he took cards in that game.

"Stay here," he said over his shoulder to Carly as he hurried out of the cell block. He looked around and spotted his gunbelt hanging on a peg on the wall next to the cabinet that held Fairmont's shotgun and a couple of Winchesters. He set Pike's gun on the desk while he took down the belt and buckled it on.

That was better, he thought. He picked up Pike's gun with his left hand and used his right to draw his own Colt. He was ready for whatever trouble might be out there.

But not for the trouble that was going on in the jail.

Carly screamed.

The sound was choked off as The Kid whirled around. He saw that Pike had made it back to his feet and grabbed the young woman. As Pike stood in the aisle between the cells, he had his left arm looped around her neck, pressing up so that the skin of her throat was drawn taut.

His right hand held a knife to that tight-drawn skin, and as he glared over her shoulder at The Kid, he said, "Drop those guns, Morgan, or I'll cut her throat!"

Chapter 14

The Kid stood absolutely still, swiftly calculating the odds of firing a shot past Carly's head and putting the bullet in Pike's brain. That would be difficult enough, but the chances of accomplishing it before the bounty hunter could plunge the blade into Carly's throat were even higher.

If he dropped the guns, though, he'd be sealing his death warrant. He knew Pike had no intention of taking him in alive. A dead man couldn't argue when somebody went to collect the price on his head.

Pike backed away, maintaining his grip on Carly.

Suddenly, the bank robber reached through the bars and grabbed Pike's right arm, jerking the knife away from Carly's throat. At the same time, he caught hold of Pike's shirt collar and jerked him back hard. Pike's head thudded against the iron bars. The impact was enough to unhinge his knees and make him collapse.

Carly pulled free of Pike and stumbled toward The Kid. Since the firing was still going on in front of the jail, he holstered his Colt, took her arm, and told her, "Go out the back door! You can't stay in here with Pike!"

"But my dad—"

"I'll find him," The Kid promised.

He gave her a push toward the door that opened into the alley behind the jail. As Carly stumbled toward safety, The Kid drew his gun again and turned toward the front door, glancing into the cell block at Pike's senseless form as he did so.

"Go on, Kid," the bank robber urged. "I'll keep an eye on this one."

The Kid wondered what the man could do from inside the cell . . . but he *had* saved Carly's life. Jerking his head in a curt nod of thanks, The Kid went to the front door. It stood ajar several inches. He hooked the toe of his boot in the gap, threw the door open, and went out fast and low in a gunfighter's crouch. His gaze darted rapidly from side to side. The street had cleared in a hurry as people hunted for cover when the shooting started, so it wasn't hard to locate the source of the shots.

Several men had ducked behind a wagon parked to The Kid's left. They were firing at somebody who had taken shelter in the alcove of a store down the block.

One of the men behind the wagon caught sight of The Kid and yelled, "That ain't Pronto! It's Morgan!"

"Get him!" another man shouted.

So Pike had partners, just as The Kid supposed. The man in the alcove was probably Marshal Fairmont. That was all The Kid had time to think about before bullets started whizzing around his head.

He threw himself off the boardwalk in front of the jail in a dive that landed him behind a water trough. Rolling onto his belly, he made himself as small a target as possible and edged one eye and the barrel of his Colt around the corner of the trough.

The wagon was about twenty feet away from him. He could see the legs of the men who had taken cover behind it.

The Kid opened fire.

Inside the cell block, Pronto Pike groaned, heaved himself onto his hands and knees, and shook his head. He didn't see the girl or Morgan anymore, but since the battle was still going on outside, he assumed that Morgan was in the thick of it.

Instinct warned him, and he ducked away just as the prisoner in the cell behind him, having reached through the bars and picked up Pike's knife, slashed at him with it.

The knife missed its target, and Pike climbed to his feet. He looked through the bars at the man standing there, still holding the knife. "You made a big mistake," Pike said coldly.

He turned and stalked into the office, confident that the men outside could handle Morgan. Taking down the shotgun from the rack, he broke it open and saw the empty barrels. He jerked open the middle drawer of the desk. Sure enough, several thick red shells lay there.

He picked up two of them and thumbed them into the greener. Then he snapped it closed and walked back into the cell block.

The prisoner dropped the knife. It clattered on the stone floor. The man backed away toward his bunk. "No!" he cried as he held out his hands toward Pike. "Jesus, no!"

"You picked your side," Pike said as he leveled the shotgun. His finger squeezed both triggers.

The roar was deafening in the cell block as it bounced back from the thick walls. The double load of buckshot lifted the prisoner and slammed him against the suddenly blood splattered wall behind him. What bounced back and pitched forward to the floor was a gory, shredded travesty of a man.

Pike turned away, his need for cruel revenge satisfied and promptly forgotten. He strode into the office and grabbed more shells from the desk drawer. With the shotgun reloaded, he headed for the front door, ready to take a hand in the fight out there.

The Kid heard the shotgun blast from inside the jail just as he saw one of the men behind the wagon go down howling in pain. The Kid's bullets had cut the man's legs out from under him.

If Pike had fired the greener, The Kid knew he'd soon be facing an even greater threat. He twisted on the ground and brought up both revolvers as Pike charged out of the marshal's office with the shotgun in his hands.

Flame gouted from the muzzles of the two guns before Pike could bring the greener to bear on The Kid. One of the bullets struck the underside of the twin barrels right where the breech joined them. The impact wrenched the weapon up and drove it out of Pike's hands. The shotgun hit Pike in the face and knocked him back through the door.

"Son of a bitch!" one of the men behind the wagon yelled. "Pronto's down, and Gomez is hit, too. We better get out of here!"

Shooting fiercely to cover their retreat, the men headed for some horses tied at a nearby hitch rail. One of them helped the wounded man limp along as fast as he could.

The Kid knew he couldn't stop them by himself, and the marshal's gun had fallen silent. Fairmont might be wounded or worse. Keeping one eye on the door of the marshal's office in case Pike reappeared, The Kid thumbed fresh cartridges into his guns.

The fleeing bounty hunters reached their horses and piled into the saddles. Still shooting and yelling, they took off down the street. The Kid risked a look, and to his surprise, he saw a figure leap out of an alley and intercept them.

"Give me a hand!" the man yelled.

The Kid recognized Pronto Pike's voice. After having the greener shot out of his hands, Pike realized luck wasn't on his side. He'd run out of the jail through the open back door and along the alley until he caught up with his partners as they tried to light a shuck out of Las Vegas.

One of the riders reached down and snagged the wrist of Pike's upthrust hand. The man slowed just enough to haul Pike up onto the back of the horse behind the saddle. Digging in his spurs, he sent his mount racing after the others as Pike hung on for dear life.

The Kid could have thrown a few bullets after them, but didn't see any point since they were already getting out of town as fast as they could. Besides, he was more worried about Marshal Fairmont.

He scrambled to his feet and ran toward the alcove. "Hold your fire, Marshal!" he called, in case Fairmont took him for one of the gunmen. "It's me—Morgan."

No shots came from the alcove. When The Kid reached it, he saw the figure slumped in the shadows. Biting back a curse, he dropped to a knee.

"Marshal! Can you hear me?"

Fairmont groaned. "M-Morgan?" he rasped. "Is that . . . you?"

"Yeah. How bad are you hit?"

"Bastards . . . shot a leg out from under me."

The Kid tucked Pike's pearl-handled gun behind his belt and reached down to feel along Fairmont's legs. He found a bloody patch on the right one, on the outside of the thigh.

"Doesn't feel like it's too bad," he told the marshal. "Probably just a deep crease, enough to knock you down and make you lose some blood, but if the bone's not broken, I think you'll be all right."

"What are you doing . . . out of your cell?"

"It's a long story," The Kid said. "We'll worry about that later. Right now, we need to get you some help."

He wrapped his free arm around Fairmont and lifted the marshal to his feet. They had taken a couple unsteady steps toward the jail, when a sudden rataplan of hoofbeats made The Kid jerk his head around.

It was only two horses, and someone was leading one, not riding it. The Kid felt a shock of surprise go through him as he recognized his own buckskin.

The person holding the reins was Carly Fairmont. "Kid!" she called to him as she dismounted. "Kid, I brought your horse from the livery stable. Take him and get out of here!"

"But your father—"

She stepped up onto the boardwalk and held out the reins toward him. "I'll take care of Dad. You can't stay here. You saw what happened tonight. Other bounty hunters are liable to show up and try to take you. Men will risk anything for that much money. You have to leave and clear your name."

The Kid knew she was right. Pike and his men might return. Other bounty hunters might hear that he was locked up in Las Vegas's jail and come for him. It was too dangerous for him to stay there, especially with Fairmont already wounded.

"He's got a bullet through the leg," The Kid told Carly as he took the buckskin's reins from her and helped her get her arm around the marshal. "He'll be all right, but he needs a doctor."

"I'll take care of him," she said. "I'm sorry all this happened, Kid . . . Mr. Browning."

"Leave it at Kid," he said. "Thanks, Carly."

Fairmont groaned. "Carly, don't . . . don't help this prisoner get away."

"I have to, Dad," she told him. "He's not a murderer. I know it."

"Blast it . . . it's not right. It's not . . . the law."

"Sorry, Marshal," The Kid said. He stepped down from the boardwalk, put his foot in the stirrup, and swung up onto the buckskin's back. "But this is better for everybody."

He wheeled the horse around and sent it galloping out of Las Vegas without looking back.

He hoped Fairmont wouldn't stay mad at Carly too long for helping him. It was the best way, and once the marshal thought about that, he might see it, too.

As he rode through the night with the wind in his face, The Kid thought about what he would do next. One thing was certain: no matter where he went, he would be in great danger as long as those wanted posters with his name and description and the ten thousand dollar price on his head were circulating.

Claudius Turnbuckle's wire had said he was going to Santa Fe to straighten everything out. That was where the true problem lay, and that was where the solution would be found as well. As he thought about it, his path seemed clear.

He would pick up that big black horse he had left hidden outside the settlement, and head for New Mexico Territory, to whatever fate awaited him in Santa Fe.

Chapter 15

Several days later, The Kid was in northern Arizona, near the Grand Canyon of the Colorado River. He had heard of the magnificent canyon but had never been there. Although he was tempted to detour to the north and have a look at it, having circled south of the imposing natural landmark, he didn't want to take the time to do so.

Since leaving Las Vegas, nobody had tried to kill him . . . but The Kid knew better than to believe his luck would last.

He was riding the black through hills covered with a thick pine forest and leading the buckskin. Flagstaff was somewhere to the south of him, but he intended to avoid the town, as he had avoided other settlements on his journey. He didn't want to run the risk of being recognized by another small-town lawman who might try to lock him up.

His plan was to steer clear of civilization as much as possible until he reached Santa Fe. By the time he got there, Claudius Turnbuckle ought to have reached the territorial capital, too. The Kid would get in touch with him somehow and find out if the lawyer had been successful in quashing the charges against him.

He didn't relish the idea of spending the rest of his life as a fugitive. But he liked the thought of being locked up even less.

Once the sun set, night fell quickly amidst the towering trees. As dusk settled down, The Kid found a clearing at the base of a rocky bluff that would make a suitable campsite.

A spring trickled from the stone wall and formed a small pool of clear, cold water. There was plenty of grass for the horses, and The Kid thought the trees were thick enough that he could risk a small fire to cook some of the supplies that Carly had stuffed in his saddlebags before she brought the buckskin to him.

Eventually he would have to pick up more provisions from a small hamlet or isolated trading post, but he had enough to last a couple more days.

The nights got cold at that elevation, so after his meager supper, The Kid was glad he had his coat as he hunkered next to the tiny fire he built. He held out his hands toward the flames to catch what little warmth they gave off.

He had ridden out of Las Vegas without his hat. When he stopped for supplies, he would see if he could find another one similar to it. A man got used to wearing a hat and felt a little naked without one.

The same thing was true of a gun. At least it was for men like The Kid.

He had guns: his own Colt, the pearl-handled revolver he had taken from Pronto Pike, which was tucked away in one of his saddlebags, the

Winchester, and the heavy Sharps carbine he normally carried, along with a good supply of ammunition for all of them.

Some might say he was armed for bear, not that he expected to encounter one. For The Kid, packing that much iron was just the usual state of things.

The buckskin pricked up his ears, and a second later, so did the black.

The Kid noted the horses' reactions and frowned. He was still nursing the last of the coffee in his tin cup. He set it aside and came to his feet. Moving over to the buckskin, he stroked the horse's shoulder and murmured to him. "You hear something, fella?" The Kid asked in a voice barely above a whisper. "Or maybe smell something?"

The buckskin couldn't answer, of course. Not in words. But the way the horse lifted his head and looked into the thick shadows under the trees, The Kid knew *something* was out there.

A mountain lion, maybe. Horses and mountain lions were mortal enemies. The same was true of wolves.

The Kid bent over and reached for the Winchester from where he had leaned both of his long guns against one of the saddles on the ground. As he closed his hand around it, a swift-moving shape leaped out of the darkness at him, teeth bared in a snarl.

The Kid snatched the rifle up quickly so the beast's teeth closed on the barrel, not on his flesh. The next second, the animal's weight slammed into him and knocked him off his feet. As he fell, he grabbed hold of the thick, shaggy coat and hung on.

In the firelight, he saw that the creature struggling to sink its fangs into him wasn't a mountain lion or a wolf or even a bear.

It was a dog, and he would have sworn it was the *same* dog he had tossed off that rock slab more than a week earlier when he encountered that gang of bounty hunters.

He had his left hand on the dog's throat, holding off the teeth, and he still clutched the Winchester in his right. He raised the rifle and brought the butt smashing down on the dog's head.

The blow stunned the dog and gave The Kid time to throw the animal off and roll to the side. He came to his feet in a blur of speed and brought the Winchester to his shoulder, the barrel lined on the dog, which had regained its feet and was gathering itself for another spring.

"You pull that trigger, mister, and I'll kill you."

The words that came from behind him, uttered in a loud, clear voice, made The Kid's finger freeze on the Winchester's trigger for two reasons.

One was the obvious threat behind them. The other was the fact they were in a woman's voice.

He heard footsteps and a crackle of brush as she stepped out of the undergrowth beneath the pines. She said, "Hold, Max," and the dog settled down on its haunches but still looked like he wanted to tear The Kid's throat out and gnaw on his bones.

"Put the rifle on the ground," the woman ordered.

"How do I know you've even got a gun?" The Kid asked.

He heard the metallic ratcheting of a revolver being cocked not far behind his head.

"That a good enough answer for you?"

"Yeah, I suppose so." The Kid bent over and placed the Winchester on the ground at his feet.

"Back away from it."

He did so, keeping his hands in plain sight. Depending on how much trigger-pull her gun required, it might not take much to put a bullet in his head.

"All right, turn around." To reinforce the order she had given a moment earlier, the woman said again, "Max, hold."

The Kid turned to face her. A shock went through him as he recognized the poncho and the broad-brimmed brown hat.

He had thought that dog looked familiar. So did his captor. "I thought you were dead," he told her.

Her mouth tightened in a grim line. "Not hardly. What you really mean is that you thought you killed me."

"You were trying to kill me at the time," The Kid pointed out.

She had a blued-steel Colt Lightning pointed at him from a distance of about four feet. Too far for him to jump her before she could pull the trigger.

While keeping the revolver leveled and rock steady, she brought her left hand up and cuffed her hat back so it hung behind her head on its chin strap, revealing a head of closely cropped auburn hair and a narrow, scabbed-over wound that started on the side of her head and disappeared into the hair above her right ear. "Your bullet just grazed me," she said. "It knocked me out cold and I had a headache for three days afterward, but I wasn't dead."

The Kid grunted. "I can see that. Where's the rest of your bunch?"

"I don't have a bunch. I was just traveling in the same direction as those men."

The Kid had a hunch there was more to it than that, but he didn't press her on it. He had more important things to worry about.

"So you're alone," he said.

"Don't let that give you any ideas," she snapped. "I've killed men before, and I won't mind doing it again if I have to." She nodded toward his gunbelt. "Unbuckle that belt and set it down, slow and easy."

The Kid knew if he allowed her to disarm him, his chances of getting away would plummet.

She was a woman, but her face held a hard competence that told him gender didn't matter a whole lot in this case. Female or not, she couldn't be soft and feminine and survive for very long as a bounty hunter. She had to be plenty tough.

He said, "All right . . . McCall."

The use of the name he guessed belonged to her surprised her enough that the gun in her hand jerked a little. It was what The Kid was watching for. He moved as soon as the reaction hit her. A quick shift to the right put him out of line for a split second—long enough for him leap forward, bat the barrel even farther to the side, and grab the woman.

"Max!" she cried.

Knowing the big dog would spring to the attack, he tightened his grip on the woman, whirled around, and took her with him. The dog was already in midair, trying to leap onto his back, but he gave the woman a shove that sent her right into the animal's path. They crashed together and both of them went sprawling.

The Kid sprang back and whipped out his Colt as the dog scrambled up again.

"Call him off!" The Kid told the woman. "I don't want to shoot him, but I will if I have to."

From her knees, the woman said sharply, "Max! Down!"

The dog subsided into a snarling crouch.

The woman had dropped her gun when she fell.

It lay a couple feet to her right. The Kid saw her eyeing it and said, "Don't try it."

"How do you know my name?" the woman demanded. "What did you do, paw through my saddlebags after you stole my horse?"

"You mean after you tried to kill me?" The Kid shot back.

"The wanted posters say dead or alive. I take prisoners in alive when I can, but if they put up a fight . . ." She gave an eloquent shrug.

"To answer your question," The Kid went on, "yes, I looked through your saddlebags. I found the envelope with the picture of the little girl in it."

"You son of a bitch," she whispered. "You had no right."

The Kid ignored that. "Who is she? She can't be your daughter. I can't imagine a woman like you ever having children."

"Why not? Because I'm a bounty hunter?"

"Let's just say you don't strike me as the maternal type."

"Go to hell. What did you do with the picture? Do you still have it?"

The Kid started to think maybe he'd been wrong. The raw edge of need in her voice as she spoke of the little girl's picture told him she might be a relative after all.

"I sent it back to the address in Kansas City," he said, softening his tone a little. "Along with the money I found in the saddlebags. I thought you were dead at the time, remember? I figured the little girl and whoever's taking care of her might need the cash."

A surprised frown creased the woman's forehead. "You did that?"

"Regardless of what you think about me, McCall—and I'm a lot of things that aren't very good, I'll admit that—I'm not a thief."

"You took my horse."

"I thought you were dead," he said again, "and I didn't have much choice in the matter."

She looked at him for a long moment, then asked, "Can I stand up?"

"Don't get too fancy about it. And don't try for any weapons you've got under that poncho. Why do you wear it, anyway?" Before she could answer, he went on, "Wait, don't tell me. It helps hide the fact that you're a woman, doesn't it? Just like the short hair."

"Go to hell," she repeated as she climbed to her feet. "Why I do things is my business."

"Like following me all the way from Nevada?"

A wolfish smile curved her wide mouth. "I want that ten grand."

"For the little girl back in Kansas City?"

"Shut up about her, would you?"

"More of your business?"

"Damn right."

The Kid shook his head. "Dress like a man, cuss

like a man . . . Do you chew tobacco and drink rotgut whiskey, too?"

"I never picked up the habit of chewing. A drink would be pretty good right now, though."

The Kid couldn't argue with that. He didn't have any whiskey to offer her, though, and wouldn't have even if he did.

"What in blazes am I going to do with you?" he asked.

"Better go ahead and kill me," she advised, "because if I get the chance, I'm sure as hell going to kill you."

Chapter 16

The dog was a problem. The Kid was going to have trouble dealing with the woman as long as he had to worry about the dog.

The simplest thing to do would be to shoot the beast. But he couldn't bring himself to do that in cold blood. The dog was doing what it had been trained to do—help capture fugitives from the law. The dog had no way of knowing that The Kid had been wrongly accused.

The woman ought to be able to understand that, though.

"Listen to me," he said. "Those wanted posters are wrong. They're all a mistake." He had made that same argument so many times in the past few months the words seemed to echo hollowly in his head. "I never killed any prison guards," he went on. "My lawyer is working on clearing my name right now."

"Yeah, the prisons are full of innocent men," she jeered.

"I was innocent. Damn it, I *am* innocent." Well, not really, he thought, but close enough in this case. "If you don't believe me, I'll have to make sure you don't follow me again."

"By gunning me down?"

And that was the problem right there, he thought with a sigh. He wasn't the cold-blooded killer he was accused of being. "I'll tie you up, leave you here, and take your horse with me. You'll be able to get loose eventually."

"Leaving me on foot in the middle of nowhere is the same as killing me, isn't it?"

"Not hardly, to use your words," The Kid said. "I'll leave your guns where you can find them. It's not more than ten miles to Flagstaff. That's a long walk, but it won't kill you." It was the best solution he could come up with.

"I'll track you down," she vowed. "You won't be able to hide your trail from me. And when I catch up to you again, I won't sic Max on you. I'll just go ahead and put a bullet in your dirty hide."

"I'm sorry you feel that way. Take off that poncho."

Her face hardened. "Try to mess with me, Morgan, and I'll kill you, I swear it. But not until I've taken a knife to you and made you wish you were already dead."

He spat out a curse. She was no lady, so he didn't worry about watching his language. "That's not what I want," he told her. "I just want to make sure you don't have any other guns or knives hidden under that thing."

Glaring at him, she took hold of the bottom of the poncho and pulled it up and over her head, revealing that she wore a butternut-colored man's shirt under the voluminous garment. Her breasts weren't overly large, but they were big enough they could be spotted easily if she weren't wearing the poncho.

"Turn around."

She did as he told her. He stepped forward and plucked a knife from a sheath on her left hip. The shirt and the buckskin trousers were tight enough for him to see she didn't appear to be carrying any other guns.

"All right, go hug that tree over there."

She cursed him in a low, monotonous voice as she followed the order.

He circled wide around the dog, which continued to stare at him with open hostility. He had some cord in his saddlebags and paused to crouch and fumble it out by feel while he kept his Colt leveled at the woman.

Approaching the tree as McCall put her arms around it, he angled in so he could still cover her. "Put your hands out as far as they'll go."

"Why should I cooperate with you?" she wanted to know.

"Because if you don't, I'll rap you on the head with the barrel of this gun, knock you out, and tie you up anyway. Do what I tell you and you'll avoid another headache."

"You are one gold-plated son of a bitch, you know that, Morgan?"

The Kid chuckled. "So I've been told."

"Anyway, you can't knock me out. If Max sees you hurt me, he'll come after you. There won't be any stopping him. He's barely controlling himself now."

The Kid knew she was telling the truth. He had seen the way the dog's muscles trembled a little with the need to attack.

"Then do what I tell you, and there won't be any need for me to shoot him."

She sighed and muttered another curse, then thrust her hands out as The Kid had told her to.

Moving fast so she couldn't pull back, he whipped the cord around her wrists, then yanked it tight.

She let out a yelp of pain. "Careful, you bastard."

"Sorry, I didn't mean to hurt you."

Oddly enough, the words were true. Despite the threat she represented, he couldn't work up any hatred for her, or any desire to cause her pain.

He holstered his gun and finished binding her wrists together, tying the knots so she would be able to work them loose, but would take her a while to do so.

"Keep the dog here with you," he warned her. "I will shoot him if I have to."

She glared at him around the tree trunk and didn't say anything.

He gathered up his gear, well aware of the hostile stares directed at him by both McCall and the dog. When he saddled the black, she broke her silence by saying, "You're stealing my horse again."

"I don't have any choice in the matter," The Kid told her. He smiled. "Anyway, it's a fine horse."

"You're going to wind up at the end of a hang rope."

"I've been worse places," The Kid said.

He mounted up and looked for her horse. It took him a while to find it. She had left it several hundred yards away and approached the camp on foot.

When he rode back up to the camp leading the chestnut gelding, he stiffened in the saddle as he looked at the tree where he had left her.

She was gone.

He thought for a second he must be looking at the wrong tree. The fire had died down and wasn't giving off much light anymore.

As he reined the black to a halt, he realized it was the right tree. McCall just wasn't tied to it anymore. There was no sign of her or the dog in the clearing.

The slight rustle of pine boughs was the only warning he had.

He twisted in the saddle and looked up as his hand flashed to his gun. The Colt hadn't cleared leather yet when McCall plunged down from a branch above and slammed into him. The diving tackle knocked him off the horse with barely enough time to kick his feet free of the stirrups.

When he hit the ground with her weight driving down on top of him, the impact knocked the breath out of his lungs and left him gasping for air as his head spun. He lashed out with a fist but didn't connect.

A second later something rough struck his head with stunning force. As he fought to hold on to consciousness, he caught a glimpse of her raising the broken branch she was using as a club. He threw a hand up in time to catch it as it descended in another blow.

McCall was like a wildcat, punching, writhing, digging her knee into his belly. She wrenched the branch out of his hand and hit him again with it. The Kid felt his awareness slipping away.

A terrible growl sounded in his ear. He felt the hot animal breath against his face.

"Give up, damn you!" McCall said. "Give up or he'll rip your throat out, and I won't stop him!"

Under the circumstances, The Kid knew he had no choice except to surrender. But he didn't get a chance to give up.

He passed out first.

It was an utterly revolting development, he thought when he regained consciousness. For the second time in only a week, he had been knocked out . . . by a woman! The memory of being tackled and then pounded into oblivion by McCall came flooding back to him, along with the pain in his head.

His arms and shoulders hurt, too, and it took

him a moment to figure out the reason why. He was sitting on the ground at the base of a tree, and his arms had been wrenched back behind the trunk so his wrists could be lashed together.

His head hung forward on his chest. His eyes were closed. But he could see a shifting red glare against his eyelids that came from a campfire larger than the one he had built earlier. He felt the warmth of the flames against his face.

He hauled his head upright. It seemed to weigh a hundred pounds. His eyelids were equally heavy, but he forced them up, then winced as the glare from the fire struck his eyes. A groan welled up his throat and escaped from his mouth.

"So, you're awake, are you?"

He recognized McCall's voice, and she sounded smugly satisfied with herself. The Kid turned his head a little and saw her sitting beside the fire. She wore her hat and poncho again, and she had a Winchester cradled across her knees.

"I was starting to think maybe I'd walloped you too hard with that branch."

He tried to talk, couldn't do it, then tried again and rasped out, "Yeah, I'm sure you'd have been brokenhearted if I was dead."

She grinned at him. "You'd have been easier to handle, no doubt about that, but you sure would have started to stink before we got to Santa Fe. I probably would've wound up cutting off your head and just taking it with me. I hate doing that."

The Kid thought she looked and sounded serious.

He heard a soft panting sound and looked toward it. The big ugly dog sat a few feet away. He would have sworn that the beast was *grinning* at him. "You two are proud of yourselves, aren't you?"

"I'll admit, we usually get what we go after," McCall said. "Don't we, Max?"

The dog let out a loud bark.

"Keep your opinions to yourself," The Kid muttered. He looked at McCall. "What happens now?"

"I take you to Santa Fe and collect that ten grand reward."

"Flagstaff is a lot closer. You could turn me over to the authorities there and put in your claim."

She shook her head. "And have to trust that some crooked lawman wouldn't try to cheat me? No, thanks. It's the Territory of New Mexico that wants you, and I intend to go as high up the ladder as I can. I'd dump you right in the governor's lap if I could. That way everybody will know I've got the whole ten thousand coming to me. I captured the notorious Kid Morgan all by myself."

The Kid glanced at Max. "You had a little help," he pointed out.

"He'll get his share, don't worry. Max and I

have been partners for a long time. We work well together."

The Kid couldn't dispute that. He said, "I figured I killed him when I threw him over the edge of that rock."

"You could have," McCall snapped, her eyes flaring with anger. "It was just pure luck he landed on Charley Hobart. Charley's a good-sized man. He broke Max's fall."

"So I came close to killing him and close to killing you on the same night."

"Yeah. You shouldn't be surprised that I don't like you, Morgan."

"I don't care if you like me," The Kid said. "I just wish you'd believe me when I tell you that this is all wrong."

"You mean that loco story about those wanted posters being a mistake?" She shook her head. "If you want to sell me a bill of goods, mister, you'd be better off trying something else. But if by some miracle you *are* telling the truth, you can straighten it out with the law in New Mexico . . . *after* I've collected that bounty."

He stopped arguing. It wasn't doing any good.

"What's your name besides McCall?"

She frowned at him and asked, "Why do you want to know?"

He shrugged as best he could with his arms tied to the tree like they were.

"Just curious, I guess."

"Well, it's none of your business."

"What's the story on that little girl in the picture?"

Her frown darkened. "That's *really* none of your business."

"Hey, I'm just making conversation here. If you're going to take me to Santa Fe, we'll be on the trail together for at least a week, probably more. It'll be a long, boring ride if we can't even talk." He paused. "I'm guessing that she's your niece."

"Well, you're wrong," McCall said. "You're so damned sure of yourself . . . sure you've got me pegged . . ." Emotions warred on her face. "She's my daughter, all right?"

The Kid looked at her, saw the pain in her eyes, and murmured, "Sorry."

"You should be," McCall said in a sullen voice. "Her name is Linda Sue, not that it's any affair of yours. She lives in Kansas City with my mother. I send money back to 'em, whenever I can."

"So I did the right thing by sending that roll of greenbacks to them."

"Yeah, you did. Although my mother's going to be worried when she gets the picture of Linda Sue with the money. She's liable to think I'm dead."

"At the time, I thought you *were* dead. I thought the picture ought to go back where it came from."

McCall looked away and shook her head. "I

reckon that was . . . a thoughtful thing for you to do. As soon as we get to somewhere I can post a letter, I'll write to my mother and let her know I'm still alive."

"Sorry if I've caused any trouble."

"Hell, you didn't know. No way you could know my life story." A bitter laugh came from her. "You wouldn't want to, even if you could."

"I wouldn't be so sure of that," The Kid told her. "I'd be glad to listen to anything you want to tell me."

Her eyes narrowed as she looked at him. Then her face twisted in a scowl and she jerked the rifle up toward him.

"What the hell are you trying to do?" she demanded. "Sweet-talk me? Is that what you think you're gonna do, Morgan? Pretend that you like the homely old gal so you can wrap her around your little finger and get her to do whatever you want?" Her finger tightened on the rifle's trigger. "Cutting the head off your corpse is starting to sound better all the time."

The Kid forced himself to stay calm, knowing he was looking death in the face. When he spoke, he told the truth. "You're not homely, and you're not old, McCall. I doubt if you're much more than twenty-five. I was just making conversation, not trying to seduce you."

"Yeah, well, you'd damned well better not try." She took a deep breath and lowered the rifle. "I don't put up with any of that stuff. Not since Pronto."

The Kid caught his breath as he recognized the name. "Pronto?" he said.

"Yeah. Pronto Pike. Used to be my partner. You must've seen him, that night we tangled before. It was his bunch I was traveling with. I knew it was a mistake. We came damn near to shooting each other when we split up a year ago, but when he asked me to give him a hand tracking you down, I said I would. Then when I was wounded—when *you* wounded me—he went off and left me, the bastard. All he was interested in was that reward."

The Kid struggled to make sense of all she had told him. He had figured that group of bounty hunters he'd encountered had continued on west in search of Kid Morgan. They hadn't gotten a good look at him that night, hadn't known he was actually the man they were after.

But for some reason they had doubled back to Las Vegas and caught up with him there, just like McCall had trailed him to the spot where she had jumped him.

He couldn't figure it all out, but he supposed it didn't really matter. He was McCall's prisoner.

He was sick and tired of being *somebody's* prisoner.

"I wouldn't have figured you for being friends with a cold-blooded bastard like Pike," he said.

McCall's eyes widened in surprise. "You know him?"

"We ran into each other in Las Vegas. He had ideas about that ten grand reward just like you do."

"But you got away from him?"

"Yeah."

She cursed and started heaping dirt on the flames to put out the fire.

"What are you doing?"

"You should have told me Pike was on your trail. I figured we had both given him the slip. You getting away from him like that will just make him more loco than ever. He'll hunt you down and try to take you away from me."

"I thought you used to be lovers."

"I never said that!" McCall blew out her breath as she extinguished the last of the flames and darkness plunged over the camp. "But it's true," she went on quietly. "And if he finds out that I've got you and he doesn't, he's liable to kill us both . . . you for the bounty, and me for the sheer fun of it."

"Do you still plan to take me all the way to Santa Fe?" The Kid asked her.

"That's right. And we're gonna get started right now!"

Chapter 17

As McCall was saddling the horses, she said, "You'd be wise not to give me any trouble from here on out, Morgan. If you cooperate, the worst I'll do is take you to Santa Fe and turn you in . . . alive. Pike won't go to that much bother."

"You mean he'll just kill me and be done with it," The Kid said.

She paused and looked at him. "Isn't that what I told you? If you doubt it, maybe I'll just leave you tied to that tree and let Pike find you."

The Kid shook his head. McCall was right. "I'll cooperate . . . for now."

She flashed a cold grin at him. "You're not making any promises for down the road, is that it?"

"Something like that," The Kid said.

"Yeah, well, right now I'll settle for putting this part of the country behind us," she said as she jerked a saddle cinch tight. She came over to him and pulled her knife from its sheath. "I have your word you won't try to escape? Because I can knock you out and tie you belly down over your horse if you'd rather."

The Kid took a deep breath and then nodded. "I give you my word," he said. It was a bitter promise to make, but seemed like the best option.

McCall returned the nod and went around to the

other side of the tree. The Kid felt the knife tug on the ropes as she cut them.

He pulled his arms back in front of him, grimacing as pain shot through the stiff muscles. His hands had gone partially numb. He rubbed them together to get feeling into them.

"You can ride that buckskin of yours," she told him. "I'm taking Blackie."

He laughed. "You named your horse Blackie? Your black horse?"

She turned sharply to glare at him. "You got a problem with that? I could still kill you and cut your head off, you know."

"No, no problem," The Kid said with a grin that he knew would annoy her. He went over to the buckskin and swung up onto the saddle.

"Move out," McCall told him as she mounted. "You're leading the way."

"You think I know where we're going?"

"You know which way's east. I want you in front of me so I can shoot you if I have to."

The Kid shook his head and heeled the buckskin into motion. Riding at night was tricky, especially in rugged terrain, so he let the horse pick his own pace.

McCall rode to the left and a few feet behind him, leading the third horse. He turned his head and said to her, "There's one thing I'm curious about."

"What's that?"

"How did you get loose when I went to find that horse you were riding? I didn't tie you up as tight as I could, but you shouldn't have been able to work your way free that quickly."

"You've got Max to thank for that," she said with a nod toward the big dog, who padded along beside them. "He chewed through that cord without much trouble when I told him to."

The Kid grunted. "I didn't figure on some damn trick dog."

"You didn't figure on a lot of things," McCall said.

The Kid didn't have a response for that, so he didn't say anything. He couldn't help but think, though, that he had never met a woman quite like the bounty hunter named McCall.

She kept them moving far into the night, explaining that if anyone had spotted the campfire, she wanted to be a long way from that location before they stopped to rest. When she finally called a halt, a faint tinge of gray in the eastern sky signaled dawn was only a few hours off.

McCall dismounted first and drew her gun. "All right, Morgan. Get down from that horse and put your hands behind you."

"I need to tend to some personal business first," The Kid said as he swung down from the buckskin.

"If you want to take a piss, there's a bush right

there that could use some watering." McCall raised her Colt Lightning and pointed it at his head. "It's short enough I can see you to shoot if you give me a good reason."

"I promised to cooperate, remember?"

"Yeah, but it wasn't much of a promise. For now, you said, and how the hell am I supposed to know how long that is?"

She had a point, he supposed. He stepped behind the bush and took care of the chore while she stood a few feet away aiming the gun at his head. The arrangement was a little awkward, but it was better than nothing, he told himself.

When he was finished, she said, "All right, hands behind your back."

"You don't need to tie me up."

"I'll rest a lot easier if I do."

"How about this? I give you my word I won't try to escape for the next twenty-four hours. That way you can get some sleep, too, while I stand guard."

She laughed humorlessly. "I'm supposed to believe an hombre who's wanted for breaking out of prison and murdering guards?"

"One of those charges is completely false, and as far as I knew until recently, the other one had been dropped because of extenuating circumstances."

"Extenuating," she repeated. "Where'd you learn a word like that?"

"You'd be surprised how much I know."

"Maybe. But you don't know how to do like you're told. Now, about putting your hands behind your back . . ." She lifted the Lightning.

"Do you know where I was going when you caught up to me?" he asked.

She shook her head. "Not really."

"I was going to Santa Fe. My lawyer's there. That's where I *want* to go. You're not taking me there as much as we're just riding together."

"This gun says different. So does Max."

The dog bared his teeth at The Kid at the sound of his name.

McCall went on, "He can knock you down and chew on you for a while if you don't want to go along with what I say. After that I reckon you won't be so quick to argue."

The Kid put his hands behind his back, but not without muttering, "One of these days you won't have that gun and that dog."

"Yeah, you just keep telling yourself that," McCall jeered.

She tied his hands, then helped him sit down at the base of a tree. After holstering the Lightning, she pulled her Winchester from its sheath and sat down where she could lean back against the trunk of another tree. She didn't make a fire, and it was cold enough that their breath fogged in front of their faces.

As uncomfortable as The Kid was, he didn't

think he'd be able to sleep. But exhaustion trumped discomfort, and even though he was leaning against the rough bark of a pine trunk, he dozed off quickly.

When he woke up, he found he had slumped onto his side while he was sleeping. The sun was up, slanting its rays through the trees.

A few yards away, McCall was lying on her side, too, and appeared to be sound asleep. Her hat had come off, and her head was pillowed on one arm. The hard lines of her face had softened some as she relaxed. She wasn't what anybody would call pretty, but as The Kid looked at her, he realized when she wasn't trying to appear fierce and intimidating, her features had a certain attractiveness to them. The lines that a hard life had etched into her face also gave her character.

The Kid's mouth tightened into a grim line as he told himself he shouldn't be thinking such things about her, or about any woman. It hadn't been long enough since he had buried his wife.

But it didn't hurt anything to lie there and look at McCall. He wondered how she had wound up with a child living in Kansas City while she wandered the frontier trying to apprehend the worst of the badmen who were wanted by the law.

The sound of hoofbeats drifted to The Kid's ears and caused him to jerk his head up as he listened intently. Several horses, he decided, and they weren't far away.

McCall still slept soundly.

Softly, The Kid spoke to her. "McCall! McCall, wake up! Riders coming."

She didn't budge. In fact, her breathing seemed to be deeper and more regular than ever. She was settling in for a nice, long sleep.

The Kid muttered a curse and sat up. He pushed his back against the tree trunk and started wiggling his shoulders as he worked his way up. After a moment, he managed to get a foot underneath him and awkwardly pushed himself into a standing position.

His legs were stiff from sleeping on the ground. He stumbled over to McCall and nudged her shoulder with a booted foot. "Wake up, damn it!" he said to her in an urgent whisper.

She woke up, all right. She sat bolt upright, snatched the Winchester from the ground beside her, and rammed the barrel into The Kid's belly, causing him to double over in pain.

As The Kid tried not to retch, McCall scrambled backward on her butt and trained the rifle on him. "What the hell are you trying to do?" she demanded in a loud voice.

The Kid hissed through his teeth at her, hoping she would understand that he meant for her to keep it down. "Riders coming," he croaked out.

McCall lifted her head and listened. An

expression of alarm flashed across her face. She had heard the horses, too.

She leaped to her feet and drew her knife. "I'm gonna cut you loose," she said as she stepped behind The Kid. "We've got to keep our horses quiet and hope those men, whoever they are, pass us by. I can count on your word not to try to escape?"

"You can," The Kid told her.

She slashed the ropes around his wrists. He massaged them, then stepped over to the buckskin and put a hand on the horse's muzzle. McCall did the same with the other two horses and told the dog, "Quiet, Max."

Max stood with his tail up and the hair on the back of his neck bristling, but he didn't make a sound.

The hoofbeats grew louder. The riders probably weren't more than fifty yards away. The Kid heard the low mutter of men's voices, but they were too far away for him to make out any of the words or recognize the voices.

That early in the morning there wasn't much breeze. With any luck, the strangers' horses wouldn't scent the four animals in the makeshift camp. The Kid and McCall waited in tense silence.

The hoofbeats began to recede as the riders passed the camp and were going on without discovering it. The Kid and McCall stood motionless until the sound of the horses faded away completely.

McCall heaved a sigh and said, "They're out of earshot now."

"Could you tell if they were Pike and his men?"

She shook her head. "No, I never could hear them well enough for that."

"If they were, they're ahead of us now. If we keep going east, we're liable to come up behind them."

McCall nodded and said, "I know. That's why we're going to cut south for a while and then head east again."

"You know, sooner or later we'll have to find out just how much you trust me."

She frowned at him and asked, "What do you mean by that?"

"If we run into Pike, there'll be trouble, you said."

"Yeah, you can count on that."

"When that time comes . . . you're going to have to give me a gun. Two of us will have a better chance against five killers."

"Those still aren't good odds." McCall grunted. "But I'll have to admit, they're better than five to one. Still, I might be a damn fool to put a gun in your hand."

"I guess if it happens, we'll find out," The Kid said.

"*When*. I know Pike. Since you got away from

him in Las Vegas, he'll feel like he's been cheated, and won't stop looking for you until he finds you. Not with ten grand at stake." McCall shoved the Winchester in its saddle boot. "So it's not a matter of *if* we have to fight for our lives, Morgan. It's a matter of *when*."

Chapter 18

They cut south for the next couple days, hitting the Verde River and following it southeast as it cut around the Mogollon Rim. The Kid had a vague memory of his father telling him about some range war he had been involved with in the area, but he didn't recall any of the details.

It was the long way around and would add days to their journey to Santa Fe, but McCall was convinced it would help them avoid Pronto Pike . . . if, in fact, Pike and his bunch of bounty killers were on their trail.

"Pike must be hell on wheels to make you as nervous as he does," The Kid commented as he and McCall rode along with the rim looming to their left. Max padded alongside them.

"There's a big difference between being careful and being nervous," she said. "Don't forget, I rode with Pike for a good long time. I know what sort of man he is. He likes killing people, Morgan. He just makes sure that everybody he kills is wanted by the law. That way he doesn't wind up at the end of a hang rope himself."

"I saw enough of him in Las Vegas to know that you're probably right."

"You can bet a hat that I am," McCall said. "Why, one time I saw Pike—"

Whatever she was going to say about Pike went

unfinished as half a dozen gunshots rang out. They weren't too far away, and the sound traveled clearly in the thin air.

The Kid and McCall reined in sharply and exchanged glances.

"Whoever that is, they don't seem to be shooting at us," The Kid said.

McCall nodded. "And it's none of our business, either."

Both riders recognized the sound of several pistols creating the burst of gunfire. A moment later, a rifle cracked a couple times, followed by more revolver shots.

"Somebody's putting up a fight," The Kid commented.

"Still not any of our business," McCall replied with a stubborn shake of her head.

"Unless Pike's mixed up in it somehow. Maybe he and his men jumped somebody they thought was us. Could be innocent people being shot at over there."

The Kid nodded toward the Mogollon Rim. The reports from the rifle and the handguns were mixed together, coming from that direction.

McCall glared at him. "You're a fugitive from the law. Men like you aren't usually worried about what might be happening to innocent people."

The Kid smiled thinly. "That's just one more indication the charges against me are a mistake."

“Still scraping out that tune on your fiddle, are you?” McCall blew out her breath in an exasperated sigh. “All right, we’ll go take a look. But that’s all. We’re not getting mixed up in any war unless it can’t be avoided.”

They turned their horses and rode toward the rim, which was nothing more than the southern edge of the Mogollon Mesa and the massive Colorado Plateau. In his days as Conrad Browning, when he took an active interest in a number of railroad lines, he had studied dozens of survey and topographical maps and knew the geography of the western states.

The rugged limestone and sandstone cliffs of the rim rose a thousand feet or more above the pine-dotted flats that stretched off to the south. Trails ran to the top, so the rim wasn’t an impassable barrier, but it was a definite dividing line that ran through the midsection of Arizona Territory. There were a lot of ranches in the area, and more than a few mines in the canyons that nature had cut into the rim.

The shots got louder as The Kid and McCall approached the dark, looming cliffs. McCall motioned for The Kid to slow down as they reached the edge of a stand of trees. She dismounted, and The Kid followed suit.

They stepped forward to where they could look across a clearing that stretched for a couple hundred yards to the base of a cliff. A rough log cabin squatted at the bottom of the cliff. A short distance to the right of it was the mouth of a narrow, steep-sided canyon.

It appeared to be choked with brush, but when The Kid looked closer, he saw that someone had built a gate across it and camouflaged that gate by tying branches to it. Somebody had closed off the canyon on purpose but tried to conceal what they had done.

Probably the same person holed up in the cabin, The Kid thought.

A puff of gunsmoke came from a loophole cut into the log wall every time the rifle cracked. The shots were directed at half a dozen men crouched behind boulders that had fallen from the cliff face in ages past. They littered the area in front of the cabin and served as cover for the gunmen. The range was a little long for Colts, but they acted like they had plenty of ammunition to spare as they continued peppering the cabin with shots.

One thing was certain: if the man inside the cabin were to step out, he would be riddled with lead in a matter of seconds. The besiegers had a grim determination about them, a resolve to wipe out the man they had trapped.

"That's not Pike and his bunch," McCall said quietly.

The Kid agreed. The gunmen were hard-looking individuals in range clothes, but they weren't the bounty hunters.

"So I was right, this is none of our business," McCall continued. "Let's go."

The Kid had been watching the cabin. The lack of return fire from other loopholes told him the defender was alone. "Six to one odds aren't what I'd call fair," he said.

McCall looked over at him in surprise. "You want us to take a hand in this game? I told you, it's none of our business."

"Sooner or later, they'll root out whoever's in the cabin and kill him."

"Do you know who it is?"

The Kid shook his head. "I don't have any idea."

"Then why do you care? For all you know, he's a son of a bitch who deserves whatever he's got coming to him."

The Kid couldn't deny that. But he said, "I still don't like it."

"And I don't give a damn what you like or don't like." McCall put her hand on the butt of her gun. "Climb back on your horse. We're getting out of here."

She hadn't been tying his hands the past couple of days. Evidently she believed his pledge to accompany her to Santa Fe, but that didn't mean she had forgotten he was her prisoner. He was unarmed, and she always kept some distance between them so he couldn't jump her and overpower her.

The Kid didn't want to ride away from the ruckus, but he didn't see what choice he had. He was about to nod and reluctantly get back on the buckskin when he heard something else. "There's a wagon coming," he said as his keen ears identified the sound.

McCall lifted her head and listened. "You're right," she said after a couple seconds. The hoofbeats of a team and the creaking of wagon wheels grew louder. "Let's get these horses out of sight."

They took hold of the reins and led the animals deeper into the trees, leaving them there along with the dog. The wagon moved up on their left, obviously following a trail they hadn't seen as they approached the scene of battle.

The wagon stopped before it left the trees. A moment later, a man called, "Make the old bastard duck, and I'll bring the stuff out to you!"

Immediately, the men behind the boulders increased their fusillade, aiming high so the bullets would carry farther. As slugs thudded into the front wall of the cabin, a man darted from the trees carrying a small wooden crate.

The Kid's jaw tightened as he recognized the markings on the crate. "That's dynamite," he told McCall. "They're going to blast the man out of there."

For a second, McCall didn't say anything. Then, "That's pretty raw. It's bad enough when you outnumber somebody six to one without resorting to dynamite." She shrugged. "But still—"

"None of our business," The Kid finished for her.

"Yeah. That's exactly right."

"You can ride away from seven hardcases trying to kill an old man?"

"How do you know he's old?"

"The one who brought the dynamite called him an old bastard."

"Could be just a figure of speech," McCall said. "Or it could be an old-timer in there. Somebody's grandfather."

"Yeah, well, my old man was somebody's grandfather, and he was the sorriest son of a bitch to ever walk the face of the earth." McCall's voice was thick with bitterness. "We're leaving, Morgan. I'm getting tired of arguing the point."

The man with the crate of dynamite had reached the rocks. He bent and put the crate on the ground before prying the lid off.

"He's lucky he didn't trip and fall while he was carrying that stuff," The Kid said. "Might've had quite an explosion if that had happened."

"I thought you had to set dynamite off with blasting caps," McCall said with a frown.

"That's the normal procedure, but it's notoriously unstable. Men who handle it are usually more careful than to run around with a box full of it."

"Maybe that fella doesn't know that. And how come you do?"

"I've spent time in several railroad construction camps while my companies were building spur lines."

McCall stared at him. "What?"

"Never mind," The Kid said with a wave of his hand. "McCall, we can't just stand by and let them blow somebody to kingdom come."

She glared at him for several seconds before shaking her head and saying, "You're right. Damn it. What do you think we should do?"

The Kid's eyebrows rose in surprise. "You're asking me?"

"I figure if you were able to break out of a place like Hell Gate Prison, you must be able to come up with some pretty good ideas."

"All right," he said. "How good a shot are you with a rifle?"

She snorted. "I've lived this long. What do you think?"

"Fine. See the fella who brought out the dynamite? He's tying three sticks of it together. He's going to throw it at the cabin."

"I see him. What do you want me to do?"

"When he draws back to let fly with it, see if you can drill his arm."

"Make him drop the stuff, you mean?"

The Kid nodded. "If you can do that, I guarantee the rest of them will scatter like the Devil himself is after them . . . because that's pretty much what it'll amount to."

"What about the one I'm supposed to wing?"

"That's why I didn't tell you to shoot him in the leg. He'll still be able to run."

"You don't think they'll turn around and come after us?"

"I think they'll be too spooked to do that," The Kid said, "but if they do, at least they'll be scattered. We can take them on one or two at a time."

"That's assuming I give you a gun," McCall said. "That's a mighty big maybe."

"We'll worry about that later." The Kid nodded toward the boulders. "Looks like he's getting ready to light the fuse. It's time for you to make up your mind, McCall."

She glared at him, but she lifted the rifle she had taken from her saddle. There was already a round in the chamber. She brought the weapon to her shoulder, snugged the butt against it, and nestled her cheek on the smooth wood of the stock so she could peer over the barrel.

"You know, there's no guarantee I can make this shot," she said. "It won't be easy."

"I never said it would be," The Kid replied.

She muttered something, squinting slightly as she settled the sights on the man who had scratched a lucifer to life and was about to hold the flame to the end of the twisted fuse dangling from the bundle of dynamite.

The Kid saw sparks fly as the fuse caught. The man drew his arm back high above his head as he prepared to throw the dynamite at the cabin.

McCall squeezed the trigger, and the whip-crack of the Winchester's shot filled the air.

Chapter 19

The man screamed as the .44-40 round tore through his arm. The three sticks of dynamite slipped from his fingers, fell to the ground, bounced once, and rolled to a stop, leaning against the side of the crate that held the rest of the dynamite.

It was a hell of a shot, The Kid thought, but the results were going to be more spectacular than he had intended.

The gunmen yelled in alarm and scattered, just as he had thought they would.

At the same time, he turned and grabbed McCall's arm to shove her deeper into the stand of pine trees.

"Move, move!" he told her. "We've got to get farther away!"

She turned and ran. So did The Kid. Glancing over his shoulder he caught a glimpse of the wounded man leaning over the crate and the dynamite he had dropped. He pawed frantically at it with his uninjured arm, trying to pluck the fuse away from the blasting caps.

He was too late.

The ground jumped up for a second under The Kid's feet as a thunderous roar filled the air and echoed from the cliffs of the Mogollon Rim. The man bending over the dynamite disappeared in a sheet of flame.

The Kid stumbled and fell as what felt like a giant hand slapped him in the back. Pine needles blown off their branches showered down around him. He pushed himself up and twisted his head to look back again.

A huge, rolling cloud of dust filled the open area in front of the cabin. The force of the explosion most likely crumbled the boulders to pebbles.

He climbed to his feet and looked around for McCall. She lay a few yards away where the blast had knocked her down. She sat up, shook her head groggily, and said something.

The Kid saw her mouth moving, but couldn't hear a word. He couldn't hear anything except an eerie, whispering hush, and realized the explosion had temporarily deafened him.

His hastily conceived plan hadn't included the whole crate of dynamite going off. At least one of the men had been killed for sure, and some or all of the others might not have gotten far enough away to escape the deadly force of the blast.

It would probably be a good idea to find out about that as quickly as they could, he thought. He bent and caught hold of McCall's arm again. He helped her to her feet and put his mouth close to her ear. "Can you hear me?" he shouted.

She nodded. She had lost her hat when she fell, and her short auburn hair was tangled around her head. "I'll take a look!" she shouted into his ear.

"I'll come with you!"

She didn't waste any breath arguing with him. Together, they moved to the edge of the trees. The dust cloud was starting to thin, but choking masses of the stuff still hung in the air here and there. The Kid peered through the gaps and saw the boulders were still there, although it looked like the one closest to the site of the explosion had been toppled on its side.

A pit five feet deep and twenty feet wide had been gouged out of the ground by the blast.

Suddenly, a man came out of the dust, the gun in his hand spewing flame and death. McCall twisted toward him and fired the Winchester from the hip, cranking off three rounds as fast as she could work the weapon's lever. The man stumbled and dropped his gun as the slugs ripped through him. He collapsed with his hands pressed to his bloody midsection.

As she faced that threat, McCall's back was turned toward another man who appeared out of the dust with no warning. His gun was swinging up toward the bounty hunter when The Kid tackled him from the side and drove him off his feet.

They sprawled on the ground as they were pelted by chunks of rock and dirt clods that had been thrown high in the air by the blast.

The Kid got a hand on the man's wrist and wrenched his arm aside just as the man tried to turn the gun toward him. The man's other hand flashed up, clenched into a fist that slammed into the side of The Kid's head.

Ignoring the pain The Kid put his hand on the man's neck, digging fingers in to cut off his air. The man thrashed under him and hammered at his head, but The Kid raised his shoulders, hunkered down, and continued to ignore the pain of the blows. He had to keep the gun pointed away from him and maintain his death grip until the man died or passed out, whichever came first.

But he couldn't ignore the pain that shot through him when the man lifted a knee into his groin, making The Kid loosen his grip. The man jerked his gun hand free.

As he saw the barrel swinging swiftly toward him, The Kid drove his head down into his opponent's face. The revolver went off, blasting close to his ear. He felt the sting of burning grains of powder as they sprayed across his cheek.

His forehead pounded the man's nose, flattening it into a pulp. Hot blood spurted across The Kid's face. He lifted his head and grabbed for the man's gun, wrenching it loose.

With savage strength, he brought the butt down in the middle of the man's already-ruined face, striking again and again and yet again, until the man went limp underneath him.

The Kid blinked blood out of his eyes and saw that the man was dead.

He pushed himself to his feet and pawed more of the gore off his face. McCall stood nearby, holding the Winchester.

"I would have shot him," she said, "but you were in the way. I couldn't ever get a clear shot."

The words sounded tinny and distorted in The Kid's ears, but he understood them well enough to know his hearing was coming back, at least on one side. It might be a while before the ear that had been so close to the barrel of the dead man's Colt recovered.

"Do you see any more of them?" he asked her.

She shook her head. "No. There are a couple lying over yonder who look like they were killed by the explosion."

That made five, counting the man who had been blown to smithereens. Two men unaccounted for, thought The Kid. They might still be running . . . or they might be lurking around trying to figure out what had happened—and who was to blame.

"Let's go take a look at the cabin," The Kid suggested. "Maybe whoever's in there can tell us what's going on here."

"Are you sure you want to do that?" McCall asked. "We stopped those men from blowing up the place. That's enough. Let's find our horses and light a shuck out of here."

The Kid shook his head. "I want to know what it was about."

"Damn it, *I'm* in charge here! I've got the gun."

"Not the only one," The Kid said, and he showed her the Colt he had taken away from the man he'd killed. The handle was still a little slick with blood, but he didn't have any trouble holding it.

For a second he thought McCall was going to shoot him with the Winchester. After that tense heartbeat—during which he didn't know what he would do if she threw down on him—she nodded and said, "All right, if it's that important to you, let's go check out the cabin."

"I think it's a good idea," The Kid said.

Most of the dust had cleared, and he was acutely aware that they were out in the open as they walked around the boulders. The cabin appeared to be undamaged. The rocks had shielded it from most of the force of the blast.

As they approached, the door swung open and the barrel of a rifle thrust out. The Kid and McCall tensed.

"Don't come any closer!" a man's voice yelled. It was reedy with age and strain. "I'll shoot if I have to!"

"We saw plenty proof of that, old-timer," The Kid called. "We're on your side, though. You don't have to be afraid of us."

"How can you be on my side?" The question came from the dark interior of the cabin. "I don't know you. You ain't got no earthly idea who I am!"

"That's true," McCall muttered. "I'm glad to see that somebody else is thinking straight around here."

"That explosion could have destroyed your cabin," The Kid said. "With you in it. Thanks to us, it didn't."

"Well, I'm obliged to you for that, I reckon. But that don't mean I'm dumb enough to trust you. Who are you, anyway?"

"My name's Morgan. This is McCall. We were riding through when we heard the shots."

"How come you got mixed up in my troubles? They ain't none o' your business."

McCall said, "Again, somebody who's thinking straight."

The Kid ignored her. "We didn't like the look of the odds. We liked them even less once the fellow showed up with the dynamite."

"Yeah, that bunch would'a been glad to blow me hell-west and crosswise," the unseen old man responded. He finally stepped into the doorway. He was twisted sideways and held the rifle in his right hand while resting the barrel across what appeared to be the stump of his left arm. That sleeve of his faded flannel shirt was pinned up where most of the limb was missing.

The ease with which the old-timer handled the rifle told The Kid the injury wasn't a new one.

The missing arm might not have been caused by an injury. He could have been born that way.

He was short, stocky, and mostly bald. A fringe of white hair circled the back of his head, running from ear to ear. A thick white beard jutted from his chin and hung down over his chest. He wore overalls, the flannel shirt, and work boots that laced up.

He stared at McCall for a second before exclaiming, "Good Lord! You're a woman, ain't you, Red?"

"That's right," she told him. "Does that bother you, mister?"

"Shoot, no. It's just that it's been a long time since I seen a female, that's all, stuck off under this rim like I am." His eyes narrowed as he peered at her. "Don't recollect seein' a gal totin' firearms since I knowed that bawdy ol' wench, Calamity Jane. Got to say you're a whole heap prettier'n Calam ever was. She had a way o' comfortin' a man, though, when he needed it . . ."

"That's about enough of that," McCall snapped. "Who are you, mister?"

"See, I done told you, you don't know me from Adam's off ox. I'm Chester Blount. Name mean anything to you?"

The Kid shook his head. "I can't say that it does."

"Well, no reason it should. I've always lived a quiet life. Until Spud Guthrie decided he had to have Dos Caballos Canyon there." He inclined his bald head toward the mouth of the canyon that had been closed off by the camouflaged gate.

"I never heard of Spud Guthrie, either," The Kid said, "but he doesn't sound like a very pleasant sort."

Chester Blount chuckled. "Oh, he ain't, and that's the blessed truth. Them was Guthrie's men tryin' to kill me. Are you claimin' that you blowed 'em up, mister?"

"We did. Some of them, anyway."

"How in blazes did you manage that? Sounded like the world was comin' to an end for a second there. Way the ground shook, I was pert near afraid the whole rim was about to come down on top of me."

"They had a crate of dynamite they were going to use to blast you out," The Kid explained. "The whole crate sort of . . . went off."

Blount let out a low whistle. "I hope to smile it did. Kill all the varmints?"

"It looks like a couple of them got away."

Blount stiffened and frowned. "The two o' you best take off for the tall and uncut, then, whilst you still got a chance to do so. Them boys'll run straight back to Guthrie, and when he hears what happened here, he'll saddle up the other thirty or forty of his gunwolves and come callin'. He ain't been too unfriendly so far, but this'll really piss him off."

That comment startled a laugh of disbelief out of The Kid. "Sending seven hardcases after you with a crate of dynamite isn't being too unfriendly?"

"You don't know Spud Guthrie. That sawed-off little runt is the meanest man to ever walk the face o' the earth. If you don't believe me, you just stick around here and see what happens."

McCall said, "If that's true, then you can't stay here, either, Mr. Blount. We have an extra horse. You can come with us."

Blount had lowered his rifle as they talked, but now he raised it again. "I ain't goin' nowhere!" he snapped. "I been prospectin' Dos Caballos for nigh on to ten years now, and I ain't leavin' just when I'm about ready to finally make a good strike!"

Those words explained a lot, The Kid thought. Blount was a prospector, always on the lookout for the bonanza of gold or silver that would make him rich, and like most of his breed, he was probably a little touched in the head. He would cling stubbornly to his belief that someday he would strike it rich.

Even though that belief might get him killed.

"Take it easy," The Kid told the old-timer. "McCall's right. If this man Guthrie shows up with an army of hired killers, you won't stand a chance. Why don't you come with us now, and you can always come back later once things have cooled off a little."

"They ain't gonna cool off," Blount insisted. "And I can't leave, 'cause if I do, when I come back Dos Caballos won't be there."

"Won't be there?" The Kid repeated with a frown. "Where is a canyon going to go?"

"Underground," the old-timer said. "Guthrie's gonna blast the sides and collapse the whole blamed thing."

Chapter 20

The Kid and McCall stared at Blount. What the old man said sounded crazy.

"Why in the world would he do that?" The Kid asked after a moment.

Blount waved a hand toward the top of the looming cliff. "Guthrie's Rafter G spread is up yonder, on top of the rim. It's a good ranch, but his herds have grown so fast he's runnin' short of grass and water. Now, it just so happens he owns some land down here on the flats with plenty o' grass and water, but there ain't no good way to get his stock to it. He'd have to drive the critters nigh on to a hundred miles to get a good-sized herd down off the rim. Only other way would be to bring 'em single file down one of the narrow trails, and that'd be a recipe for disaster." Blount shook his head. "That's when he brung in some engineerin' fella who told him that if he blasted the sides of the canyon and made 'em collapse into the canyon itself, he could haul in some dirt and make a nice, wide trail out of it. Then his herds could get up and down off the rim without no trouble."

It was an audacious scheme, The Kid thought, and fraught with obstacles, but he'd had enough engineering training in college to know that it might actually work.

"But Guthrie's main problem is that *you* own Dos Caballos Canyon, right?" he asked Blount.

The old-timer nodded. "Dang right. I filed on it more'n ten years ago, when I decided I was gonna prospect. I got a nose for gold. I know it's in there."

"If you own the canyon, why don't you just sell it to Guthrie?" McCall asked. "If it's that important to him, he'd probably give you a good price."

Blount snorted. "No offense, ma'am, but wasn't you just listenin'? I'm gonna make a good strike in there, and it'll make me a lot richer than Spud Guthrie ever could."

"And how long did you say you'd been looking for that strike?"

"Ten years," Blount replied proudly.

"Didn't you ever stop to think that if you haven't found it in that amount of time, you probably never will?"

The old man glared at her. "You say that 'cause you ain't got no faith. I do."

"There's a difference between having faith and being muleheaded," McCall said as she returned the glare. "Come on, Kid. Let's get out of here."

"Hang on," The Kid said. "Did Guthrie offer to buy you out, Mr. Blount?"

Blount nodded. "He did. I turned him down flat."

"What did he do then?"

"Well, he tried to run me out, o' course. Several times whilst I was workin' up in the canyon, somebody took potshots at me. They come close enough I could tell they was tryin' to scare me, not kill me. When I didn't leave, they started comin' closer."

"Until today, when he sent men to kill you."

"Yep. I seen them varmints comin' and hotfooted it for the cabin. Barely made it here 'fore they started shootin' at me. I guess Guthrie figured I might fort up, so he sent along that fella with the dynamite, too."

"That backfired on him," The Kid said with a glance toward the crater behind the boulders.

"Thanks to you two," Blount said. "I reckon if you hadn't come along when you did, I'd be tryin' to kick down the Pearly Gates right about now. Either that or shakin' hands with the Devil."

"You're welcome," McCall said. "But from here on out, you're on your own, old-timer. If you were smart, you'd light a shuck and put this place far behind you."

Blount shook his head. "It's too late for that. Some of Guthrie's men are dead. He ain't gonna stand for that. I told you he was a mean sidewinder. He'll have to kill me now. I wouldn't never be able to run far enough or fast enough to get away from him."

"Then what *are* you going to do?" The Kid asked.

"Stay here and fight," Blount declared. "Do as

much damage to the son of a buck and his hired guns as I can until they get me." He shrugged. "It ain't been that good of a life, I reckon, but it's sure enough been a long one. I ain't got no kick comin'. At least I'll go out scrappin'."

"There's something else you can do," The Kid said.

"What's that? 'Cause I ain't seein' it."

"Sell a half-interest in Dos Caballos Canyon to me."

"Damn it!" McCall exploded. "Have you forgotten that you're my prisoner, Morgan?"

"Not anymore," The Kid said. "Not unless you want to shoot me and cut my head off, like you keep threatening to do. I'd have to try to stop you from doing that."

She glanced at the gun in his hand, and he knew she was trying to gauge just how serious he was.

Blount looked back and forth between them, a baffled expression on his leathery face. "What the hell are you folks talkin' about? Buyin' the canyon? Takin' folks prisoner and cuttin' off their heads? That's loco!"

Without taking her eyes off The Kid, McCall said, "Morgan's a fugitive from the law. He's wanted for breaking out of prison and killing a couple guards over in New Mexico Territory. There's a ten thousand dollar reward for him."

"The part about killing the guards is a lie," The Kid said. "I never did that. And the only reason I broke out of prison was because I'd been locked up by mistake. They thought I was somebody else."

Blount scratched at his beard. "That's a pretty wild story," he said dubiously.

McCall grunted. "It gets even wilder. Morgan claims he's really some sort of tycoon who just pretends to be a gunfighter."

"I never used the word *tycoon,*" The Kid said. "But my real name is Conrad Browning, and I do have a lot of lucrative business interests."

"If that's true," Blount said, "then what in blazes are you doin' runnin' around the frontier lookin' like some sort o' saddle tramp?"

"It's a long story."

McCall snorted to indicate her disbelief. She said, "You gave me your word, Morgan."

"That I'd go to Santa Fe with you. I still will . . . but only after we help Mr. Blount settle his troubles."

"It ain't that I don't appreciate the offer," Blount said. "But why would you want to help an old codger like me? An hour ago, you hadn't ever laid eyes on me."

"That's true," The Kid admitted. "I guess you could just say . . . I used to know somebody who would have wanted me to help you."

That was the way it had been since Rebel's death. Once his need for revenge had been satisfied, at least as much as it could be, The Kid had wanted nothing more than to be left alone with his sorrow.

Time and again, he had run into people who were in trouble, usually through no fault of their own. He knew Rebel would have wanted him to help them. He even seemed to hear her voice at times, speaking to him and urging him to do the right thing, even though it went against what he really wanted.

It had happened enough that he was growing to accept it. He had wanted to be a loner, holding the world at arm's length . . . but it kept crowding in on him, refusing to allow him to sink into an abyss of solitude and grief.

When you came right down to it, he thought, trouble might well be the only thing that was keeping him alive. Maybe he had to risk his life in order to save it.

It was too much for him to figure out. All he really knew was that he couldn't ride away and leave Chester Blount to face death alone.

"You can't do anything to help him," McCall argued. "You heard what he said. Guthrie has dozens of gunmen working for him. And you've got an appointment with the law in Santa Fe."

"One that I'll keep when the time comes," The Kid said. "Think about it, McCall. This is a pretty isolated area. Pike's not going to be looking for us here. If we hole up here for a while, maybe he'll get tired and stop searching for us."

"Who's Pike?" asked Blount.

"An added annoyance," McCall snapped. "You might have something there, Kid. We lay low for a while, then make a run for Santa Fe. There's just one problem with the idea."

"What's that?"

She gestured curtly toward the rim. "Guthrie's gunhawks will probably kill us!"

"Well," The Kid said, "we'll just have to make sure that they don't."

Chapter 21

Claudius Turnbuckle was a tall, burly, balding man with muttonchop whiskers. Dressed in an expensive suit and bowler hat, he made an impressive figure as he strode determinedly across the plaza in front of the Territorial Courthouse in Santa Fe.

For the past few years, the imposing brick building had served as the territorial capitol. The previous capitol building had burned down, and a new one was being built. According to one of the clerks in the hotel where Turnbuckle was staying, the fire's origin was mysterious and likely arson, motivated by the fact that nearly everybody in town had thought the old capitol building with its Victorian design was ugly as sin and out of place in the predominantly Spanish architecture of Santa Fe.

Turnbuckle didn't give a damn about any of that. He wanted to see Governor Miguel Otero face to face to plead Conrad Browning's case. It was absurd to think that a man such as Conrad should be a wanted fugitive, but so far, Turnbuckle hadn't had a chance to persuade the territorial governor of that fact.

Turnbuckle went into the building and proceeded down marble-floored hallways to the governor's spacious office. Otero's aides had turned him away a couple of times since he'd been in Santa Fe, but Turnbuckle wasn't going to be stopped any longer, even if he had to pick up one of those slick-haired political flunkies and toss him out a window.

In fact, he almost hoped that would happen. It would feel good to cut through some of the red tape by force. Of course, he couldn't give in to that impulse. And in the long run, it probably wouldn't help Conrad.

Turnbuckle took off his hat as he entered the outer office. The clerk who sat at the desk there recognized him and sighed. "Governor Otero doesn't have any time available today to meet with you, Mr. Turnbuckle," he said. "As I've explained to you, and the governor's aide Mr. Blanton has explained to you, you'll need to make an appointment to speak to the governor, and the earliest you'll be able to do that is the middle of next month."

"The middle of next month is too late," Turnbuckle said. "My client could be dead by then, murdered by bounty hunters who are after him on false charges."

"I realize that's your claim, but you'll have to present proof to the governor."

"Which I can't do without seeing him."

"Which you can't do until next month, yes," the clerk said with an exasperated glare. "I fail to see what the confusion is."

Turnbuckle glanced out the window and thought about how good it would feel to toss the smarmy little slug through it. Reaching into his coat he took out an envelope. "I have a letter here from Lew Wallace asking Governor Otero to meet with me right away."

The clerk's eyes widened. "Governor Wallace?" he asked.

"That's right." Lew Wallace had been the governor in New Mexico more than fifteen years earlier, but he was still a well-known figure in the territory because of his personal involvement with Billy the Kid, Pat Garrett, and the Lincoln County War. The fact that he had authored the phenomenally successful novel *Ben-Hur* while serving as governor only increased his prominence. Even after all that time, his name carried considerable weight in Santa Fe.

The clerk was clearly torn about what to do. Finally, he stood up, held out his hand, and said, "I'll give the letter to Mr. Blanton. If he chooses to pass it on to the governor, I'll let you know."

Turnbuckle shook his head. "Not good enough. I want you to put the letter in the governor's hand personally."

The clerk looked shocked. "I can't do that. Mr. Blanton—"

"I'm tired of hearing about Mr. Blanton."

It hadn't taken long for a man as skilled as Turnbuckle to find out how things worked. Charles

Blanton, though he didn't hold an official position in the territorial government, was Governor Otero's most trusted aide. Although Otero was the son of a prominent New Mexico family with considerable wealth and influence, no one had expected the president to appoint him to the governorship. He had little in the way of broad support from the often squabbling factions battling for control in the capital. Therefore Otero relied heavily on Blanton, who had business connections with the governor's family.

The few times Turnbuckle had met Blanton, he had instinctively disliked and distrusted the man. The feeling seemed to be mutual.

Turnbuckle swung his heavy body toward a door at the side of the office. It was smaller than the ornate door leading into the governor's private office, but Turnbuckle knew that beyond it was where most of the real power lay. Blanton's office was on the other side of that door.

"I'm going to talk to him myself, damn it," Turnbuckle growled.

The clerk shot up from his chair, saying, "Sir, you can't—"

He was too late. Turnbuckle already had hold of the knob. He twisted it and shoved the door open.

The chair behind the desk in Blanton's office was empty. Turnbuckle glanced to his left and saw the man standing next to a sideboard with a decanter of liquor in one hand and a glass in the other.

Charles Blanton was a rawboned man with a squarish head and graying fair hair. He frowned at the lawyer and asked, "What's the meaning of this, Turnbuckle?"

"A bit early in the day, isn't it?" Turnbuckle asked with a nod toward the liquor.

Blanton flushed and set the decanter and glass back on the sideboard. "What do you want?"

Turnbuckle held up the envelope. "I have here a letter from Lew Wallace requesting that Governor Otero see me immediately and grant me every possible consideration."

"General Wallace is no longer in a position of authority in New Mexico Territory."

"I'm aware of that, but he's asking Governor Otero to cooperate out of personal courtesy, as one statesman to another."

"You can't see the governor," Blanton snapped. "He's much too busy. You'll just have to wait—"

"Every day this matter waits is another day my client is in needless danger."

"Perhaps if your client hadn't escaped from prison, he wouldn't be in danger."

"If Conrad Browning hadn't escaped from prison, he never would have exposed the crimes of some powerful men." Turnbuckle's rather bushy eyebrows raised. "Perhaps that's why you don't want me to see the governor. You don't want the stench of official corruption to rub off on him."

"The governor is an honest man," Blanton said. "His reputation is beyond reproach. And *he* didn't appoint that crooked warden. His predecessor did."

"Then he should be anxious to undo the damage that was done, including the injustice to my client."

"The circumstances don't matter." Blanton's voice was flat and hard, unwilling to budge an inch. "The man known as Kid Morgan broke out of prison. Two men died in that escape. Until these matters are properly dealt with in court, the charges against him will remain in place. That's my final word on the subject, counselor, and I don't care how many letters you have from Lew Wallace or anybody else."

"So *you're* the governor now, is that it?" Turnbuckle asked.

"Of course not. But he's given me great latitude to deal with administrative matters as I see fit. If you want to petition for a pardon for your client after he's been tried and convicted, feel free to do so."

Turnbuckle's free hand clenched into a fist. "With a ten grand bounty on his head, dead or alive, he'll never make it to trial, and you know it!"

"That's regrettable, but nothing can be done about it."

"You mean you *won't* do anything about it."

Blanton sighed. "Get out, Turnbuckle, or I'll call the guards and have you removed."

The two men glowered fiercely at each other for a moment before Turnbuckle jabbed the envelope toward Blanton.

"This isn't over," he said. "I'll go to the newspapers. From what I've heard, the governor's support is rather shaky to begin with. A scandal like this can't help him."

"Following the rule of law is not a scandal," Blanton said archly. "Do your worst, counselor."

Turnbuckle continued glaring for a second, then swung around and lumbered out of the aide's office. The clerk, who had been watching from the doorway, stepped aside hurriedly to let him pass.

If Blanton wanted war, Turnbuckle thought as he left the capitol, then, by God, it was war he would have!

Late that afternoon, Charles Blanton slipped through the side door of a cantina located on one of Santa Fe's narrow, twisting streets. He pushed aside a beaded curtain and stepped into a small, windowless room lit only by a single candle. The sound of a guitar being strummed drifted through the curtain from the front part of the cantina.

A young, handsome man with sleek blond hair sat at a table. The table and a couple chairs were the only pieces of furniture in the room. The young man had a bottle of tequila and two glasses in front of him.

"Come in, Blanton," he said as he poured drinks for both of them. "Why did you want to see me?"

Without sitting, Blanton picked up one of the glasses and tossed back the tequila without batting an eye.

"It's Turnbuckle," he said. "He's threatening to go to the papers."

"I don't see how that's a problem," the young man said. "You assured me that nothing illegal was going on."

"It's not . . . technically. But some of the papers are very opposed to Governor Otero. If they play up this affair, it could erode his support. And he can't really afford that."

"What do you want me to do?"

"Take care of it," Blanton said with a harsh, savage edge in his voice. "I've had a man following Turnbuckle for the past few days. He always has supper at the same café near his hotel. If he was waylaid by a thief while he was walking to the café . . ."

The young man sipped from his glass and smiled. "That would solve the problem for both of us, eh?"

"That's right. It would be a tragedy, of course, but it's not that uncommon for people to be killed by thieves."

"Indeed it's not." The young man downed the rest of his tequila and pushed the bottle toward Blanton, who still stood nervously. "Don't worry about it. I have a feeling that everything will work out for us. Unfortunately for Claudius Turnbuckle, he won't be able to say the same thing." Abruptly, the man's face twisted into lines of utter hatred. "But that's what he gets for trying to help a son of a bitch like Conrad Browning."

Turnbuckle frowned as he paced along the narrow street paved with flagstones. It had been a damned frustrating day, he thought. He had made appointments with the editors of the local newspapers but hadn't been able to speak with any of them. Tomorrow would be different.

At least he could look forward to a good meal. Being from San Francisco, he had eaten very little of the sort of cuisine favored in Santa Fe. He had discovered that he had a great liking for food seasoned with the hot peppers that were so popular, especially when he had a mug of beer to temper the spices in his mouth and throat.

Since his thoughts were occupied not only with the impending meal but also the legal problems he was struggling with on behalf of Conrad, he almost didn't notice the man who stepped out of the shadows at the mouth of an alley.

"Señor," the man said urgently, "señor, please help. My child, she is very sick—"

Instantly, Turnbuckle was suspicious, but the man was already too close to him. An arm shot out, and Turnbuckle felt the hot bite of cold steel into his body.

Grunting in pain, Turnbuckle stumbled forward, but managed to stay on his feet. The knife flickered back. Turnbuckle lunged at the man as the blade darted toward him again.

The thrust was hurried and scraped against his side. Turnbuckle's right hand closed around the throat of the would-be assassin, while his left caught the wrist of the man's knife hand.

Despite his rather sedentary profession, Claudius Turnbuckle was a big, strong man. He squeezed so hard the bones inside the man's wrist ground together. The man would have screamed in pain if Turnbuckle's other hand hadn't closed off his throat.

Hot, wet agony flowed from the wound in his belly. He knew he was losing a lot of blood and would soon pass out because of it.

But his instincts as a fighter wouldn't let him surrender. He shoved his attacker deeper into the shadows of the alley and rammed him against the adobe wall of one of the buildings. The man struggled desperately against the grip Turnbuckle had on his throat, but he couldn't get free.

Turnbuckle pulled him away from the wall, then slammed him against it repeatedly, until the man went limp in his hands.

The lawyer let go and staggered back. The assailant collapsed on the dirty floor of the alley and didn't move. Turnbuckle wheeled around and looked at the rectangle of faint light that marked the alley mouth.

He stumbled toward it, pressing his hands to his wounded midsection. "Blanton," he muttered. He had no doubt the governor's aide was behind the attack. Blanton wanted him out of the way so he couldn't continue trying to get the charges against Conrad Browning dropped. That made Turnbuckle more convinced than ever there was something shady behind the ten thousand dollar bounty.

But he had to live in order to prove it. His legs moved, putting one foot in front of the other. He had to remain conscious until he could get some help. If he passed out in the alley, he would bleed to death.

He was only a few feet short of his goal when the world suddenly turned a black deeper than the shadows in the alley. Turnbuckle pitched forward, groaned once, and lay silent and motionless as his life's blood continued running out onto the dirt.

Chapter 22

The Kid and McCall fetched Max and the horses from the trees, skirting wide around the crater and the bodies of the dead men as they did so. Blount told them they could put the horses in the small pole corral behind the cabin where he kept his mule.

They had been keeping an eye out for the pair of Guthrie's gunwolves who had gotten away, just in case the men returned. Blount thought it was more likely the men would hightail it back to the Rafter G with the news of what had happened, and The Kid agreed with that.

Sooner or later, more trouble would show up, and he wanted to be prepared for it when it did. "I'll take my guns back now," he told McCall. The revolver he had taken away from one of Guthrie's men was tucked behind his belt.

"I guess I might as well go along with that," she agreed with a sigh. "We've sort of gotten past the point of considering you my prisoner, haven't we?"

"I'd say we're partners . . . for now."

She shook her head and sounded disgusted with herself as she said, "This is the first time something like this has happened. I don't know what's wrong with me."

"It seems to me like you're just being reasonable," The Kid said as he took the Colt she handed to him. They carried all the rifles into the cabin, including his Winchester and Sharps.

Blount said, "First time I've seen one of those Big Fifties in a while. Used to know a fella who hunted buffalo with a carbine like that. It's a hell of a gun if you need to make a long-range shot. Packs a mighty big wallop close up, too. Almost like bein' shot with a cannon."

The Kid had actually shot a man once with a cannon, but he didn't mention that.

"What are we going to do about those bodies out there?" McCall asked. "I can't help but wonder if any of them have rewards out for them."

"Spoken like a true bounty hunter," The Kid said.

Anger flashed in McCall's eyes. "It's a job like any other," she said.

"Any other that pays in blood money."

"You two best save your squabblin' for later," Blount advised. "Guthrie will be back here before the day's over, more'n likely, and we got to figure out what we're gonna do about it. He can take them dead hombres with him when he goes, if he wants to."

"I was looking at the cliff earlier," The Kid said. "There's a ledge up there, about a hundred feet above the cabin. Is there any way to get to it?"

"Yeah . . . if you're a durn mountain goat!"

"What are you thinking, Kid?" McCall asked.

"That a man on that ledge could keep anybody from getting close to the cabin if he had a rifle and plenty of ammunition. It'd be like a target shoot from up there."

McCall nodded. "Yeah, that's true. Are you volunteering?"

"I could take the first shift, anyway. You and I could take turns guarding the place." The Kid frowned in thought. "That won't solve Mr. Blount's problem in the long run, though."

"Nothin's gonna solve that except puttin' a bullet through Spud Guthrie's head," Blount said. "I don't much cotton to cold-blooded murder, though."

"If he's attacking you, it wouldn't be murder," The Kid pointed out. "This is your land. It would be self-defense."

"Yeah. Problem is, all them hardcases workin' for him would try to grab the range for themselves as soon as Guthrie was dead."

The Kid didn't have a solution for that. For the time being, however, he and McCall could protect the old-timer and try to figure out something else as they went along. He picked up his Winchester and said, "Show me the trail to that ledge."

"Callin' it a trail is bein' mighty generous. But I'll show you where to climb."

The Kid stuffed a box full of .44-40 cartridges into his coat pocket and followed the old man out of the cabin. McCall came along, too, and said, "I'll keep an eye out for trouble."

The Kid and Blount went around the cabin and walked over to the cliff face. Blount started pointing out the footholds and handholds The Kid would need to use to reach the ledge, which had a slab of rock perched on it that he could use for cover.

"I'll head on up," The Kid said when he was sure of the route. He took off his belt and used it to rig a sling for the rifle so he could carry the weapon over his shoulder.

The climb took almost a quarter of an hour. When The Kid finally reached the ledge, he rolled onto it and waved a hand to let Blount know he was there safely. He unslung the Winchester and scooted into position behind the rock.

He could see the entire open area in front of the cabin, as well as the band of trees on the other side of it. In fact, the view was spectacular, stretching for several miles of green, pine-covered landscape. Sitting up there and looking out over the vast swath of Arizona Territory would have been pretty peaceful, he thought . . .

If he hadn't been waiting for a small army of gunmen to show up and try to kill him, McCall, and Blount.

The Kid wondered if McCall was starting to believe that he was innocent of the charges leveled against him. She had agreed to give back his guns with much less argument than he had expected.

Of course, the fact that he was already armed might have had something to do with that. It was easier for them to cooperate than to try to kill each other.

Having her as an actual ally would make it easier for him to get to Santa Fe and set the record straight. From all indications, they had given Pike and the other bounty hunters the slip, but The Kid had believed that before and turned out to be wrong.

He didn't let his mind wander too much. His attention stayed focused on the approaches to the cabin. About an hour had passed since his climb to the ledge when he spotted riders approaching from the east.

It was a large group, approximately twenty men, but according to Blount, that was only about half of Guthrie's force. The rancher probably thought that was more than enough to overwhelm any defense Blount might put up.

The Kid had no doubt that Spud Guthrie believed his word was law in those parts. The Kid had run into that sort of arrogant cattle baron before, and he had heard about others from his father. Men who believed they could run roughshod over anyone who opposed them, even to the point of murder, simply because they had more land and cattle than anybody else in the area.

Sometimes they had to be shown the error of their ways at the point of a gun.

The Kid's eyes followed the riders as they circled to the far side of the trees. They disappeared from his sight there, but he was confident that they would show up again.

Twenty minutes later, three of the men rode out of the trees and reined in where they could see the cabin. One of the riders edged his horse slightly in front of the other two. Even from far away, The Kid could tell that he was on the small side. That was probably what had gotten him the nickname Spud.

The man cupped his hands around his mouth and shouted, "Blount! Blount, can you hear me?"

His voice was surprisingly deep for a man of his size and carried like a foghorn.

"I hear you, Guthrie!" Blount replied through the single window in the front of the cabin.

"You killed some of my men!"

"Only because they tried to kill me first!"

The contrast between Guthrie's bullfrog-like bellows and Blount's rather high-pitched voice would have been humorous if the situation hadn't been so deadly serious, The Kid thought.

"I'm gonna give you one more chance!" Guthrie said. "Get on that mule of yours and ride away, and you can have safe passage out of here. Just don't ever come back!"

"You can go to hell!" Blount responded. "Dos Caballos is mine and always will be!"

"I've got twenty men out here, you old fool! If we charge that cabin, I don't care who you've got helping you! We'll overrun you and kill you!"

"Not without a whole heap o' you buzzards dyin' first!" Blount shouted defiantly. "And I reckon I'll be aimin' at you first thing, *Spud!*"

The scornful tone of the old-timer's voice told The Kid that Guthrie probably didn't like being called by his nickname. Probably didn't care for being reminded of his lack of stature. Another indication of that was the tall crown on the hat Guthrie wore.

That hat was a mighty tempting target, and a faint grin tugged at The Kid's mouth as he lined the Winchester's sights on it.

"All right, Blount!" Guthrie roared. "You called the tune, now you can damned well dance to it!"

He lifted an arm to signal for his men to attack. Even though The Kid couldn't see them, he knew they were probably spread out through the trees in a skirmish line. Blount and McCall couldn't hope to pick off more than a few of them as they charged.

But The Kid could see the whole field, and he thought it was time to send a signal of his own.

He squeezed the Winchester's trigger.

Chapter 23

As the rifle cracked, Spud Guthrie's hat leaped from his head. Guthrie leaped, too, bouncing in the saddle and clapping a hand to his suddenly uncovered cranium. As he came back down on leather, he grabbed the reins and whirled his horse around to dash back into the timber.

At the same time, the two men who had ridden out with him whipped their rifles to their shoulders and started blazing away at the ledge where the shot had come from.

The Kid ducked low behind the rock. From their angle, the two gunmen couldn't get a clear view of him, nor could they ricochet their slugs off the cliff face behind him.

He waited until their weapons fell silent, then thrust his Winchester over the top of the rock again and cranked off four swift shots, aiming just short so the bullets kicked up dust under the hooves of the horses.

The animals spooked. The men had to fight to get them under control. The Kid probably could have picked them both off, but instead he held his fire and allowed Guthrie's men to retreat into the woods.

The message he had sent was clear. With a field of fire commanding the entire area in front of the cabin, he could kill the men at will if they charged. Combined with the damage that McCall and Blount would do by firing from inside the cabin, it was possible they might be able to wipe out the whole party.

Guthrie was smart enough to know that, too. He came back to the edge of the trees and called, "Blount! Blount!"

"Speak your piece!" Blount shouted back from the cabin.

"Tell your man to hold his fire!"

"He already is, ain't he? Hurry it up, 'fore we get impatient!"

"I want the bodies of my men!" Guthrie said.

Blount hesitated in answering, but after a moment he called, "All right! You can take 'em! There ain't nothin' left of the one who was standin' right over that dynamite when it blew, though!"

"We'll come out and get the others! Hold your fire!"

Several men emerged from the pines and cast nervous glances toward the ledge where The Kid had them covered. They hurried forward, picked up the bodies of the two men who had been killed in the explosion and the two who had died in the fighting afterward. They carried the corpses back into the cover of the trees.

"I'm leaving!" Guthrie yelled. "But I'll be back! You can't win, Blount! You can't hold out against all of us!"

"Maybe not, but a bunch of you will die before you root me out!" Blount followed the declaration with a cackling laugh.

Guthrie didn't respond to that. The Kid kept watching, and a few minutes later, the group of riders reappeared, moving away from the area. Some of the men had doubled up, so their horses could be used to carry the bodies.

"They're gone!" he shouted down to the cabin when Guthrie and his men were out of sight.

McCall and Blount emerged and waved up at him to show they had heard. "You need me to spell you?" the bounty hunter called.

"Not yet," The Kid replied. "I'm fine."

He settled back to keep watch. As his eyes scanned the landscape, he muttered, "I hope you're satisfied, Rebel. I've gotten myself mixed up in trouble that's none of my business . . . again."

A warm breeze blew past him. It was almost like the caress of fingers against his cheek.

The rest of the afternoon passed quietly. As the sun was setting, The Kid climbed down from the ledge. Once night had fallen, he wouldn't be able to see well enough from up there to do any good.

That same thought had probably occurred to Guthrie.

When he made it to the bottom of the cliff, he went into the cabin and said, "We all need to get out of here."

"What are you talkin' about, Kid?" Blount asked from the stove, where he was cooking some flapjacks.

"Guthrie and his men are liable to come back as soon as it's good and dark," The Kid explained. "If we let them catch us here in the cabin, we won't be able to hold out against them."

"Dadgummit, this has been my home for ten years! I can't just abandon it."

The Kid shook his head. "You can take anything of value with you, but it's a bad idea to stay."

McCall asked, "Where do you think we should go, Kid?"

"I was thinking we could hole up in the canyon. The entrance is pretty narrow. They can't come at us all at once if we're in there."

McCall thought it over and nodded. "That's not a bad idea."

"It's a terrible idea!" Blount said. "Guthrie's such a snake, he's liable to burn the cabin down!"

"Let him," The Kid said. "I know you don't like the idea, Mr. Blount, but Dos Caballos will be a lot easier to defend."

"Damn it!" Blount sighed. "I reckon you're right. But I don't have to like it."

"We've got three horses and a mule. We'll gather up as many of your belongings as we can and take them with us."

They postponed supper for the time being and

got busy. Blount didn't say much and obviously was still upset, but he didn't argue anymore. Within half an hour, they had the old-timer's gear loaded and were ready to make the move.

A red glow remained in the western sky. The Kid knew they didn't have much time. He led the buckskin and the extra horse McCall had brought from Las Vegas. McCall followed, leading the black, and Blount brought up the rear with the mule. Max bounded ahead of his human companions, on the alert for any sign of danger.

When they reached the mouth of the canyon, Blount unlatched the brush-covered gate.

"How did you build such a thing with only one arm?" McCall asked.

"Lots of time, sweat, and determination," Blount replied. "Gimme a hand here, Kid. I can open and close this gate by myself, but it's a heap easier with two people."

They swung the gate back and took the animals into the canyon, then pulled the gate shut behind them. It wouldn't keep out anybody who really wanted in, but it would slow down an attack. Somebody would have to open the gate, and after a few of Guthrie's men got picked off trying to do that, it might discourage them into giving up.

The Kid didn't believe it, though. Guthrie's pride had been wounded too badly to turn back now.

"Is there any way to climb down these walls?"

The Kid asked as they moved deeper into the canyon.

"Nope," Blount replied. "Maybe in daylight, if a fella was half fly. But sure as sin, nobody could do it in the dark."

"What about the other end of the canyon?"

"Ain't no way out there, or in, neither. We're boxed up good an' proper in here."

McCall said, "Maybe this wasn't such a good idea, Kid. Guthrie can just lay siege to the place and starve us out."

"He can try. We'll have to hope fate deals us a trump card."

McCall's snort made it clear just how unlikely she thought that was.

The Kid already had the glimmering of a plan drifting around in the back of his mind.

Blount led them to a trickle of a creek where they built a campfire. A big rock jutted out from the canyon wall to shield the fire from the canyon mouth. The old man boiled coffee and they ate the flapjacks they had brought with them. It was a meager supper, but they might have to make their provisions last for quite a while.

From the other side of the rock next to the fire, they could see the entrance to the canyon and agreed to take turns standing guard. Blount suggested that he take the first watch and McCall the second, since The Kid had spent most of the afternoon hunkered on the ledge. "That way you can go ahead and get some rest," the old-timer said.

The Kid agreed. He was tired, and it would feel good to stretch out on his bedroll.

Even though he hadn't been born and bred a frontiersman—far from it, in fact—he had developed many abilities over the past few years, including the ability to fall asleep almost instantly when he had the chance. He dropped into a deep, dreamless slumber that didn't end until McCall touched him on the shoulder long after midnight.

The Kid came awake just as quickly as he fell asleep. He was fully alert as he sat up and asked quietly, "Any trouble?"

"Not a bit. Guthrie hasn't tried anything."

The Kid was a little surprised to hear that. He hadn't thought the rancher would wait very long to launch another attack on the cabin.

Blount snored loudly from his bedroll nearby. McCall laughed and said, "I'm not sure how you slept through that."

"Just tired, I guess." The Kid buckled on his gunbelt and picked up his rifle. "I'll take over now."

"I'll come with you for a minute."

The Kid wondered why McCall would do that, but didn't argue. They walked around the rock, and Max followed them.

"I sat on that log there," McCall said, pointing

to the deadfall that was barely visible in the starlight. "It's not real comfortable, but when you lean back against the rock, it's better than the ground."

"When you're standing guard, you don't need to be too comfortable," he said.

"That's what I thought."

They settled themselves on the log. Max lay down at their feet, resting his head on his paws.

The Kid sensed that McCall had something on her mind. He didn't press her. If she had something to say, she could get around to it in her own way and in her own sweet time.

After a couple minutes of silence, she asked, "What did you say your real name is, Kid?"

"Conrad Browning," he replied. "You believe that now?"

"Well, I don't know. But after being around you for a while, I can tell that you're not like any of the other fugitives I've ever gone after. It's not just that you're an educated man. Some of them were, too. But there's a gentleness about you that I never saw in any of them."

"I'm not a gentleman."

"That's not what I said. I said you had a gentleness. I don't think you want people to see it, but it's there. If it wasn't"—her voice caught for a second—"if it wasn't, you wouldn't have gone to the trouble of sending that picture and the money to my mother in Kansas City."

"It wasn't mine," The Kid said with a shrug.

"No, but most men wouldn't have done it." She paused. "Anyway, you've told me your real name, so I reckon I ought to tell you mine."

"It's not McCall?"

"That part of it is. But my first name is Lace."

The Kid didn't say anything for a second. Then he repeated, "Lace. Sort of a soft name for a hard-as-nails bounty hunter."

"I wasn't always a bounty hunter. My mama . . . she worked in a house in St. Louis. You know?"

"I know," The Kid said. "You don't have to tell me any of this if you don't want to."

"If I didn't want to, I wouldn't be telling you," she snapped. Her tone softened again as she went on, "I was born there. She wanted a better life for me than she had, so she moved to Kansas City and tried to find a real job there. It was hard for her, though, and after a while . . . well, she went back to it. With all that, I don't guess anybody would be real surprised to hear that I turned out the same way."

The Kid didn't say anything, although actually he was a little surprised.

"I wound up in a family way," she went on. "One of my customers, a man named McCall, offered to marry me. I took him up on it. I wanted my child to have a name. He turned out to be a pretty bad sort, though. He didn't treat me good. After a while I found out he was even worse than

I thought when I happened to see a wanted poster with his picture on it. The man on the poster had a different name, but McCall was one of the names he was said to use sometimes. I went home, and the next time he raised his hand to me, I was ready. I shot the son of a bitch."

"You killed him?" The Kid asked.

"No, I just put a bullet in his knee, and while he was rolling around on the floor screaming, I went and found a policeman and told him there was a wanted fugitive in my house. They hauled him off, and I claimed the reward. I got it, too. That was enough for me to be able to set my mama and my little girl up so they'd be all right." She laughed. "That was how I found out I liked bounty hunting a lot better than I liked being a whore."

"And that's what you've been doing for the past few years?"

"Five years," she said. "I already knew how to fight. I taught myself how to ride and shoot and found that I really took to it. Then I met Pronto, and he made me even better at it."

"Pike?"

"Yeah. We got along just fine at first, before I realized how loco he really is. That seems to be a failing of mine, Kid. I can't see what a man's really like until I've been with him for a while." She turned to look at him. "I'm hoping it'll be different with you."

"You're not with me," The Kid pointed out.

She cuffed the hat off her head and leaned toward him.

"The hell I'm not," Lace McCall said, and a second later her arms were around his neck and her mouth was pressed hotly to his.

The Kid's first instinct was to pull away from her. But something kept him from doing it, and after a moment, as an old familiar arousal surged up inside him, he realized he was feeling things that he hadn't experienced in months—an unexpectedly urgent need to slide his arms around Lace and pull her to him so their bodies came together with an intensity that set the blood pounding in his head.

It wasn't right, a part of his brain insisted. It wasn't right at all.

But he couldn't deny what he felt, couldn't ignore the need. It had been too long. Lace might be hard as nails most of the time, but she softened in his embrace.

He didn't get the chance to find out what was going to happen next.

At that moment an explosion lit up the night and shook the earth . . . literally.

Chapter 24

Lace sprang away from him and jumped to her feet, her hand going to the gun on her hip.

The Kid was up, too, with his Colt in his hand. His eyes searched the canyon mouth, but evidently the explosion hadn't come from there.

Chester Blount came running around the rock, yelling, "My cabin! The bastards blowed up my cabin!"

The old-timer was right, The Kid decided. A garish orange glow in the sky to the west of the canyon marked the location of a fire, where Blount's cabin was . . . or had been, The Kid thought.

Spud Guthrie's men had come back to finish what they had started earlier in the day. The Kid wondered how long it would take Guthrie to discover that nobody was in the cabin.

The rancher probably wouldn't explore the ruins until morning. When he realized there were no bodies in the charred debris, he might figure that Blount and his allies had abandoned the cabin and the canyon. Guthrie wouldn't find out different until he and his men tried to waltz into Dos Caballos and got a hot lead welcome.

Then they would lay siege to the canyon, and it would be only a matter of time before the three defenders were starved out.

There had to be a better way, and The Kid thought he had an idea what it might be.

But it required acting immediately, not waiting for morning.

"Take it easy, Mr. Blount," he told the old-timer. "The cabin can be rebuilt. One way or another, I'll see to it that it is."

"You can believe him," Lace added dryly. "He's a rich man, after all."

Blount snorted. "No offense, Kid, but that's mighty hard to believe."

"None taken," The Kid assured him. "You'll see, once we get out of here and Guthrie is dealt with."

"Who's gonna deal with him?"

"I am."

Lace and Blount both looked at him. Lace asked warily, "Just what are you up to, Morgan?"

Instead of answering her directly, The Kid asked Blount, "Can you tell me how to get to the Rafter G?"

"Well, yeah, I reckon. You ought to be able to find the trail, even in the dark. Just what is it you got in mind doin'?"

"I thought I'd pay a call on Spud Guthrie."

"Wait just a damn minute," Lace said. "It sounds to me like you're talking about running out on us, Kid."

He shook his head. "Not at all. I'm going to grab Guthrie and bring him back here. With him as a hostage, his men won't dare attack the canyon, and they sure won't dynamite the walls and cave them in."

"How's that gonna solve things in the long run?" Blount asked as he raked his fingers through his long beard. "Can't they still wait us out?"

"As soon as I get back with Guthrie, you're going to take our extra horse and ride to Phoenix as fast as you can," The Kid explained. "McCall and I will hold Guthrie and the canyon until you get back with the law."

"You really think the law's gonna side with an old prospector like me over a rich rancher like Guthrie?"

"When you get to Phoenix, send a wire to a lawyer named John Stafford in San Francisco." Claudius Turnbuckle was probably still in Santa Fe, The Kid thought, but his partner Stafford could handle this. "Use my name, and have him wire the governor of Arizona Territory and request his assistance in the matter."

Something was obviously off-kilter in New Mexico Territory, otherwise those wanted posters would have been quashed by now, but Conrad Browning had been on good terms with the territorial governor in Arizona. His name should still carry some influence.

"If necessary, Stafford can contact the Justice Department in Washington and have a deputy

United States marshal sent in," The Kid went on. "We'll stay here and protect the canyon until you get back with the authorities, and they can deal with Guthrie."

Lace said, "You sound mighty confident that these friends in high places will be glad to help out."

"I think they will," The Kid said. "The Browning financial holdings and business interests wield considerable influence."

"If that's true, how come there's a ten grand bounty on your head?"

The Kid raked a thumbnail along his jaw and admitted, "That's something I can't answer. Someone who's pretty powerful must be pulling the strings behind the scenes in Santa Fe. But I don't know who or why."

"You know," Lace mused, "the more I listen to you talk, the more I start to believe that you're actually telling the truth about who you are."

The Kid smiled. "Good. Because it's true."

"All right," Lace said. "Your plan's a longshot, but it's the only one we have other than sitting here and letting Guthrie starve us out. You're going to Guthrie's ranch to grab him?"

"That's right."

"I'm coming with you," she declared.

The Kid shook his head. "That's not a good idea. Somebody needs to stay here with Mr. Blount."

"Hey, I can take care of myself," the old-timer objected.

"I'm sure you can, but two people can defend this canyon better than one, if something happens to me and it comes down to that." The Kid held up a hand to forestall Lace's protest as she opened her mouth. "And one person will be able to slip in and out of the Rafter G easier than two."

"This would be a perfect chance for you to ride off and never come back," Lace said.

"I'm not going to do that." The Kid shrugged. "You can believe me or not."

She stared at him for a long moment before saying, "Damn it, I do believe you . . . whether I want to or not. All right, Kid . . . Conrad . . . whatever the hell your name is. When are you going?"

The Kid glanced at the midnight sky. "No point in waiting. As soon as Mr. Blount tells me how to get to the Rafter G, I'll be on my way."

It was possible Guthrie had left guards watching what was left of the cabin, although judging from the size of the blast, nothing could have lived through it. The Kid would have to take that chance.

He led the buckskin to the gate. Lace came with him. They opened it together. When The Kid had taken the horse through the narrow gap, he turned back to Lace for a moment and whispered, "Keep your eyes and ears open. When I get here with Guthrie, I'll give a hoot owl call. I may need some help with the gate."

"I'll be waiting," she said. "Kid, be careful. You're our best shot at getting out of this alive."

"Don't worry. I'm not going to die until I've cleared up those charges against me."

He wasn't sure why that had become so important to him, but it had. In months past, he wouldn't have cared very much one way or the other. His reputation meant nothing to him. Kid Morgan was nothing but a fictional creation meant to help Conrad Browning achieve his revenge.

But somehow, the identity had taken on a life of its own. Whenever he thought of himself, it was almost always as The Kid, and seldom as Conrad.

It was all right for people to think of Kid Morgan as a gunfighter, but not as a murderer and outlaw. Why that was, The Kid didn't know, but he didn't doubt the authenticity of the feeling.

Lace leaned toward him, put her arms around his neck, and kissed him. The Kid didn't try to stop her. In fact, he returned the kiss with an eagerness he hadn't felt in a long time.

"You just haven't given up on collecting that ten grand," he whispered when they parted.

"Damn right," Lace whispered back.

With that, he gave her shoulder a squeeze and

turned away. He heard her shove the gate closed behind him as he led the buckskin eastward, along the face of the towering cliffs that formed the Mogollon Rim.

He moved as carefully and quietly as possible, and no one tried to stop him. Either Guthrie hadn't bothered putting any guards on the destroyed cabin, or else he had slipped past them unnoticed.

Blount had said there was a trail leading to the top of the rim about half a mile east of Dos Caballos Canyon. It was a narrow path, barely wide enough for one man on horseback. Too narrow for cattle, even moving single file, which was why Guthrie wanted to blast the canyon into a wider trail. The next path to the top was a good five miles farther east, and it wasn't fit for cattle, either.

The wagon that had brought the dynamite to Blount's cabin earlier in the day must have gone a long way around, The Kid mused. He supposed they hadn't wanted to risk carrying the explosives down the narrow trail. Guthrie was probably mad enough that he hadn't worried about that tonight.

The Kid watched for the landmark Blount had mentioned, a boulder flanked by a couple of pine trees. The trail started its climb right behind that boulder. The Kid had only starlight to navigate by. A moon would have helped, but it also would have made it easier for him to be spotted by his enemies.

In that part of the country, other than Lace McCall and Chester Blount, all he had were enemies.

He found the trail without much trouble, mounted up, and started on the twisting path to the rim. The surefooted buckskin moved carefully. One misstep could have sent both man and horse plunging hundreds of feet into the darkness.

He heaved a sigh of relief when they came out on the top of the rim. The headquarters of the Rafter G was a couple miles due north from there, Blount had said.

The Kid steered by the stars and headed in that direction.

A chilly wind swept down from the Colorado Plateau and blew in The Kid's face. It would help keep the horses in the Rafter G's corrals from scenting the buckskin and raising a ruckus.

The men who had blown up Blount's cabin had had plenty of time to get back to the ranch and report the success of their mission to Guthrie. The Kid expected that everybody had turned in, secure in the mistaken belief their enemies had been blown to kingdom come.

As he approached the ranch headquarters, he spotted a yellow glow. Lamplight through a window. Somebody was still up and awake.

Stealthy as an Apache, The Kid dismounted and stole closer to the big ranch house on foot, leaving the buckskin tied in some trees. It was too dark to make out all the details, but the Rafter G's headquarters appeared to a sprawling, two-story log structure, with a bunkhouse and several smaller outbuildings off to one side, near a big barn and some corrals.

The light he saw was on the first floor of the ranch house. An office, maybe. Guthrie might be burning the midnight oil, trying to come up with some more deviltry now that he thought he had gotten rid of Chester Blount.

More than likely, he was figuring out his plans to turn Dos Caballos Canyon into a cattle trail. Men had an infinite capacity for convincing themselves they weren't evil, The Kid mused. In Guthrie's mind, his actions were justified. If Blount had accepted the offer to buy the canyon, then Guthrie wouldn't have been forced to blow him sky-high.

Or maybe he *knew* he was a ruthless son of a bitch and just didn't care. It didn't really matter. Either way, he had to be stopped.

And it had fallen to The Kid to stop him.

He crouched beneath the lighted window and raised himself until he could peer through the glass, which was lowered against the night chill. His guess that the room inside the window was an office proved to be correct. Guthrie sat at a massive rolltop desk, pawing through papers. Maps and engineers' reports, The Kid thought.

From the window, The Kid had a good view of his profile. The rancher was short and wiry, with a high forehead, thinning brown hair, and a soup-strainer mustache that hung over his mouth. He didn't look all that impressive at first glance, but there was a vitality about him, a force and drive that went a long way toward explaining how he had been able to carve a ranch out of the wilderness and seize as much power as he could hold.

He might have been an admirable man, The Kid thought, if his pride and arrogance hadn't gotten out of control.

Slipping along the wall in the shadows, The Kid came to a porch and climbed onto it, being careful not to make the boards creak. His hands found the front door. West of the Mississippi, few people locked their doors except those who lived in the big cities, and Spud Guthrie was no exception.

The knob turned under The Kid's fingers, and the door swung open with only a faint rasp of hinges. He held his breath, hoping the noise hadn't been loud enough to penetrate into the office where Guthrie was working. When he didn't hear any response, he stepped inside and eased the door closed behind him.

The office was to his right, down a hallway. The

door was open a crack, just enough to let a narrow band of light slant through it. The Kid started toward it.

He had taken only a couple steps when a voice behind him said, "Do not move, or I will kill you."

Chapter 25

The voice belonged to a man, and it had a soft, sibilant accent The Kid couldn't place at first. Then he realized that it sounded Chinese. He guessed that Guthrie had a Chinese cook who also took care of the house. The man must have heard the noise the door had made when it opened.

The Kid didn't want to hurt the man, but he couldn't afford to let anyone stop him from accomplishing his mission. The lives of Lace and Blount might well depend on it.

He started to raise his hands, said quietly, "Take it easy, friend," and whirled around, ducking so that if the man fired a gun, the bullet would go over his head.

No shot blasted. The Kid heard the hiss of cold steel through the air and felt something brush across the top of his head, stirring his sandy hair. The son of a gun had tried to cut his head off with a meat cleaver!

Swiftly, The Kid threw his right arm up to block any backhanded stroke. Stepping forward he hooked his left fist forward in a short but powerful punch, aiming at where he thought the man's midsection ought to be. His knuckles sunk deep into the man's belly, causing him to grunt in pain. The Kid reached out, found the man's arm, and slid along it to the wrist. He twisted hard and heard the clatter as the cleaver slipped out of the man's fingers and fell to the floor.

Knowing he didn't have much time before Guthrie came to investigate, he struck again with his left fist, aiming at the man's head. The first blow slid off the man's ear, but the second landed solidly on his jaw.

The man collapsed onto the floor with a heavy thud.

Guthrie couldn't have missed that one, The Kid thought. As he turned back toward the corridor where the office was located, the door swung open, letting more light splash out. Guthrie's short, slender figure was silhouetted against the glow as he called, "Wing? Is that you?"

The name confirmed The Kid's hunch about the Chinese cook, but he didn't waste time congratulating himself. He rushed across the space separating him from Guthrie. The rancher saw him coming and clawed at a gun holstered on his hip.

The Kid had been lucky in avoiding gunshots that would alert the whole ranch to the fact that something was wrong. Wanting to keep it that way, he struck with blinding speed, driving a punch into the jaw of the startled Guthrie. The blow had all the strength of The Kid's rangy, trouble-hardened body behind it, and it lifted the rancher from his feet and threw him back against the rolltop desk.

Guthrie was tough despite his size. He stayed on his feet, grabbed a heavy paperweight from the desk, and flung it at The Kid's head.

The Kid had to duck, giving Guthrie time to clear leather with his gun. As the revolver swung up, The Kid kicked out. The toe of his boot caught Guthrie's wrist and knocked the gun loose. It spun out of the rancher's fingers.

Guthrie opened his mouth to yell, but The Kid was too fast. His left hand clamped over Guthrie's mouth while his right hammered into Guthrie's body.

The Kid felt a twinge of guilt at physically attacking a man who was a head shorter and fifty or sixty pounds lighter, but it didn't last long when The Kid remembered how Guthrie had sent his men to kill Chester Blount. Guthrie would kill him, if he had the chance, and never blink an eye.

The Kid slammed a haymaker into the middle of Guthrie's face and put the man down and out. Guthrie didn't look very threatening, crumpled on the floor in front of the desk, but The Kid knew that some of the most venomous snakes in the world were small, too.

After standing for a few seconds with his heart slugging heavily in his chest, he bent and got hold of Guthrie, hoisting the rancher over his left shoulder. At least Guthrie didn't weigh very much.

As The Kid turned toward the door, a stocky figure appeared in the doorway. The Chinese cook had regained consciousness and stood poised to throw the cleaver like a Barbary Coast hatchetman. He hesitated at the sight of Guthrie draped over The Kid's shoulder.

The Kid's gun flickered out of its holster. "Drop it," he warned in a low voice.

The man's dark eyes stared down the Colt's barrel. An ugly smile spread across his face as he said, "You would not dare shoot. The sound would bring twenty men running from the bunkhouse."

"That's true," The Kid said, "but you wouldn't be alive to see them get here, now would you? And what could they do as long as I've got hold of their boss?"

The cook's smile disappeared. A string of syllables came from him that The Kid figured were Chinese curses. But the cleaver hit the floor as the man dropped it.

"Good," The Kid said. "Turn around."

Fear appeared in the cook's eyes. "Do not kill me," he said. "I ask you—"

"Turn around," The Kid said again.

Nervously, the man turned. The Kid stepped up close behind him. He flipped the gun around in his hand and struck, rapping the cook sharply on the head just above the black braid.

The cook folded up, out cold. The Kid knew he

wouldn't regain consciousness for several minutes. Balancing Guthrie on his shoulder, he went to the front door of the ranch house and slipped out into the night.

He could have killed Guthrie, but he wasn't a cold-blooded murderer, and anyway, there was no guarantee that would solve the problem. One or more of the hired guns working for the rancher might decide it was time for them to take over the Rafter G.

It was going to take a true cleanup, and for that The Kid needed the law. Even if it meant being recognized by the badge-toters and risking his own freedom.

Moving at a trot, The Kid headed for the trees where he left the buckskin. Before he got there, a man stepped out of the bunkhouse and called, "Hey! Who's there?"

Ignoring the challenge The Kid kept going. He figured the good luck couldn't last, and he was right.

"Hold it!" the man yelled. "Damn it, I'll shoot!"

The Kid didn't stop or even slow down. A moment later, muzzle flame stabbed through the night as the man fired twice. "Everybody out!" he shouted. "Something's wrong!"

The Kid reached the trees as Guthrie's men piled out of the bunkhouse, yelling questions and curses. More guns began to roar. It was too dark for accurate shooting, and The Kid heard slugs whip through the pine needles, but none of them came close to him and Guthrie.

He reached his horse and slung Guthrie's senseless form over its back. As he jerked the reins loose and swung up into the saddle, he heard a bullet smack into a tree trunk only a few feet away.

The Chinese cook shouted, "Stop shooting! Stop shooting! He has Mr. Guthrie! Stop!"

The guns fell silent.

The Kid turned the buckskin and moved as fast as he could through the trees. He couldn't risk a full-tilt gallop in the darkness.

Within minutes, Guthrie's men would be mounted up and coming after him. The Kid's brain worked swiftly as he tried to figure out what to do next. If he headed for the rim, taking the narrow, back-and-forth trail down the cliff face would give the pursuers a good chance to catch up to him.

The gunmen believed that Chester Blount and his mysterious allies had died in the explosion that destroyed the old-timer's cabin. The timing of Guthrie's kidnapping was suspicious, of course, but they wouldn't naturally assume that whoever had grabbed their boss was heading for Dos Caballos Canyon.

When The Kid came out of the trees into an open stretch, he heeled the buckskin into a run that carried them east, roughly parallel to the edge of the Mogollon Rim a couple of miles to the south.

With him fleeing in that direction, Guthrie's men likely wouldn't think that he had any connection to Blount and the canyon that Guthrie craved. The Kid wanted to keep it that way.

All he had to do was outride a couple dozen hardcase killers who wanted to see him dead.

As if that wasn't going to be enough of a chore, Spud Guthrie chose that moment to wake up, twist around, and drive an elbow into The Kid's belly as hard as he could.

Chapter 26

The sudden attack took The Kid by surprise. He bent forward in the saddle, the breath knocked out of his lungs by Guthrie's vicious blow.

Guthrie was squirming like a wildcat, almost toppling The Kid out of the saddle. He grabbed the horn at the last second and managed to stay mounted.

Still gasping for air, he launched a left uppercut that caught Guthrie under the chin as he spewed obscenities. The rancher's teeth clicked together, and he screeched in pain as he bit through his tongue.

The Kid hammered another punch into Guthrie's face. Guthrie sagged backward. The Kid wrestled him around, looped his left arm around the rancher's throat, and drew his gun. He pressed the barrel into Guthrie's back.

"Settle down, you little snake!" The Kid hissed into Guthrie's ear. "I'm damn close to blowing your spine in two and being done with it."

Guthrie stopped fighting. He couldn't talk very well with The Kid's forearm pressing into his throat like an iron bar, but he managed to rasp, "Who . . . who the hell are you? What do you want with me?"

"Right now I want you to stop fighting so I don't have to kill you. As for who I am, let's just say I'm a friend of Chester Blount's." The Kid paused, then added with grim humor, "How's your hat, Spud?"

"You!" Guthrie said. "You son of a—You were the maverick up on that ledge this afternoon!"

"That's right. I could have killed you then. I drilled your hat on purpose. Don't make me regret deciding to let you live."

"But . . . but that cabin . . ."

"We weren't in it," The Kid said. "Blount's fine."

Guthrie cursed bitterly at the news.

The Kid had kept the buckskin moving, guiding the horse with his knees since both his hands were occupied. But he knew he couldn't keep on that way. Guthrie's men weren't far behind him, and they would be riding hard.

"Take off your belt and put your hands behind your back," The Kid ordered.

"Go to hell."

"I'll kill you if I have to," The Kid warned. "If I keep you propped up in front of me, your men won't know you're dead. They'll have to hold their fire for fear of hitting you. So you can be a live hostage or a dead one, Guthrie. It's up to you."

Guthrie realized The Kid meant it. He fumbled with his belt and pulled it off. The Kid holstered his gun but kept his tight grip around Guthrie's neck. He looped the belt around Guthrie's wrists and jerked it tight, binding the rancher's arms behind his back.

With that done, The Kid was able to take hold of the reins and urge the buckskin into a gallop again. They made better time, but when he looked back, he spotted a dark mass in the distance—the riders from the Rafter G giving chase.

Coming to an area of more rugged terrain cut by rocky ridges and gullies, The Kid was forced to slow down and ride back and forth to avoid some of the obstacles. He worked the buckskin into a brush-choked ravine. The shadows were so thick no starlight penetrated. Taking a bandanna from his saddlebags, he wadded it up, and forced it into the mouth of a bitterly protesting Guthrie to serve as a gag.

"Take it easy," he whispered into the rancher's ear. "I can cut your throat without making a sound."

He could have if he'd had a knife . . . which he didn't. But Guthrie didn't have to know that.

They waited in silence for about fifteen minutes. Then The Kid began to hear hoofbeats not far away.

The riders came closer. The Kid knew they had to be the hired killers from the Rafter G. The men passed close enough to the ravine for him to hear them arguing.

"Damn it, Nebel, we don't know that he came this way," a man protested.

"He was headed in this direction when he left the flats," another man replied.

"Why would he grab the boss in the first place? Ransom, maybe?"

"Could be. Spud's the richest hombre in these parts." The gunman called Nebel laughed. "Hell, his wallet's damn near as big as he is."

Guthrie made angry noises until The Kid closed a hand around his throat.

The voices faded as the searchers rode on past, but The Kid heard one of the men say, "I think we ought to check out that canyon."

"Dos Caballos?" Nebel asked. "We blew up that old codger and his friends. They didn't have anything to do with this."

The Kid smiled grimly. That was exactly what he wanted them to think.

After a moment, he couldn't make out the voices anymore, and the hoofbeats soon faded to nothingness. The Kid waited another half hour, then, satisfied that his decoying tactics had worked, he emerged from the ravine and sent the buckskin back toward the Rafter G.

When he came to the trail that led down off the rim, he dismounted and hauled Guthrie down from the horse's back. "You're going in front," he told the rancher. "Try anything funny, and you'll be the one who makes it to the bottom of the rim in a hurry."

With The Kid leading the buckskin and

prodding Guthrie along, the three of them started the descent. It was bad enough having to follow the trail in darkness, but with his hands tied behind him, Guthrie had it even worse. He had to move very slowly to keep his balance and find each spot to place his feet.

It seemed to take forever to reach the bottom. The Kid lifted Guthrie onto the horse and felt the man trembling as he did so. Likely Guthrie didn't want to live through anything like that again any time soon.

For that matter, neither did The Kid.

The eastern sky was gray with the approach of dawn by the time they reached the entrance to Dos Caballos Canyon. The Kid gave the cry of a hoot owl, something Frank Morgan had taught him how to do, and a moment later the brush-covered gate began to swing open.

"Kid!" Lace called softly. "Kid, is that you?"

"Yeah," he replied, "and I've got Guthrie."

"Good Lord!" The exclamation came from Chester Blount. "I didn't really believe you could do it."

The Kid took hold of the heavy gate and helped Lace open it. Then he led the buckskin through with the prisoner on its back. He and Lace closed the gate while Blount glared up at Guthrie in the gray gloom.

"Bet you thought I was blowed to smithereens, didn't you, you snaky little varmint?" Blount demanded. "Well, I ain't, and pretty soon you're gonna be answerin' for all the no-good things you done. Some o' them fellas who disappeared just before you gobbled up their range was friends o' mine. I'll bet once the law starts pokin' around, they'll find that them skallyhooters who work for you are mighty good with a runnin' iron, too!"

Blount hadn't said anything before about suspecting Guthrie of being behind a wave of murder and rustling in the area, but The Kid wasn't surprised.

Guthrie still had the gag in his mouth. He made angry sounds through it at Blount's accusations.

"Let's get him back to the camp," The Kid said. "I want to get him tied up good and proper, so he can't get away."

"I got that other horse o' yours right here," Blount said as he led the animal forward. "The names I need to remember when I get to Phoenix are John Stafford in San Francisco and Conrad Browning, right?"

"That's right," The Kid told him. He shook hands with the old man. "Good luck."

"You two are the ones who're gonna need it," Blount said. "You'll be stuck here in this canyon with a viper in your midst and a whole heap o' killers right outside just waitin' for a chance to ventilate you."

"We won't give them that chance," The Kid promised. "You'd better get started. It'll be a while before they decide to come look here, but there's no point in waiting."

Blount mounted up, and The Kid and Lace opened the gate again. The Kid kept one eye on Guthrie while they were doing that, but the rancher didn't try anything. His shoulders seemed to droop in defeat.

It could be just a ruse. The Kid wasn't going to let down his guard.

When Blount was gone and the gate was securely fastened again, The Kid and Lace escorted Guthrie to the camp on the other side of the big rock. While The Kid covered him, Lace used several pieces of rope to hogtie Guthrie. They set him down with his back against the rock, confident that he couldn't get loose.

"You've had some practice at tying up prisoners," The Kid commented.

Lace smiled. "Yeah. Once I've got my hands on a man, he doesn't get away . . . unless I want him to."

The Kid didn't ask what she meant by that. He had a hunch he might find out.

Chapter 27

It was the middle of the morning before The Kid heard horses approaching the canyon. "Riders coming," he called to Lace.

She hurried around the rock to where he was standing watch, leaving Guthrie trussed up on the other side and the dog to keep an eye on him. "I told Max if Guthrie opens his mouth to yell, he can chew on him a little," she informed The Kid with a grin.

Carrying their Winchesters, they trotted up to the gate to look out. A group of about a dozen men came into sight, riding toward the canyon from the east. The Kid knew they had probably come down the treacherous trail he and Guthrie had descended the night before. He didn't actually recognize any of them, but the hard stamp of their faces told him they were some of Guthrie's hired killers.

"That whole gun crew's probably split up to search in all directions for Guthrie," Lace said quietly. "You think they'll ride on past?"

"They might," The Kid said. "But in case they don't, we'd better get behind some cover." He nodded toward a couple thick-trunked pine trees that would give them a good view of the gate. In a crouching run, he and Lace moved over and got situated behind them. They waited as the hoof-beats got louder.

The riders stopped just outside its entrance, as The Kid thought they would. One of them ordered, "A couple of you get down and open that damn gate the old man built."

The voice was familiar. The Kid thought it belonged to one of the gunmen he'd heard talking the night before, while he and Guthrie waited in the brushy ravine.

That was confirmed a second later when someone asked, "What would the boss be doin' in there, Nebel?"

"Damned if I know," Nebel replied, "but we're gonna look every place we can find."

From the way he gave orders, Nebel was probably Guthrie's *segundo*, or at least the boss of the hired hardcases. There might be a regular foreman who supervised the cowboys doing the actual work of running the ranch.

From The Kid's position, he could see the latch that held the gate closed. He drew a bead on it with his rifle and waited. A moment later, through a gap in the brush, he saw a hand reach for the latch.

He drilled a .44-40 slug right through the hand.

The man screamed and jerked it back. A second later, shots roared as the men outside the gate acted instinctively, pulling iron and blazing away through the brush.

The Kid had already ducked back behind the tree, and Lace was safely behind the trunk of the other pine. A few bullets knocked bark off the trunks, but that was all. Most of the slugs whined off harmlessly up the canyon.

"Hold your fire! Hold your fire!" Nebel roared, cutting short the fusillade. "We don't know who's in there!"

"Must be that old codger," one of the other men said.

"We blew him up," a third gunnie protested.

Nebel said, "We blew up his cabin. We don't know for sure that he was inside it. Besides, he had some help yesterday, and we don't know who or how many." He paused. "We gotta get that gate open."

"And get shot like Benson?" a man asked. "He may not ever be able to use that hand again."

There was a moment of silence while Nebel thought about it. Then he said, "Rope it. We'll pull the damned thing down."

That would probably work, The Kid thought, and if it did, the gunmen could charge through and overwhelm him and Lace before they could stop all of them. They couldn't run that risk, so he called out, "Nebel! Can you hear me?"

Surprised silence greeted the shout. After a moment, Nebel said, "Who the hell is that?"

"It doesn't matter who I am," The Kid said. "The important thing is that I've got your boss in here, and if you try to come through that gate, he's a dead man!"

Again, Nebel didn't respond right away. Seconds dragged by before the gunman said, "You've got Guthrie?"

"That's right," The Kid said.

"How do we know you're telling the truth?"

"Somebody took him right out of his own ranch house last night, didn't they? And knocked out the cook while they were there. How would I know that if it wasn't me who grabbed him?"

Nebel didn't have an answer for that. When he spoke up again, it was to ask, "What do you want?"

"Turn around and ride away," The Kid said. "Leave this canyon alone. If you bust in or try anything else, Guthrie will be dead long before you can get your hands on him."

"You'll die, too, you son of a bitch, you and whoever else is in there with you!"

"Maybe. So will a lot of your men."

"That's a dead end canyon. You can't get out. You've trapped yourself in there, you fool. We can sit out here until you starve."

"Guthrie will starve first," The Kid pointed out. "You don't think we'll be sharing our rations with him, do you?"

"I don't know for sure that he's even still alive. I want some proof you've got him, damn it!"

The Kid had been expecting that. He looked over at Lace and nodded. She dashed back around the rock to the campsite, and when she reappeared, she was prodding Guthrie ahead of her at the point of her Winchester.

His feet were untied so he could walk, but his hands were still lashed tightly behind his back. He didn't have a gag in his mouth, so when Lace poked him in the back with the rifle, he was able to yell, "Nebel!"

"Is that you, boss?" Nebel sounded slightly surprised to hear Guthrie's voice.

"Damn right it's me," the rancher replied. "I want you to come in here and kill this bastard who kidnapped me! Not the girl, though. I got something special planned for her."

Guthrie grunted in pain as Lace jabbed him hard in the kidney with the rifle barrel. "You don't *have* anything special, you weaselly little varmint," she told him.

"There's a girl in there, too?" Nebel called.

"And she can shoot just as good or better than any of you," The Kid replied. "If you don't believe me, just try to get in here. You know now we've got Guthrie, so back off!"

Nebel hesitated again. "Boss?"

Guthrie sighed through clenched teeth. "Do what they say, I reckon . . . for now. They're both loco enough to kill me."

"You mean there's only two? Where's the old man? Is he dead?"

"No, he rode off—"

The Kid motioned to Lace, and she drove the

barrel of her Winchester into Guthrie's back again, hard enough to knock him to his knees as well as silencing him. She put a boot in his back and shoved him down onto his face.

The Kid didn't want Nebel thinking too much about where Chester Blount might have gone, or else the gunman might realize Blount was fetching the law from Phoenix. To forestall that, The Kid called, "The old-timer was plenty glad to sell me his claim and be shut of all the trouble! He's halfway to Mexico by now!"

He heard some muttering from the men outside the gate. They knew that Blount had refused Guthrie's offer to buy him out, otherwise the rancher wouldn't have resorted to attempted murder to get his hands on Dos Caballos Canyon.

But it was possible Blount could have accepted someone else's offer, as much to spite Guthrie as anything else, so they couldn't discount the possibility The Kid was telling the truth.

After a few minutes, Nebel called, "We're leaving, but this ain't over. If you're smart, you'll let the boss go and then light a shuck out of here! You might get clear with your lives that way."

The Kid didn't believe that for a second. Nebel would leave riflemen hidden in the trees to watch the canyon mouth. If he and Lace so much as showed their faces, they would be gunned down instantly.

Hoofbeats thundered away. Lace reached down, grabbed Guthrie's arm, and hauled him to his feet.

"Now what do we do, Kid?" she asked.

"Now we wait," he said.

The siege was on.

Chapter 28

By late afternoon, Guthrie was raving like a lunatic. He couldn't stand being tied up and started cursing The Kid and Lace, spewing vile profanities. Even the threat of setting Max on him didn't shut him up.

So The Kid stuffed the gag in Guthrie's mouth again. He had to jerk his hand back to keep Guthrie from biting him.

"If I ever saw a man who could pass for a hydrophobic skunk, it's him," Lace said with a nod toward the rancher. "How does anybody get so twisted and evil?"

The Kid didn't answer. In the days after Rebel's death, he had come so close to giving in to his despair that he could have wound up just as warped as Guthrie. Clinging to the memories of his wife had kept him sane.

"I guess I shouldn't talk," Lace went on. "I was mixed up with Pronto Pike, after all. If anything, he's even worse than Guthrie."

"Hard to believe, but I'll take your word for it," The Kid said. "He's quiet now, anyway. I'm grateful for that."

Guthrie couldn't do anything except make grunting noises through the gag, but his eyes continued to follow them around the camp, lit by the hellish glare of murderous hatred.

They kept guard most of the time, one watching the gate, the other scanning the tops of the canyon walls, looking for sharpshooters Nebel might send up there to try to pick them off.

The Kid was watching the opposite rim when he spotted movement. A moment later, his keen eyes saw the barrel of a rifle thrust around a rock. The bushwhacker leaned out a little to aim.

It was enough of a target for The Kid. His Winchester snapped to his shoulder and cracked. The bullet struck the rock only inches from the man's head and made him jerk back, exposing more of him.

The Winchester's lever was a blur as The Kid worked it and fired again, the bullet boring through the man's head. He jerked as death claimed him and pitched forward, dropping his rifle and landing so his arms and head and shoulders hung off the edge of the canyon rim. Blood dripped in a steady stream from his shattered skull.

"Kid?" Lace called from the other side of the rock. "You all right?"

"Yeah," he replied. "Keep an eye on the gate. They might try hitting us from two directions at once."

After a few minutes, somebody The Kid couldn't see took hold of the dead man's feet and hauled him back, away from the rim. That was fine with The Kid. He didn't need the grisly sight as a reminder of the danger he and Lace were in, and hoped the bushwhacker's death discouraged any other gunman from trying the same tactic.

By nightfall, nothing else had happened. Not wanting to risk a fire, The Kid and Lace had a cold supper. They would build one in the morning so they could have coffee . . . if they were still alive.

Guthrie had settled down some, and when he made noises indicating he wanted the gag removed, The Kid obliged. Guthrie didn't try to take a finger off.

"Don't I get something to eat?" the rancher asked wearily.

"You heard Nebel. He's planning on starving us out. We have to make our supplies last as long as they possibly can."

"You know it's not gonna come to that," Guthrie said. "You sent Blount to Phoenix to fetch the law, didn't you?"

The Kid didn't see any point in denying it. "That's right. He'll be back in another three days or so, and your little reign of terror will be over, Guthrie."

Guthrie laughed and shook his head. "I don't know how you figure that. I'm an important man in these parts. The authorities won't believe an old fool and a couple of drifters over me."

"That's where you're wrong, Guthrie. My real name is Conrad Browning."

Guthrie stared up at him in the darkness. "Seems like I've heard that name before."

"You should have. I own an interest in a number of banks in Arizona Territory, as well as the railroad and several mines."

A curt laugh came from Guthrie. "I'm supposed to believe that? You're nothing but a fast-gun saddle tramp!"

"Appearances are deceiving. Not only that, I've made an offer to Mr. Blount for half interest in Dos Caballos Canyon. We haven't worked out the details yet, but he's going to take me up on it. So for all intents and purposes, this is my land, too, and I'm not going to let you steal it."

"You're loco," Guthrie muttered, but there was some doubt in his voice. He was starting to realize he might have bitten off a bigger chunk than he could handle.

A few minutes later, he tried to salvage the situation. "Listen to me. If you take me with you as a hostage, you can ride out of here in the morning. My men won't have any choice except to let you go. I'll order them to stay here and not follow you, and when you've got a five or ten mile lead, however much you want, you can let me go and ride on. You've killed some of my men and annoyed the hell out of me, but I'm willin' to call it square."

"I'm not," The Kid said. "I hold a grudge."

He knew that Guthrie was lying. The rancher

would never let them go unscathed. One way or another, he would have to have his revenge, unless he was locked up.

Or dead.

Leaving Max to keep an eye on the prisoner, The Kid and Lace moved to stand guard on the gate. One of them would stay awake at all times to listen for anyone trying to sneak up. They used the pine trees for cover again.

They planned to alternate two-hour shifts. The Kid would stay awake first, letting Lace get a little sleep. He stood with his back against the tree, the rifle cradled across his chest, and listened intently. Guthrie's men might be able to slip up to the gate on foot without being heard, but they couldn't unfasten the latch without making the brush rustle.

The night was quiet, cool, and peaceful. It would have been mighty pleasant, The Kid thought, if he hadn't been listening for a bunch of cold-blooded killers who wanted to wipe out him and Lace.

After a couple hours, she called softly, "Kid! I'm awake. Get some shut-eye."

"Thanks," he told her. He slid down to sit at the base of the tree with his back against the trunk. Sleep claimed him within seconds of closing his eyes.

He hadn't completely mastered the trick of waking up when he wanted to, but he was able to come pretty close to the allotted amount of time.

When he opened his eyes again, he was confident that not much more than two hours had passed. If he had overslept by too much, Lace would have called to him and woken him.

"All right—" he started to say as he got to his feet, but she shushed him instantly.

"Somebody's out there," she called in a half whisper.

He brought the rifle to his shoulder and swung around the tree so he could aim at the gate across the canyon mouth. He listened and didn't hear anything at first, but a moment later the soft scrape of boot leather on the ground came to his ears. He knew Lace was right.

Somebody was creeping up on the gate, and they couldn't be up to anything good.

A faint rasp and a sudden small flare of light sent alarm stabbing through The Kid's veins like ice. Damn them and their fondness for dynamite!

Sparks sputtered at the base of the gate as The Kid dashed out from behind the tree and sprinted toward the canyon mouth.

He hadn't anticipated them trying to blow up the gate, but he should have, he thought bitterly, racing toward the gate to reach the bomb and pull the fuse before it exploded.

"Kid!" she cried behind him.

"Cover me!" he shouted over his shoulder as he threw himself forward in a long dive that carried him to the bottom of the gate.

Lace sprayed rifle slugs over his head, through the brush tied onto the wooden framework. At the same time, Guthrie's men opened fire from outside the canyon. Bullets whined around The Kid's head.

Focusing on the bundle of dynamite and the sputtering fuse just on the other side of the gate, he shoved brush aside and thrust his arm through the opening he had created. The dynamite was just out of his reach. He threw his shoulder against the gate and stretched his arm out as far as he could, far enough that he felt bones creaking in their sockets.

His fingers brushed the burning fuse. He pushed aside the pain as sparks bit into his hand. The fuse was too short for him to pull, so he did the only thing he could.

He closed his hand around it, smothering the fire with his flesh.

The sparks died out, but a second later bullets began to smack into the ground around him. Guthrie's men were trying to detonate the explosives by firing into them.

Not wanting to take the chance it might work, he strained forward again, and closed his hand around the three sticks of dynamite that had been tied together. He pulled them through the gate and rolled away from the slugs that were whipping around him. It was possible a few sticks of dynamite could come in handy later on.

He tossed them over to the far side of the canyon, then snatched up his Winchester, which he had dropped when he dove for the explosives. He scrambled back behind the pine tree and joined Lace in returning the fire of Guthrie's men. In the dark, all they could do was aim at muzzle flashes. It was impossible to know if their bullets found their target.

After a fierce exchange of shots that lasted for several minutes, Lace suddenly cried, "Kid! On the rim!"

The Kid twisted and looked up, saw the flare of another match. They were going to try dropping dynamite from up there. He brought up his rifle and fired three shots as fast as he could, aiming at the lucifer.

A man staggered forward, silhouetted against the starlight. With a scream, he pitched forward off the rim, plummeting toward the canyon floor far below. An ugly thud, like that of a watermelon breaking open, silenced him in mid-scream.

The Kid held his breath for a few seconds, waiting to see if any dynamite was going to go off. When there was no explosion, he knew he had winged the man before he'd been able to light the fuse.

The shooting from outside trailed off. As Lace's gun fell silent, The Kid took a chance and yelled, "Nebel! You out there?"

"What do you want, you son of a bitch?" the gunman answered.

“Call it off now, or Guthrie dies! I’ve got a gun to his head!”

That wasn’t strictly true, but all it would take was a shouted command by Lace for Max to rip Guthrie’s throat out, so it was almost the same thing.

After a moment, Nebel shouted, “All right! We’re leaving! But this ain’t—”

“Yeah, it ain’t over,” The Kid called back mockingly. “I’ve heard that before. If you and the rest of Guthrie’s crew have any sense, you’ll ride out now and save your own hides. The sweet deal you had here . . . *that’s* over.”

Nebel didn’t say anything. After a minute, the sound of hoofbeats drifted through the night. Maybe Guthrie’s crew of killers were really pulling out, or maybe it was another trick.

Either way, The Kid thought as he thumbed fresh cartridges through the Winchester’s loading gate to replace the ones he’d fired, he and Lace would be ready. If it came down to it, they would go out fighting.

It was as good a way to die as any.

And better than most, The Kid told himself grimly as he worked the rifle’s lever and jacked a round into the chamber.

Chapter 29

The retreat of Guthrie's men was no trick. The rest of the night passed quietly, as did the next two days and nights after that.

"Looks like Nebel and the rest of your bunch have decided you're not worth fighting for," The Kid told Guthrie on the morning of the fourth day. With any luck, it was the day Chester Blount would be back from Phoenix with a posse of lawmen.

Guthrie glared at The Kid. They had taken pity on him and given him coffee and something to eat every day, but it hadn't improved his disposition any.

"They're just biding their time," Guthrie insisted. "They won't let me die, and they sure as hell won't let me be turned over to the law." His glare turned into a smirk. "I know too much about too many of those boys. They won't want me testifying."

"Sounds like a good reason for them to decide they're better off with you dead," Lace commented.

Guthrie looked surprised and a little worried. Obviously, he hadn't thought of that.

"Max, guard," Lace told the dog. He planted himself on his haunches in front of Guthrie and gazed intently at the prisoner, mouth open a little so Guthrie could see the sharp teeth. If The Kid hadn't known better, he would have said Max was grinning at Guthrie in an attempt to unnerve the rancher.

Lace inclined her head toward the other side of the rock as an indication that she wanted The Kid to follow her. He did so with his Winchester tucked under his arm. His gaze roved constantly over both canyon rims and the gate. Just because Guthrie's hired killers hadn't tried anything for a couple of days didn't mean the trouble was over.

"What is it?" he asked quietly when he and Lace had put the big rock between them and the prisoner.

"The old-timer's liable to be back today."

The Kid nodded. "I know. If nothing happened to delay him, and if he was able to get the authorities in Phoenix to listen to him."

"If he was able to use your name to make them listen, that's what you mean."

The Kid shrugged. "Influence isn't worth having if you're not willing to use it in a good cause."

That was the sort of altruistic statement the old Conrad Browning never would have made. To him, influence was only good for increasing his own wealth and power. Being around Frank and Rebel had changed him, and then Rebel's death had tempered the steel inside him even more. There was no longer any point in denying it.

"You see, that's not the sort of thing I'd expect

to hear a hunted fugitive say," Lace said. "If that wild yarn of yours is true and you really are this rich fella Conrad Browning, I think it's time you told me how you went from that to being the man you are now. What's this Kid Morgan business all about, anyway?"

The Kid's jaw tightened. "That's sort of personal."

"Damn right it is. You think those things I told you about *my* life weren't personal? You think it was easy to tell you that my mama was a whore, I was a whore, and I'm gonna make damn sure *my* daughter doesn't grow up to be a whore? Because I'll tell you right now, Kid . . . it wasn't. It wasn't easy at all."

He didn't know what to say to that. She was right, of course. She had been honest with him. Did he owe her the same sort of honesty? They were comrades-in-arms, after all. They had fought side by side, risked their lives for each other, heard the same bullets whipping past their heads.

But she was asking him to reveal things no one else knew except Frank Morgan and Claudius Turnbuckle. And even those two had never heard *all* the details of that horrifying night in Carson City.

As he hesitated, she went on, "If we get out of this mess with Guthrie alive, we'll be heading on to Santa Fe pretty soon. Will we be going there as partners, to clear your name, or do I have to take you prisoner again and turn you in for that ten grand bounty?"

The Kid smiled. "Do you think you could?"

"For ten thousand dollars, I'll give it a damned good try," she said flatly, and he knew she was telling the truth.

"All right," he said, reaching a decision. "If you want to know the ugly story of Kid Morgan's birth, then so be it." He thought about how he had put the barrel of a rifle against the head of an unarmed man and pulled the trigger. "But you may not like everything you hear."

"Try me," she said. "It's not likely you'll be able to shock me."

"I'm not trying to shock you. I'm just doing what you asked, telling you the truth."

For the next half hour, that's what he did, speaking quietly so Guthrie couldn't overhear. It was bad enough opening himself up to Lace without letting the evil little rancher in on it.

She tried to keep her face expressionless at first, but as the tale unfolded of Rebel's murder, the injuries he had suffered, and the stark, unrelenting vengeance he had exacted on those responsible for the tragedy, he saw both shock and pity in her eyes.

The shock didn't bother him so much. He didn't want any part of the pity. "If you're feeling sorry for me, forget it," he snapped. "There's no need."

She shook her head. "But it was so unfair—"

"It was life," The Kid said harshly. "You want to know the biggest truth I ever learned?"

She waited in silence.

"Anything can happen to anybody at any time," The Kid said. "People won't admit that to themselves or even think about it too much, because if they did, it would drive them mad. But it's still true. You go along, and you think you've got a good life, and it can be snatched away from you in a second, with no warning at all. Everything you've ever worked for can disappear, just like that." He snapped his fingers. "And it doesn't do a damned bit of good to talk about fair or unfair. It just is. If you're going to mourn what you've lost or the bad breaks that have happened to you, you might as well mourn the sun coming up in the morning, because it's all part of the same thing."

She stared at him as he finished his bleak pronouncement. He had put into words the feelings that had ridden with him over the past year. He had never really been alone, no matter what he thought. The stark horror of life had always been at his side.

Finally she said, "Don't you think . . . don't you think that sometimes people can get good breaks, too?"

"Sure," he said with a shrug. "That's part of it. There are probably some people who go through life without anything bad ever happening to them. But it's not because of anything they did. It's just the luck of the draw. They might go along just fine for fifty years and then lose it all. Or they might go to their grave still thinking the world's a wonderful place. It doesn't change anything."

Lace shook her head. "I feel sorry for you, whether you want it or not, Conrad."

He smiled. "You believe me now?"

"Yeah. Nobody could spin some crazy yarn like that without it being true." She turned away from him. "And don't worry, I'll try to help you clear your name, but I won't waste any pity on you from here on out. You're already getting plenty of that from yourself."

His hand shot out and gripped her arm. He jerked her around toward him, saying, "You think I feel sorry for myself?"

Her gun came up. The barrel pressed under his chin as she eared back the hammer. "Let go of me," she told him between clenched teeth.

The Kid saw the anger in her eyes and felt the tremble that went through her muscles. He opened his hand and released her arm.

She stepped back and lowered the gun. After easing down the hammer, she pouched the iron on her hip. "Damn right you feel sorry for yourself," she said. "You had every right to, for a while. The way you've helped people out along the way, despite how you felt, well, I can admire you for that. But for God's sake, you can't let what happened ruin you for life. You can't just shut yourself off from everything that's good out there."

"Why the hell not?"

She looked at him and said, "Because Rebel wouldn't want you to."

His first impulse was to slap her, to warn her not to dare tell him what Rebel would or wouldn't have wanted him to do. The fact that he didn't wasn't solely due to the fact that she might shoot him if he did.

He knew she was right.

He had fought, again and again, with the things his heart had tried to tell him. His brain acknowledged the grim uncertainty of life, but he had refused to allow himself to see the hope that his heart urged on him.

"You talk about the truth," Lace whispered. "The truth is somewhere in the middle. You're not just Conrad Browning or Kid Morgan. You're both of them. And that adds up to a good man, whether you believe it or not. *That's* why I'm going to help you, Kid."

"I thought you were going to call me Conrad."

She shrugged. "I like Kid a little better. But it doesn't really matter."

"No," he said. "I suppose it doesn't."

He took hold of her arms again, but he was

gentle as he drew her toward him. His mouth found hers as her arms went around his neck.

The parts of his being that had been locked in mortal combat with each other could take up their struggle again later.

The rest of him was going to be busy for a while.

They were sitting at the base of one of the pine trees near the canyon mouth. The Kid's arm was around Lace's shoulders, and her head rested against his arm. She wore her poncho again, but her hat hung by its neck strap.

She chuckled and said, "It's a good thing Nebel and the rest of that bunch of gunwolves didn't come along a little while ago."

"Yeah," The Kid agreed, "but I was keeping an eye and an ear out for them."

"Sure you were," she said, laughing again.

Actually, it was true, but he wasn't going to argue the point.

The afternoon was still and quiet, so he didn't have any trouble hearing the horses in the distance. From the way Lace suddenly stiffened against him, he knew she heard them, too.

"Sounds like a big bunch of riders," she said.

"Yeah, and they're coming closer."

"Maybe it's the old man and a posse from Phoenix," Lace suggested.

"It could be," The Kid agreed. He got to his feet

and helped her up. "But we'd better make sure."

Carrying their rifles, they hurried toward the canyon mouth and stopped at the gate. As The Kid peered through the screen of brush, he spotted a cloud of dust in the distance to the east, not to the south as it likely would have been if it heralded the return of Chester Blount.

"That doesn't look good," Lace said quietly.

"No, not at all. It appears that Nebel and some of the rest of Guthrie's crew are paying us a visit again."

But not all of the gunmen, The Kid saw as the riders came closer and he began to be able to make them out. There were about a dozen men in all. Six to one odds, he thought. He had faced worse. But as the grim side of his nature knew all too well, good luck always ran out. "Check the rims," he told Lace.

She stepped back and lifted her head to let her gaze search along both sides of the canyon. "Nothing," she reported. "Nobody's moving around up there."

"Well, that's something to be thankful for, anyway," The Kid muttered. "Maybe the rest of Guthrie's men gave up and left after their last try. Those could be the only ones he has left."

"That's still pretty long odds against us," Lace pointed out.

"Yeah, but as long as they're out there and we're in here, we can hold them off."

"I hope you're right." Lace bent over to look through a gap in the brush again. *"Son of a bitch!"*

The Kid tensed at the sudden note of alarm in her voice.

"What is it? What's wrong?"

"Those aren't all Guthrie's men," Lace said. "Look at those two hombres riding in front. Do you recognize the one on the right?"

The Kid's breath hissed between his teeth. "Good Lord," he said. "That's—"

"Yeah," Lace said. "Pronto Pike. And all the rest of his men are with him, too."

Chapter 30

"I thought we gave Pike the slip days ago," The Kid said bitterly. "How did he manage to find us?"

Lace said, "Back when I was riding with him, sometimes I thought he could *smell* the men we were after, even from miles away. It was uncanny the way he could find them. Sort of spooky, too."

"Some predators have a nose for blood. Maybe that extends to blood money, too."

"Could be," Lace agreed. "However he did it, he's here. And here he comes."

Most of the men had reined to a halt a couple hundred yards away from the canyon mouth. Pike and the man with him kept riding until they were only a hundred yards away. Then they stopped as well.

The Kid wondered if the man with Pike was Nebel, the chief of Guthrie's hardcases. It wouldn't surprise him if that were true.

"Morgan!" Pike called. "Morgan, is that you in there?"

"Don't answer him," Lace said. "If he knows for sure it's you, he'll never give up."

"I don't think he's going to, anyway," The Kid said, but he didn't respond to Pike's hail.

After a moment, the bounty hunter went on, "Hello, the canyon! I know good and well *somebody's* in there! Nebel here tells me that one of you is a woman! Lace? If that's you, come on out! Bring Morgan with you, and we'll partner up again, honey!"

From the corner of his eye, The Kid saw the shudder that went through Lace at the idea of "partnering up" with Pronto Pike.

"I know you deserted me," Pike went on, "but I'm willing to forgive you for that! All you've got to do is turn Morgan over to me! You don't really think you can claim that ten grand all to yourself, now do you? Better to get a nice share you can send to that little gal of yours back in Kansas City! That'll help keep her from growing up to be a whore like her ma and her grandma!"

Lace thrust the barrel of her rifle through the brushy screen. "That dirty son of a—I told him to never talk about my daughter!"

The Kid said, "Lace, no!" but before he could reach over to grab the rifle, she had squeezed the trigger. The Winchester cracked.

Anger caused her to miss the shot. The bullet kicked up dust a few yards to Pike's left. He and Nebel wheeled their horses and dashed back to join the other men. Lace worked the lever of her rifle and sent several more slugs after them, but the horses didn't break stride.

She muttered an exasperated curse as she lowered the Winchester. She glanced over at The Kid and saw the frown on his face. "What?"

"Pike knows for sure it's us in here now," he said. "That's why he was trying to goad you into shooting at him. He must have suspected it, but you confirmed it for him."

"Damn it, he's not that tricky." Lace hesitated. "Well, maybe he is."

The Kid put it together in his head. "Pike figured out we were behind him somewhere, instead of ahead of him, so he doubled back to look for us. He probably decided we were trying to circle around him, so he cut south, too. When he got to the Rafter G, he heard about how a man and a woman were forted up in this canyon, holding Guthrie hostage, and thought it might be us. For all I know, that Chinese cook got a good enough look at me to tell Pike what the man who grabbed Guthrie looked like, and Pike recognized the description."

"How does that bring me into it?" Lace asked. "Pike didn't know I'd captured you."

"No, but when the two of you split up, he could have figured that you'd still be trying to find me." The Kid shrugged. "It's all hunches and guesswork, but it could have happened that way, and the important thing is that Pike's out there . . . and he knows we're in here."

"What happened to the rest of Guthrie's men?"

"I don't know. They gave up and rode away to find some other job?" The Kid shook his head. "Hired guns like that are loyal only as long as they're getting paid. If they figured Guthrie wasn't going to make it out of this mess, they might have decided to cut their losses and move on."

"Leaving Nebel and a handful of men to team up with Pike and his bunch." Lace nodded. "It sure could have happened that way, Kid. What are we going to do now?"

"The same thing we've been doing: stay alert and wait for Blount to get back from Phoenix with a posse. The situation hasn't really changed that much."

An ugly suspicion was roaming around in the back of The Kid's head, though. The situation *had* changed, and it might make all the difference in the world.

Nebel and the remaining men from Guthrie's crew of gunfighters knew about the ten thousand dollar reward for The Kid. Pike had mentioned it when he was shouting at the canyon a few minutes earlier, so it couldn't be a secret.

If Pike had promised them a share of the ten grand, they might not care any more about Spud Guthrie's safety. They might have decided it would be better to take what they could get, and Guthrie be damned.

In that case, the rancher was now worthless as a hostage. Pike, Nebel, and the other men could attack the canyon without any thought for Guthrie's continued existence.

"Come on," The Kid said to Lace as those thoughts coalesced in his head. "We need to fall back."

"What about defending the canyon mouth?"

He shook his head. "We can't stop them from getting through here if they want to badly enough. If they attack us head-on, we'll kill some of them, but that'll just leave more money for the survivors to split up once we're dead. We'll fall back to the other end of the canyon and make our stand there."

Lace thought about it for a second and then nodded. "We'd have all of them in front of us that way. We wouldn't have to worry about some of them getting up on the canyon rims and getting behind us."

"That's what I was thinking," The Kid agreed. He turned and headed toward the campsite. Lace trotted alongside him.

As they came around the big rock, Guthrie asked, "What the hell was all the yelling about?"

"Looks like most of your boys have headed for the tall and uncut," Lace told him as she bent to cut the ropes around his ankles. The Kid grasped his arm and hauled him to his feet. Lace went on, "Nebel and the few others who are left have thrown in with a bounty hunter named Pronto Pike."

"That's loco!" Guthrie blustered. "My men would never betray me."

"It looks like you're wrong about that," The Kid said. "I'd say they don't give a damn anymore whether you live or die, Guthrie."

The rancher paled. If what The Kid and Lace were telling him was true, his life wasn't worth a plugged nickel at the moment.

They gathered up their gear in a hurry and loaded it on the buckskin and the black. Lace told Max to go watch the gate. The dog bounded off to follow the order.

"Where are we going?" Guthrie asked. "What are we gonna do?"

"Since when are we partners, you little snake?" Lace snapped at him. "It'd be a whole hell of a lot simpler if we just shot you in the head right now."

The Kid took hold of Guthrie's arm again. A shove sent him stumbling toward the far end of the canyon.

"Get moving," The Kid ordered.

They led the horses as Guthrie stumbled along awkwardly in front of them. Max started barking loudly and angrily, so Lace put a couple of fingers in her mouth and whistled shrilly for him. The dog came racing back and joined them.

The canyon twisted and turned as it penetrated for half a mile into the Mogollon Rim. As the far end came in sight, The Kid saw a steep, rocky wall seamed with fissures. Those cracks had been created in ages past by slabs of rock splitting off from the cliff face and toppling to the floor of the canyon. The slabs were heaped up in grotesque formations.

"We'll fort up in there," The Kid said. "The rocks will give us some cover."

"They can still try to starve us out," Lace warned.

"You think Pike will have the patience for a siege?"

"Well . . . maybe not. Especially as much as he hates the two of us."

"You didn't give some thought to taking him up on his offer?"

Lace gave a disgusted snort. "What offer? He was lying. If I'd gotten the drop on you and turned you over to him, he'd have cut my throat in a second and then put a bullet in your head—unless he decided to keep us both alive and have some fun with us first. It would have been fun for him, not us."

The Kid knew what she meant. He wouldn't put a little torture past Pronto Pike.

They led the horses as deep into the jumble of rocks as they could. The Kid put Guthrie in a little alcove formed by a couple of the stone slabs and said, "You'll be as safe from flying lead here as anywhere, I suppose."

The rancher's face was still pale and drawn. "If you let me go, I'll call off Nebel and the rest of my men," he offered. "We'll go back to the Rafter G. I don't care about this damn canyon anymore. That way you'll only have to deal with those bounty hunters."

The Kid knew Guthrie was lying. He shook his head curtly and said, "Forget it."

"Morgan! Morgan, listen to me. I'll make it worth your while—"

The Kid ignored him and went to find a good place to make his stand.

Lace was already lying on one of the tilted slabs of rock with her rifle thrust over the top of it. "This was a good idea, Kid," she told him. "We can see a couple hundred yards down the canyon, and we've got a good view of the rims, too."

"Yeah, but there are enough trees and rocks that they'll have some cover, too," he pointed out as he settled down on another of the slabs. "It'll be a good fight."

She grinned over at him. "You got anything better to do today?"

"As a matter of fact, I do," he said as he returned the smile. "But it'll have to wait."

Chapter 31

Time stretched out. As the sun rose higher, the temperature in the canyon rose as well. The Kid wondered if Pike was waiting to attack in order to make their nerves draw tighter.

"Hey, Conrad," Lace said after a while.

"Yeah?" The Kid replied. He answered to the name, even though he didn't think of himself that way anymore.

"Let's say you get out of this alive and are able to get those charges against you dropped."

"That's being a little optimistic, under the circumstances, don't you think?"

"Yeah, maybe, but let's say that's what happens."

He shrugged. "All right."

"What are you gonna do then?"

"What I've been doing, I suppose."

"You mean just drifting around, calling yourself Kid Morgan? Being a saddle tramp and a gunfighter?"

He didn't much care for the direction the conversation was taking. She was asking him about things he preferred not to think about.

"What's wrong with that?"

"It's not who you are," Lace said.

"You've known me for less than two weeks," he pointed out. "How do you know who I am?"

"We've fought side by side, and against each

other, remember? You get to know somebody in a hurry when you're mixed up in something like that."

She was right, he supposed. He felt like he had known her a lot longer than he really had.

"You told me about the man you used to be," Lace went on.

"You think I could go back to that?" he asked harshly. "To being Conrad Browning? To sitting in an office and worrying about whether I was going to make as much money this month as I made last month?" He shook his head. "I don't think so."

"Well, maybe not. But you can't keep on pretending to be somebody you're not. You just made up Kid Morgan. Hell, you came up with the name because it sounded like something out of a dime novel. You told me that yourself."

"I needed the men I was after to believe that Conrad Browning was dead. That gave me an edge when I tracked them down."

"But that's over," Lace said. "It's been over for a year. When you were done with it, why'd you keep on being Kid Morgan?"

His jaw was clenched so tight a muscle jumped a little in his face. "I couldn't . . . couldn't . . ."

"Couldn't face life as Conrad without Rebel?"

His eyes stung—probably because the sun was directly overhead and beating down into the canyon.

"Time and again, you've ridden right into trouble," Lace persisted. "Why'd you do that?"

He answered her honestly. "Because Rebel would have wanted me to help those people, like Mr. Blount."

"You mean because she would have wanted Conrad to help them." Lace paused. "Rebel never knew Kid Morgan. But she loved Conrad Browning."

Why the hell wouldn't she shut up, he asked himself savagely. They were going to be fighting for their lives any minute, and yet she kept hammering away at him, asking questions he didn't want to answer, making him ponder things he didn't want to think about.

He saw a flicker of movement as a man darted around the nearest bend of the canyon and threw himself behind a tree. The Kid whipped his rifle to his shoulder and fired, but he was a split-second too late. The slug knocked bark off the tree trunk.

A heartbeat later, the man opened fire, and slugs careened off the rocks around The Kid and Lace, forcing them to duck. In that moment, more of the enemy raced around the bend and flung themselves behind cover.

Shots began to ring out from behind other trees and rocks. The Kid and Lace risked returning the fire, and as they did so, The Kid saw puffs of powder smoke from several locations.

It was a simple but effective strategy. Pike, Nebel, and the other killers would work their way forward in the canyon, taking turns giving each other covering fire. They would lose some men along the way, but they would reach the rocks where The Kid and Lace had taken cover.

Their only chance was to kill as many of the attackers as possible before the final assault, so the odds wouldn't be too overwhelming. Even if they were able to do that, the likelihood of The Kid and Lace surviving was slim.

The ball had started, and all they could do was dance to the tune. He snugged the butt of the Winchester against his shoulder and waited for a target.

A second later, as shots roared and bullets sizzled through the air and whined off the rocks, one of the men darted into view, trying to make it from one tree to another that was about ten feet closer.

The Kid put a .44-40 round into his chest that spun him off his feet and dropped him in a limp heap on the canyon floor.

One down.

But a fresh volley from the attackers forced him to duck his head and pull the rifle back. When he risked a look again, they were a few feet closer.

Lace's rifle cracked twice. The Kid saw a man pulling himself back behind a rock, dragging a bullet-shattered leg. That one might not be out of the fight completely, but at least he couldn't charge them.

Call it one and a half.

Guthrie started cursing shrilly. The Kid figured some of the ricochets were coming close to the rancher, and Guthrie's next words proved the hunch right.

"I'm gonna get killed back here, damn it, the way those slugs are bouncing around! A man shouldn't die with his hands tied behind his back!"

"Yeah, I might worry about that if you were a man instead of a snake!" Lace called back to him. She grinned over at The Kid again. "Maybe I'm starting to see your point," she told him. "Conrad Browning wouldn't know what to do in a little dust-up like this, would he?"

"Probably not," The Kid muttered as he saw a flash of a man's shirt and instantly slammed a shot at it. The bit of color disappeared, and he didn't know if he'd hit the man or not.

The air inside the canyon was thick with smoke. The Kid ignored the way the stuff stung his eyes and the reek of it filled his nose. He blinked rapidly to clear his vision, and a bullet spanged off the rock beside him.

That shot had come from higher up. He jerked his head back and lifted his gaze to the canyon rim. The rifleman up there was on the move, trying to reach a spot where he would have a better angle at the defenders.

He should have been more patient and waited until he was there before attempting a shot. The Kid's Winchester barked, and the slug clipped the man's thigh.

That was enough to throw him off stride. He lost his balance and lurched toward the rim. Too close to the edge he toppled over the brink with a shriek, pinwheeling through the air for several hundred feet before he crashed into some rocks at the bottom with a bright crimson splash of blood.

Two and a half men out of the fight, The Kid thought. They were whittling down the odds.

But not fast enough. The rest of the attackers were only about fifty yards away.

Lace let out a yelp of pain. The Kid looked over at her in alarm and called, "Are you hit?"

She waved to show that she was all right. As she grimaced in pain, she pulled the poncho up and showed him a bloody patch on the right sleeve of her faded men's shirt, about halfway between the elbow and shoulder. From the looks of it, a bullet had grazed her.

"Hurts like hell," she told him, "but I can still use the arm, so nothing's broken."

He nodded and turned his attention back to the attackers. One of them burst out from behind a tree and tried to cover his advance by emptying a six-shooter as fast as he could.

But The Kid and Lace fired at the same time, the reports sounding like one, and both bullets ripped through the man and flung him off his feet.

Three and a half. Four if you counted the man with the busted leg who'd been left behind.

But that still left eight cold-blooded killers who were almost within spitting distance of the rocks.

Pretty soon it was going to be close quarters gun work, The Kid thought. During a brief lull, he drew his Colt and slid a cartridge into the usually empty sixth chamber in the cylinder. He was going to need a full wheel. He set the gun beside him on the rock where he could reach it easily. He did the same with the pearl-handled Colt he had taken from Pike back in Las Vegas, on that night that seemed like ages ago.

"Hold your fire! Hold your fire!"

That was Pike's voice, and The Kid was somewhat surprised to hear the order. The attackers' guns fell silent. He and Lace stopped shooting as well.

"Lace, if you're still alive, listen to me," Pike said into the hush that seemed to echo eerily after all the gun thunder that had filled the canyon for what seemed like hours though it had been only fifteen minutes or so. "Lace, you don't have to die. Shoot Morgan right now. End this. If you don't, you'll never see your daughter again."

"Damn you, Pike," she said thickly. "Keep your

dirty tongue off my little girl! Don't you talk about her, you son of a bitch!"

"I'm just tryin' to help you here, Lace," Pike said in oily tones. "You and me, we go back a long way."

"Too far," Lace muttered. She raised her voice and said, "You think I believe you? I know you'll kill me just as soon as you get the chance, Pike! You're loco, and you always have been!"

"Is that your last word?"

"No, this is: go to hell!"

"Take 'em!" Pike roared even as Lace's words echoed back from the canyon walls, and a storm of lead broke over the rocks where she and The Kid were crouched.

Chapter 32

The Kid rose up on his knees, knowing that the time for sharpshooting was over. It was going to be bloody slaughter, and devil take the hindmost.

He brought the rifle to his shoulder and swung the barrel from left to right, spraying out slugs as fast as he could work the Winchester's lever. He was throwing lead and hoping it landed in the bodies of his enemies.

He felt bullets tug at his coat. A slug passed so close to his cheek it left a hot streak along the skin. The Winchester's hammer clicked on empty. He flung the rifle aside and snatched up the two revolvers as he rose to his feet. The guns roared and bucked in his hands.

From the corner of his eye, he saw Lace doing the same. Guns filled both her hands, and thunder rolled from them as she fired, left, right, left, right.

The Kid couldn't see much through the clouds of gunsmoke swirling around him, but he caught glimpses of men falling and blood welling from bullet-torn flesh. Then what felt like a blow from a giant hammer knocked his left leg out from under him, and he rolled out of control down the slab of rock.

He crashed to the hard ground at the base of the rock and landed on his belly. He'd managed to hold on to both guns, and tried to scramble to his feet, but his leg folded up underneath him and dumped him on his belly again. Crawling forward, guns up, pushing with his good leg he dragged himself along with his elbows.

Two men ran past the rock. The Kid yelled, "Hey!" and they wheeled toward him, their Colts swinging into line.

The Kid's guns roared first. Traveling at an upward angle, the slugs caught the men just above their belts and bored up through their guts. As they doubled over in agony, their fingers clenched on triggers, but the slugs blasted harmlessly into the ground at their feet as they collapsed.

The Kid rolled against the rock and braced his shoulders on it. He got his good leg under him and shoved, sliding up the rock until he was in a roughly upright position, balanced on his right leg.

He couldn't see Lace. Smoke and dust clogged the air and half blinded him. The gunfire had stopped, but the echoes were still bouncing back and forth between the canyon walls.

A red haze filled The Kid's vision. As he tried to blink it away, he realized that blood was dripping into his eyes from a cut on his forehead.

Out of that gory haze, a dark figure loomed. "Lace . . ." The Kid whispered.

"Afraid not, Morgan," Pronto Pike said. Clad in

black and red, he looked like Satan himself stepping out of the fires of hell. "Lace is dead," he said, "and you're about to be."

The Kid lifted his guns and squeezed the triggers. The hammers fell on empty chambers.

Pike laughed as he lifted his Colt and took deliberate aim at The Kid's head.

The shape came out of the smoke behind Pike and crashed into his back, knocking his arm up just as he pulled the trigger. The bullet smacked into the rock several feet above The Kid's head.

Lace wrapped her arm around Pike's neck and drove him forward. They fell, and Pike's gun hand struck a rock, jarring the revolver out of his grip. It skittered away.

The two of them rolled over, wrestling desperately. The Kid saw that Lace's poncho was gone, and her shirt was covered with blood. Somehow, she clung to life even though she'd been riddled with bullets.

The Kid gritted his teeth and hobbled toward the gun Pike had dropped, forcing his wounded leg to hold him up. Ignoring the hot flood of blood down it he focused all his attention on the gun.

Lace was too weak to put up much of a fight. Pike threw her off, slammed a fist across her face, and rammed his knee into her belly. He hit her again and again, driving her head against the hard ground.

The Kid reached for the gun, knowing that if he lost his balance and fell, he'd never be able to get up again.

Pike reached out, caught up a rock almost the size of a man's head, and lifted it as he straddled Lace's limp form. "Now you'll die and stay dead!" he growled as he raised the rock above his head, poised to crush her skull and smash the life out of her.

"Pike," The Kid said.

Pike looked up, found himself staring down the barrel of his own gun from a distance of about a foot.

The Kid pulled the trigger.

The shot blew Pike backward off Lace. The rock sailed out of his hands and thudded to the ground. The spray of blood and brains that exploded out the back of Pike's head settled on it like droplets of crimson rain. The bounty hunter lay on his back, staring sightlessly at the sky with the bullet hole in the center of his forehead looking like a third, red-rimmed eye.

The Kid dropped the gun. His strength and his balance deserted him at last, and he fell beside Lace, close enough that he could stretch out his arm and put it around her. He pulled himself closer to her and called her name. "Lace! Lace, can you hear me?"

Her eyelids fluttered open. "K-Kid?" she whispered.

"Don't you die!" he told her between clenched teeth. "Damn it, don't you die! You've got a little girl waiting for you to come home to her!"

The tip of Lace's tongue came out and swiped over lips covered with a paste of dust and blood. "Conrad," she husked. "Conrad, you . . . you gotta promise me . . . you'll see that she . . . that she's taken care of."

"You'll take care of her," he urged.

"You got to . . . promise me . . ."

"I promise," Conrad Browning whispered. "I give you my word."

"You're a . . . good man . . . Conrad . . . and so's . . . The Kid . . ."

"No!" he howled, pulling her even closer. "No!"

He was still shouting Lace's name and holding her limp form when Chester Blount and the posse of sheriff's deputies and U.S. marshals from Phoenix found them five minutes later.

"I figure the Alamo must've looked like that, or the Little Big Horn," Blount said an hour later as one of the marshals who had plenty of experience at patching up wounds wrapped a bandage around the bullet hole in Conrad's thigh. He had cleaned the wound with a liberal application of whiskey and proclaimed that Conrad would live . . . probably.

Blount went on, "Bodies a-layin' ever'where

and the ground awash with blood. Lord, what a battle that must'a been!"

"It was bad enough," Conrad said, looking toward the blanket-covered form lying under a pine tree nearby, with the big dog sitting beside her. The marshal had spent most of his time trying to save Lace. "Were they all dead?"

"Dead as could be," the old-timer confirmed with a nod. "Except for Guthrie, and I ain't sure he's ever gonna be the same. He's plumb loco."

The members of the posse had found Spud Guthrie still in the little space between the rocks where The Kid had put him. Chips in the stone and splashes of color showed where numerous bullets had struck the rocks. Guthrie himself, however, was untouched.

But sitting there helplessly as hot lead flew around him for minutes that must have seemed like hours had done something to his mind. So far all he had done was stare straight ahead, wide-eyed, and hadn't made a sound. The Kid thought Guthrie had gone mad and might never recover.

He wondered if it was a fitting punishment for a man whose pride and arrogance had set so much killing in motion. But he was no longer in the business of punishing anyone, so it was none of his affair, he told himself.

The marshal finished tying off the bandage around his leg. "There you go, Mr. Browning," he said as he straightened. "You'll be able to walk on it a little, but I wouldn't go runnin' around if I was you. It'll heal a lot better and a lot quicker if you'll stay off it as much as you can."

"You're welcome to stay here for a while," Blount offered. "I ain't got a cabin no more, but I can pitch a couple o' tents here in the canyon and we'll be mighty comfortable. The fresh air'll do you good, I'm thinkin'."

Conrad nodded. "I'm obliged for that, Mr. Blount. I may just take you up on it."

Blount glanced toward the figure under the pine tree. "I kinda had a hunch you might."

The marshal said, "I hope you'll stop by Phoenix when you're well enough to travel and say hello to the governor. The way he set the telegraph wires to burnin' when he heard you were in trouble tells me he sets a lot of store by you, Mr. Browning. He had the county sheriff and the chief marshal in Denver hoppin', tryin' to get help for you."

"If you see him, tell him how grateful I am," Conrad said. "But yes, I'll be sure and tell him myself, too."

None of the lawmen who had galloped back to Dos Caballos Canyon with Blount had any idea that Conrad Browning, friend of the territorial governor, was also Kid Morgan, a wanted fugitive with a ten grand bounty on his head in New Mexico. Blount had kept his mouth shut about that, showing keen wisdom.

The old-timer caught a moment alone with Conrad and said quietly, "If you still want a half interest in Dos Caballos, Kid, you don't have to pay for it. I'll give it to you, free and clear, for what you done."

Conrad shook his head and waved away the offer. "I only suggested that in case it ever came down to having to fight Guthrie in court. It would have given me some legal standing. Now there's no need for it."

"No, I don't reckon there is," Blount agreed. "I don't know what'll happen to the Rafter G now that Guthrie's gone loco, but I reckon the canyon's safe from now on."

Conrad hoped that turned out to be the case. He said as much, then added, "If it ever turns out otherwise, you just get in touch with me through my lawyers."

"I'll sure do it," Blount promised. He grinned. "Now, you better go tend to the rest o' your business. I see somebody stirrin' around."

It was true, Conrad saw as he limped toward the pine tree, using a borrowed Winchester as a makeshift crutch. Lace's eyes were open, and her head turned toward him as he approached.

He tried to kneel beside her but sat on the ground instead. Her hand moved on the blanket that covered her heavily bandaged body. He took hold of it, entwining his fingers with hers.

"Kid?" she whispered. "Conrad?"

"One and the same," he told her.

"You're . . . alive?"

"Yeah. So are you, in case you hadn't noticed."

"But . . . I got shot so many times . . ."

"Four, to be exact. But the marshal who patched you up doesn't think any of the slugs hit anything *too* vital. That's the way he put it. You'll probably be laid up for weeks, and your bounty hunting career is over, more than likely, but you'll live to see your daughter again."

He squeezed her hand, and weakly, she squeezed back.

"What about . . . Max?"

She hadn't seen the dog yet. He leaned over, whined softly, and licked her face. She let out a pleased laugh.

"He's . . . all right?"

"A few bullet scrapes, but he was lucky. He wouldn't leave your side, all the time the marshal was patching you up."

"Thank God." She paused. "I guess . . . I won't have to hold you . . . to that promise you made . . . to look after . . . my little girl."

"Don't worry about that," he assured her. "You'll have plenty of money to take care of her yourself. I'll see to that."

Even in her weakened condition, anger flashed in her eyes. "Damn it, you don't have to—"

"We'll talk about that later. Right now, just concentrate on recovering."

"Conrad, what happened to . . . to Pike?"

"He's dead," Conrad said. "He'll never bother you again."

"You killed him."

"He had it coming."

She closed her eyes for a second and murmured, "Damn right." Then she looked at him again and asked, "Are you hurt?"

"A bullet through the leg. I'll be fine. In a couple weeks, I ought to be able to start for Santa Fe."

"You're . . . still going?"

"As you said, damn right." He thought about the envelope in his pocket that contained a telegram from John Stafford. One of the marshals had delivered the grim message to him. "I've got a job to finish there."

Chapter 33

Three weeks later, Conrad Browning walked into the best hotel in Santa Fe with only a slight limp. He could have managed just fine without the heavy, silver-headed walking stick he used, but he liked it.

It would also make a fine, close-quarters weapon in a pinch, if he needed one.

He wore a restrained, dark brown suit and matching bowler. The suit was tailor-made, and the coat was cut especially so that it concealed the short-barreled .38 revolver Conrad wore in a cross draw rig on his left hip.

He had never used a cross draw until recently, but over the past couple weeks, since he'd been back on his feet, he'd been practicing with it until he was fairly proficient. He wasn't as fast with it as he was with a standard draw—yet—but the instincts and reflexes he'd inherited from Frank Morgan had stood him in good stead. He was confident of his ability to handle himself in most gunfights using the .38, as long as they were at close range. The short-barreled gun had enough stopping power, but it wasn't much for accuracy.

Conrad crossed the hotel lobby to the desk confident no one was going to recognize him as Kid Morgan. The simplest thing would have been to go back to his life as Conrad and let all memories of The Kid fade away. The charges against him and the bounty that had been placed on his head would be moot.

He couldn't do that. Not until he had found out who was responsible for those wanted posters . . . and why they had wanted to make his life a living hell.

He gave the clerk his name, and the man gave him a toothy smile and said, "Of course, Mr. Browning. We weren't sure exactly when you would arrive, but we've been holding a suite for you. I'll have a boy take you right up. Your bags . . . ?"

Conrad inclined his head toward the entrance. "Out front in the hack that brought me from the station."

"Yes, sir, we'll take care of them."

"I believe John Stafford is staying here as well."

"That is correct, sir."

"Let him know that I'm here, will you?"

"Of course. Right away."

A bellboy took Conrad up to the luxuriously furnished suite on the second floor. A bottle of cognac was already there waiting for him, as he had specified in his telegram.

He had just poured two drinks when someone knocked on the door. He left them sitting on a beautifully carved table as he went over to the door and put his hand on the butt of the pistol under his coat.

"Who is it?"

"Stafford."

Conrad opened the door to let the lawyer in. He thought John J. Stafford bore a certain resemblance to his partner, Claudius Turnbuckle, and wondered if all lawyers just looked alike to him.

The two men shook hands. Stafford said, "By God, it's good to see you, Conrad. I wasn't sure if I ever would again. How's the leg?"

"Healing fine. It doesn't give me much trouble except in damp weather. Then it aches a little." Conrad stepped over to the table. "Do you want a drink?"

"Definitely."

The cognac was smooth and went down like liquid fire. Stafford smacked his lips appreciatively and then said, "I don't suppose you're interested in making small talk."

"Not at all," Conrad said. "You've taken care of everything?"

"Of course. The coffin was shipped back to San Francisco. The last important thing Claudius did before he was attacked was to speak with a man named Charles Blanton, who's a special aide to Governor Otero."

"What have you found out about Otero?"

"He seems to be an honest man, or at least as honest as any politician."

Conrad smiled. "People say the same thing about lawyers."

"And successful businessmen," Stafford shot back. "None of us rate very highly as far as trust goes."

"Is there any reason Otero would be holding a grudge against me or my family?" It wasn't common knowledge that there was a connection between Kid Morgan and the notorious gunfighter Frank Morgan, or between Conrad Browning and Frank, or Conrad and The Kid, for that matter. But someone could have uncovered those links, he supposed.

"I haven't been able to uncover anything like that. Otero's been busy enough trying to hold together the fragile political coalition he formed when he was appointed governor. He doesn't seem to have had the time or the inclination to be carrying out a campaign of vengeance against you, Conrad."

"And yet he refused to do anything about those wanted posters."

"He might not have known about them," Stafford pointed out. "Claudius wasn't able to speak directly with the governor. This man Blanton kept him from meeting with Otero."

"What do we know about Blanton?"

Stafford shrugged. "An old friend and ally of the Otero family. He wasn't appointed to any official position but serves as a special aide to the governor. He's paid out of Otero's personal funds, not the territorial budget."

"And yet he has enough power to determine who sees the governor and who doesn't?"

"That's right."

Conrad swallowed the rest of his drink. "I never heard of the man. Why would he conspire against me?"

"There's only one good reason I can think of," Stafford said. "Money."

"He was paid off?"

"It's certainly a possibility. Or perhaps he was blackmailed into acting against you. I'm still looking into that, but if it's true, the chances are that he's covered up his trail so well I may not be able to find it."

Conrad nodded slowly. "What about the rest of it?"

"I have a sworn deposition from Miss Jillian Fletcher explaining how you were mistakenly imprisoned because of your resemblance to the outlaw Benjamin Bledsoe. It also goes into detail about what happened after that and how you're innocent of the charges against you. I expect that it will carry considerable weight since Miss Fletcher is the daughter of the late warden of Hell Gate Prison. I also have letters from the governor of Arizona Territory, from General Lew Wallace, and from President McKinley, all asking Governor Otero to issue a pardon absolving you of all charges."

Conrad's eyebrows rose. "President McKinley? I don't even know the President."

"But he knows who you are."

Conrad grunted and shook his head. "With ammunition like that, it's going to be difficult for Otero to refuse, I would think. But it still doesn't answer the questions of who and why such a thing was done in the first place."

"No, it doesn't," Stafford admitted. "I hate to say it, Conrad, but you may never know."

"Oh, I'll find out," Conrad said. "There's a ball at the Palace of the Governors tonight, and Otero and Blanton will both be there. So will I. One of them is bound to have the answers I want."

A look of alarm appeared on Stafford's face. "You can't just burst in on something like that and start causing trouble. There'll be guards—"

"I have an invitation." Conrad held up a small envelope. "It was sitting on the table, next to the cognac, when I got here."

Stafford drew in a sharp breath of surprise. "But why—"

"Why invite me to the governor's ball?" Conrad smiled. "Someone must have heard that I was on my way to Santa Fe, and they're ready for a showdown."

Stafford's fingers tightened on his glass. "What you're saying is that it's a trap."

"Possibly," Conrad replied with a shrug.

"Which you'll walk right into, just to get to the bottom of this."

"Gladly."

The lawyer shook his head. "You don't have to do this, Conrad. As one of your attorneys, I have to advise you to act in what I consider to be your best interests. Don't attend the ball. Leave this alone. Go back to Boston, or San Francisco, or wherever you'd like to live from now on, and go on with your life. Let this . . . this whole Kid Morgan business die!"

"I can't do that," Conrad said without hesitation. "Whoever is responsible for it has a definite grudge against me. He's not going to give up that easily. I'll be in danger until I ferret out whoever it is, and so will everyone connected to me." His voice hardened. "I would think you'd understand that, John, after what happened to Claudius."

"Damn it, I'm just as upset as you are about what happened to Claudius. He's my partner, and more than that, he's my friend. But we can't change things now—"

"I know as well as anyone that we can't change the past," Conrad broke in. "But we can have an affect on the future, and I intend to."

Stafford tossed back the rest of his drink. "Maybe you never should have started this blasted Kid Morgan business in the first place."

The two men traded angry, level stares for a moment before Conrad said, "Maybe I shouldn't have. I was trying to . . . I don't know . . . put my life as Conrad Browning behind me, I suppose.

Kid Morgan was just a useful fiction at first, but I found that it was easier being him. For a while I even tried to change the way I thought and spoke, to be more like what I thought a frontier gunman would be like." He shrugged as his anger eased. "But in the end, I couldn't escape reality. I am who I am."

"Not entirely. You've changed, Conrad. Claudius told me that you had, and now I see it for myself. I'm afraid there's a part of you that *is* Kid Morgan."

Lace McCall had said much the same thing. Conrad was still turning that over in his mind, trying to come to terms with it.

But such pondering could wait for another day. For now, he had an enemy to find . . . and deal with, whatever it took.

And that would begin at the ball, at Santa Fe's Palace of the Governors.

Chapter 34

The long, shaded walk in front of the Palace of the Governors was thronged with people on that warm, pleasant evening, and more were walking across Santa Fe's main plaza toward it.

Conrad's suit was black, with a matching vest. Like the outfit he had worn earlier, the clothes were cut to conceal the gun he carried. He wore a flat-crowned black hat and had an unlit cigarillo clenched between his teeth. His left hand gripped the silver-headed walking stick.

A guard in a fancy blue uniform with a scarlet sash stood at the entrance to the palace. Conrad held up his invitation. The guard looked at it, handed it back, and said, "Go right in, sir. Please enjoy the ball."

"Thank you." Conrad strolled into a lobby with several sets of large double doors that led into a ballroom. The palace was largely devoted to governmental offices, but the ballroom was used for official gatherings and soirees thrown by the territorial governor.

An attractive young woman with a brilliant smile took Conrad's hat. "What about your cane, sir?" she asked.

"I'll hang on to it," he told her. "I was injured not long ago, and I might need it."

"Oh, I'm sorry to hear that."

Conrad smiled at her, appreciating her dark, sultry good looks.

At the same time, he couldn't help but think of a woman with short, auburn hair who wasn't nearly as pretty but was even more beautiful in his eyes. Lace was recovering from her injuries in Phoenix, and when she was healthy enough to travel, she would be going back to Kansas City to be reunited with her mother and daughter. Conrad had promised to come and see her when he could.

But first he had a job to finish.

Holding the walking stick, he moved into the crowded ballroom. The cream of Santa Fe society was there, along with the rich, powerful, and influential from Albuquerque and elsewhere in the territory. Conrad recognized several men he knew from business dealings in the past, and they knew him as well. All of them had heard about Rebel's tragic death, so as he shook hands with them, he also graciously accepted the condolences they offered.

"For a while there was a rumor going around that you were dead, too, Browning," one of the men commented bluntly.

"To paraphrase Mark Twain," Conrad replied with a faint smile, "the rumors of my death were greatly exaggerated."

And he was the one largely responsible for that exaggeration, he thought, since he'd left a body in the Carson City mansion to be discovered in its ruins after it burned down.

Now all of that had been put to rest. Kid Morgan wouldn't do him any good there. Getting to the bottom of who was behind the wanted posters was Conrad Browning's job.

"Have you met the governor yet?"

"No, but I hope to, soon."

The man Conrad was talking to took his arm. "Well, come on. I'll introduce you."

The man led him toward a group of well-dressed men engaged in an animated discussion. One of them looked too young and handsome to be a territorial governor, but he was the one Conrad's acquaintance came up to and said, "Governor Otero, I'd like to introduce you to an old friend of mine, Conrad Browning."

Otero turned toward them, and so did a man who stood close beside him. The second man was older, with graying sandy hair and piercing eyes.

"Mr. Browning," Otero said as he shook hands with Conrad.

"Governor."

"Your name is familiar to me for some reason."

"Companies in which I have an interest have done a good deal of business in New Mexico Territory," Conrad explained. "Or perhaps you've heard of me in some other connection . . ." He left that hanging, to see how Otero would react.

The governor shook his head and appeared to

be genuinely puzzled. "No, I can't think of it right now," he said, "but I'm very glad to meet you, anyway." He turned to indicate his companion. "This is my good friend Charles Blanton."

Conrad put out his hand. "Mr. Blanton." He saw the suspicion and nervousness in Blanton's eyes as he shook hands with the man.

Blanton gave him a curt nod and said, "Browning. What brings you to Santa Fe?"

"A mystery," Conrad said. "A mystery I have to solve."

Otero said, "That sounds intriguing. What sort of mystery, Mr. Browning?"

The nervousness in Blanton's eyes had turned to outright alarm. The man knew something, all right. For one thing, he had to be aware that Conrad Browning and Kid Morgan were one and the same.

"Someone here seems to have a grudge of some sort against me," Conrad bluntly told the governor. "I want to find out who, and why, and see what I can do to resolve the problem."

"That's terrible," Otero said with a slight frown. "Is there anything I can do to help?"

More and more, Conrad was convinced that Otero didn't know anything about the wanted posters that had been issued for Kid Morgan. His ignorance could only be explained by the fact that someone had kept him from being informed.

That someone was standing right beside him, Conrad sensed. Charles Blanton was behind what had happened, or at least he had conspired with someone to make it happen. Since Conrad had never met Blanton before or had any connection with him, he knew that was the case.

"Thank you, Governor," Conrad said in response to Otero's offer. "As a matter of fact, I might need your assistance in this matter. Could I call on you at your office, say, tomorrow, and explain everything to you?"

"Of course," Otero answered without hesitation. "I remember now where I've heard your name. You've been heavily involved with the railroads in this part of the country, haven't you?"

Conrad nodded. "That's right."

"Well, of course I'll do anything I can to help."

Blanton, looking a little sick at his stomach, said, "Uh, Miguel, your schedule tomorrow is full—"

"I can find a few minutes for Mr. Browning," Otero broke in. He held out his hand. "I look forward to it."

"So do I, Governor," Conrad murmured as he shook hands with the man again.

The man who had introduced him had wandered off elsewhere in the crowd. Governor Otero excused himself, pleading a need to say hello to some of the other guests. He said to Blanton, "Are you coming, Charles?"

"In a minute, Governor," Blanton replied. "I want another word with Mr. Browning here."

"Of course."

Blanton moved closer to Conrad, and though they were surrounded by people, it was as if they were alone in the ballroom, considering the intensity of the look Blanton fastened on him.

"No offense, Mr. Browning," Blanton said in a low voice, "but how is it that you're here tonight? I handled the guest list, and I don't recall sending you an invitation—"

"That's because I did," a new voice said.

Conrad looked over and saw a sleekly handsome young man. He wore a charming smile, but his eyes were like chips of blue ice. Something about him was so familiar Conrad felt a shock of recognition go through him, but the feeling was followed a second later by the certainty that he had never seen the man before in his life.

"Roger, what are you doing?" Blanton demanded under his breath. "This is the governor's ball. You can't . . . you can't—"

"Take my revenge right here in the middle of a crowd of such rich, powerful people? Is that what you mean, Charles?" asked the young man called Roger. "Of course I wouldn't do that."

He took a sip from the drink he held in his hand.

Conrad kept his face expressionless and tried to ignore the way his heart had started slugging in his chest. "You speak openly of revenge," he said. "I take that to mean you know who I am."

"You're Conrad Browning, of course. Also

known as the notorious gunfighter Kid Morgan. Whom no one had ever even heard of until a little over a year ago, by the way, despite the fact that they're now writing dime novels about you."

Conrad couldn't keep the strain out of his voice as he asked, "Who the hell are you?"

"That's right, we've never actually met, despite the fact that for a short time there, we were almost related."

That was enough to make the pieces fall together in Conrad's brain. Like a flash of lightning, he knew why this man looked familiar to him. "You're a Tarleton," he said.

"Roger Tarleton. Pamela was my cousin . . . until you murdered her."

Tarleton . . . My God, was he never going to be finished with that family and their twisted need for vengeance?

He had done business with railroader and financier Clark Tarleton. He had been engaged to Tarleton's daughter Pamela.

But Clark Tarleton had wound up dead because of his criminal dealings, and Pamela had blamed Conrad Browning for that, as well as for breaking his engagement to her and marrying Rebel Callahan. Pamela's attempts to settle the score with him had led to numerous tragedies, including her own accidental death.

And yet another member of the Tarleton family was smirking at him with cold hatred in his eyes.

"I don't know what you think happened," Conrad said, "but I didn't murder Pamela. I wasn't responsible for her death. You've got it all wrong, Tarleton."

"I don't think so," Roger said. "I loved my cousin very much, Browning, ever since we were children." He cocked an eyebrow. "And not just as cousins, if you understand what I mean."

"You son of a bitch," Conrad said through clenched teeth.

"That's why I couldn't allow her death to go unavenged. Someone has to pay the price for it, and that someone is you. If you hadn't betrayed her, she'd still be alive."

Conrad shook his head, but he knew that nothing he said would do any good. From everything he had seen of the Tarleton family, there was a flaw in their brains, an inability to accept the truth, a hatred that knew no bounds when they felt wronged, a need for revenge that bordered on insanity.

Blanton moved closer and hissed, "This is not the place for this, Roger—"

"I agree, it's not," Tarleton cut in. "That's why we're going out into the plaza, where we'll have room to settle things once and for all."

"A gunfight?" Conrad asked, his lips curving thinly.

"That's right. Only I won't be taking on the infamous Kid Morgan. That would hardly be fair, now would it? I have several . . . surrogates, if you will . . . to stand in for me."

"Hired killers, you mean. You're going to have them murder me."

Tarleton shrugged eloquently. "Call it what you will. I call it justice."

"And why would I walk into a trap like that?"

"Because if you don't, Lace McCall won't live to see the sun come up tomorrow morning."

Chapter 35

It was all Conrad could do not to reach under his coat, pull his gun, and put a bullet in Roger Tarleton's brain at that moment.

He controlled the urge and forced his brain to remain level as he said, "What are you talking about?"

"Unless they receive a telegram from me calling them off, several men in my employ will kill Lace McCall tonight."

"And you won't send the telegram unless I walk out in the plaza and face your gunmen."

"That's right. If you do, then I'll let the slut live."

"You've really found out a lot about me, haven't you?"

"A suitable revenge requires suitable preparation," Tarleton said. "How do you think I found out about your little misadventure in Hell Gate Prison?"

"That gave you the idea of paying off Blanton to see that those phony reward posters were put out?"

"There's nothing phony about them," Tarleton snapped. "If someone had succeeded in killing you, the bounty would have been paid as promised."

"But that didn't happen, so you decided to come out into the open to take your revenge."

“That’s right. I’m tired of waiting for Pamela’s death to be avenged.”

“You know,” Conrad said, “those hired guns of yours might not kill me. I just might beat them. What happens then?”

“Why, I’ll keep my part of the bargain, of course. I’ll send word to my men in Phoenix to leave Miss McCall alone.”

Conrad didn’t believe Tarleton for a second, but he could only play the game one hand at a time. Tarleton seemed to hold all the cards at the moment.

“All right,” he said. “You want a showdown, I’ll give you a showdown.”

Blanton was so nervous he was practically wringing his hands together. “This is *not* the time or place for this, Roger,” he said as he leaned toward Tarleton.

“Stop it, Charles,” the young man said. “You’ve been well-paid for your part in this, so you have no room for complaint. Besides, this is a matter of honor. The Spanish influence is still strong here in Santa Fe, isn’t it? And the Spanish are a people who know the importance of a family’s honor.”

“There’s been enough talk,” Conrad said. “Let’s get this over with.”

Tarleton smiled. “You really do sound like a gunfighter, Browning. I agree. Let’s go.”

“You’re going to come along and watch?”

"I wouldn't miss it," Tarleton said. "I've dreamed of nothing else for months."

The two men turned and started toward the doors. Blanton hesitated for a second, looking torn, and then started after them.

From the corner of his eye, Conrad noticed that Governor Otero had noticed them leaving and wore a curious frown on his face as he watched them walk out of the Palace of the Governors.

There were still quite a few people in the plaza, although it wasn't nearly as crowded as it had been earlier. Most of the guests who were on their way to the ball had already gone in. Conrad spotted three men lounging near a fountain. One wore a suit much like his own, only not nearly as expensive, while the other two wore range clothes and long dusters.

All three men straightened from their casual poses as they spotted Conrad and Tarleton coming toward them, with Blanton trailing behind. Grins of anticipation stretched across their faces.

Conrad glanced to his left. The large carriage that had brought him from the hotel was parked nearby. He hadn't been the only passenger, and he signaled unobtrusively to the men waiting inside the vehicle.

The door swung open, and John Stafford stepped out.

People began to take notice of the three gunmen

and the way they stood next to the fountain, obviously waiting for trouble. Men grabbed hold of their wives' arms and hustled them out of the way. A babble of concerned voices rose as the plaza began to clear.

It wouldn't be the first gunfight that had taken place there.

Stafford turned back to the carriage to help another man step out of it. He held tightly to the second man's arm, supporting him.

Conrad came to a stop facing the three killers at a distance of about twenty feet. That range was too far for the short-barreled .38 to be very accurate.

"Blanton," he said without looking around, "if you'll take a glance to your left, you might see something interesting."

A second later, he heard Blanton's shocked gasp and knew the man was looking at Claudius Turnbuckle, who stood next to Stafford. Turnbuckle was pale and drawn from his injury.

"But . . . but . . ." Blanton stammered.

"You thought I was dead, didn't you, Blanton?" Turnbuckle called. He might not be strong at the moment, but his voice still was. "You thought the assassin you hired to kill me had succeeded and that I was dead. Well, not hardly, you scurrilous skunk! Neither is your hired killer!"

Conrad didn't dare take his eyes off the three gunmen, who were starting to look a little confused. The confrontation wasn't going exactly the way they had thought it would.

Though he couldn't see it, Conrad knew what was happening. The chief of Santa Fe's police force was climbing out of the carriage and hauling the man Blanton had hired to kill Turnbuckle with him. A policeman had found Turnbuckle in time to save his life, and the lawyer had persuaded the authorities to put out the story that he and the would-be assassin were dead. He had gotten in touch with Stafford, who had hurried to Santa Fe, and they had hatched a plan to expose Blanton. Faced with prison, the knife wielder had confessed that the governor's aide had hired him.

Conrad had gone over all of it with his lawyer that afternoon. He had planned to have Stafford, Turnbuckle, and the police come into the ball and confront Blanton with the proof of his villainy, but the evening hadn't developed that way.

In fact, it might be even better. The plaza was almost deserted except for the participants in the little drama. There wouldn't be as much of a crowd around when all hell broke loose.

"We planned to use your henchman's testimony against you to force you to tell us who you were working with, Blanton," Conrad said, "but now that's not necessary. We know who's really to blame for everything that's happened."

He risked taking his eyes off the gunmen, in

order to look at Roger Tarleton. "Looks like you'll be going to prison, too, right along with Blanton."

Lines of horror and disbelief had etched themselves onto Tarleton's handsome face over the past few moments. His features twisted into an expression of insane hatred.

Before Tarleton could say anything, Governor Otero called from the porch of the palace, "Charles! What's going on here?"

Tarleton shrieked, "Kill them! Kill them all!"

His hired guns did their best to follow that order. Their hands stabbed toward their guns.

But Conrad was faster. Ignoring the .38 on his hip, his hand swept behind his back, under his coat, and pulled the Colt revolver tucked behind his belt. The gun came out and leveled in a blur of speed and began to roar just as the three killers cleared leather.

The man in the suit never got a shot off. He went over backward, clawing at his chest where Conrad's first bullet had ripped into his heart. The second man raised his gun and jerked the trigger, but he had already been spun halfway around by a .44-40 slug through his left lung. His shot smacked harmlessly into the paving stones next to him as he crumpled.

The third gunfighter fired into the air as he went over backward, blood spurting from his bullet-torn throat. He landed in the fountain with a splash and slowly sank beneath the reddening water.

Conrad heard a gun being cocked and spun around. Panicking, Blanton had fumbled a pistol from under his coat and was trying to bring it to bear. Conrad lashed out with the walking stick, bringing it down across Blanton's forearm. Bone snapped with a sharp crack under the impact. Blanton cried out in pain and dropped the gun.

Roger Tarleton stared at Conrad in shocked surprise. His eyes widened as Conrad lifted the gun and pointed it at his face from a distance of a few feet.

"Tell me who you're supposed to send that telegram to and what you're supposed to say," Conrad ordered. "I'll give you ten seconds, and then I'm pulling this trigger."

"You . . . you'll hang for murder! I'm unarmed! You can't shoot me!"

Conrad smiled. "I think I'll risk it."

"No!" A look of sly cunning appeared in Tarleton's eyes. "You can't kill me. If you do, then that whore will die."

Turnbuckle and Stafford had come up behind Conrad. Turnbuckle said, "That *lady* is currently surrounded by a dozen or more deputy United States marshals, sir, and is in no danger whatsoever. I don't know who you are, but you've seriously underestimated your enemies."

"Claudius?" Conrad said.

"I'm sorry John and I didn't make you aware of that, Conrad, but to tell you the truth, there wasn't time. We just thought of it a short time ago and asked one of the detectives to send the wire."

"The way somebody had been striking at people close to you, we figured it would be a good idea to get some protection for Miss McCall," Stafford added.

"Thank you," Conrad said. "It was an excellent idea." He looped his thumb over the Colt's hammer and pulled it back. "Now I can just go ahead and shoot this mad dog."

"Mr. Browning," Governor Otero said. "Please. I don't know what's going on here, but there's already been enough blood spilled tonight. Hasn't there?"

For a long moment, Conrad didn't answer. Then he took a deep breath, let the Colt's hammer down gently, and lowered the gun.

"Yes. There's been enough blood spilled to last a lifetime. As for what's happened here, Blanton can explain all that. I'm sure he will to save his own skin as much as possible. I'm done." Conrad turned away from Roger Tarleton. "I'm going home."

Tarleton laughed. "Where is that, Browning?" he called as Conrad began to walk away. A policeman moved in and gripped his arm, but that didn't silence him. "You don't have anywhere to go! You've lost it all! Home! You don't have a home! *You don't have anything! You just don't know it yet!*"

Chapter 36

"Tarleton and Blanton will be in prison for a good long time," John J. Stafford said.

"You won't have to worry about them anymore, my boy," Claudius Turnbuckle added.

Conrad shook his head as he looked out the window of the suite at Santa Fe. "I'd feel better if Tarleton was dead. If you let a snake live, it can come back to bite you."

"Not in this case," Turnbuckle insisted. "The other good news is that Miss McCall is fine. The men Tarleton hired to kill her never got within a hundred yards of her before they were caught and arrested. It's a clean sweep."

Stafford reached under his coat and brought out a document. "Not only that, but here's the pardon Governor Otero signed this morning, absolving the man known as Kid Morgan from any and all charges relating to his escape from Hell Gate Prison. The Kid would be a free man . . . if, of course, he really existed."

Turnbuckle said, "Yes, no offense, Conrad, but I'm very glad that Mr. Kid Morgan has been permanently retired."

Stafford placed the pardon on the table next to his armchair and said, "There's just one more thing. The lawyer representing Roger Tarleton had this delivered to me this morning." He brought an envelope from his pocket. "Evidently it's a personal letter to you from Tarleton." He hesitated before holding it out. "You don't have to read it if you don't want to. I'm sure it's just more hateful venom spewed by that lunatic."

Conrad turned away from the window and stepped over to take the envelope. "No, I'll look at it," he said. He tore the envelope open, extracted the folded sheet of expensive notepaper inside, and opened it. The faintest hint of a familiar scent came from it.

The blood seemed to turn to ice in Conrad's veins as he recognized the handwriting. It didn't belong to Roger Tarleton.

Pamela Tarleton had written this letter.

Conrad,

If you're reading this, it means I'm dead. I'm entrusting this letter to my beloved cousin Roger with instructions that he should make certain that you receive it, should my efforts to avenge my father's life and my own honor go unrewarded. There is something I want you to know.

As I am sure you recall, you and I were intimate before our marriage, Conrad. Committing those words to paper should shame me deeply, but I am beyond shame. What you did not know is that when you broke our engagement, I was with child by you.

Yes, Conrad, you are a father . . . not once, but twice. I gave birth to twins, your children, not long after you married that other woman. They were healthy, happy infants, and now they are hidden away where you will never find them, somewhere in the vast frontier for which you deserted me.

You are a father, Conrad, but you will never know your children and they will never know you. And this . . . is my final revenge on you.

The letter was unsigned.

His fingers clenched involuntarily on the paper, crumpling it. Turnbuckle and Stafford both started up from their chairs, staring at him.

"My God, Conrad, what is it?" Turnbuckle asked. "You look like whatever is in that letter is the most horrifying thing you've ever read."

Conrad didn't answer the question directly. He said, "You were wrong a few minutes ago, Claudius."

"Wrong? Wrong about what?"

"About Kid Morgan being retired." Conrad turned to look at the coiled gunbelt and holstered Colt that lay on a side table, alongside a Stetson he had bought earlier. "Kid Morgan is going to ride again."

Center Point Large Print
600 Brooks Road / PO Box 1
Thorndike ME 04986-0001 USA

(207) 568-3717

US & Canada:
1 800 929-9108
www.centerpointlargeprint.com